PRAISE FOR
Brazilian Odyssey

"Positiva a iniciativa de identificar as personagens na *Brazilian Odyssey*, através de uma visão a partir de fora, mas por quem possui um conhecimento vivencil do país, em particular dos que dedicaram a sua vida à Amazônia. Atenção."

—**Anonymous author,** senior reporter,
and sociologist of the Amazon region

"I have known the author since we were both budding young international bankers decades ago. Stephen E. Murphy has always projected himself— head, heart and soul—vigorously into whatever activity he was involved in, financing projects like Ludwig's Amazon venture or helping Brazilian street kids in Rio de Janeiro. He brings that same intensity, local knowledge, and creative imagination to his writings. His newest book, *Brazilian Odyssey,* is no exception."

—**Steven Bavaria,** author, *The Income Factory* and *Too Greedy for Adam Smith;* contributor, *Seeking Alpha;* retired international banker

"Stephen Murphy's *Brazilian Odyssey* is a fast-paced trip through the Amazon, packed with intriguing plot twists and colorful characters who are both enchanting and treacherous. Woven into the story are two major themes: the search for redemption for the land and its people; and the struggle for justice in the fight against the forces of economic and political exploitation."

—**Professor T. Noble Foster,** Business Law, Seattle University;
co-author, "Legal Strategies for Combatting Online Terrorism,"
Atlantic Law Journal; host, international students

"*Brazilian Odyssey* takes the reader on a wild ride throughout my vast homeland. Feel the pain of Tatiana seeking justice for her slain cousin and of journalist Lucio battling vigilantes in Belém. Meet Vera, the social worker, who faces down a drug lord in São Paulo and a crafty Colombian kingpin who plies the corridors of power to expand his Amazon trade. Based on eye-witness testimonies, the author weaves a chilling yet hopeful story of Brazil today."

—**Professsor Claudio V. Furtado,** DBA, Fundação Getúlio Vargas (São Paulo); co-author, *The Private Equity and Venture Capital Industry, Second Brazilian Consensus* (2012); CEO, Brazil's National Institute of Industrial Property (Rio de Janeiro)

"In *Brazilian Odyssey*, Stephen Murphy draws us skillfully into a web of motivations and relationships, underscoring the current battle for the Amazon's rainforests. Not only does the book educate us about the forces at play in modern Brazil; it's a cracking good story of drama and intrigue."

—**Jim Hessler,** author, *Land on Your Feet, Not on Your Face*; president, Path Forward LLC

"Stephen Murphy's *Brazilian Odyssey* has all the hallmarks of a fine novel of intrigue and romance: an exotic setting that Murphy clearly knows well, beautiful women, villainous bad guys and weighty issues in contemporary Brazil."

—**Stephen W. Holgate,** author, *Tangier, Madagascar, To Live and Die in the Floating World*

"Having read and much enjoyed the twists and turns of *Havana Odyssey*, I am savoring *Brazilian Odyssey* even more. Its hero comes face to face with the deforestation brigade, a different kind of Trojan War fought in the Amazon jungle. Let's just hope this Odysseus manages to get out with his body and mind intact."

—**Kas Kalba, PhD,** author, *The Global Adoption and Diffusion of Mobile Phones* and academic articles; founder, international digital consulting network, including many projects in Brazil

"Parabéns ao autor, por ter criado *Brazilian Odyssey*, uma ficção inspirada em situações e desafios reais. No movimento dos que não querem mais esse modelo predatório de ocupação da Amazônia, que gera pobreza em meio a tantas riquezas, que premia quem vive de ilícitos e pune os que querem fazer a coisa certa. Em plena emergência climática, a Amazônia é futuro. E é pelo futuro que temos que nos mobilizar. O livro livro capta este desafio, atraves dos olhos dos 'heróis desconhecidos.'"

—**Caetano Scannavino,** co-author, *Adehauer Notebook* ("Amazonia: Development for Whom?"); columnist and member of socio-environmental team, *Folha de São Paulo;* Coordinator, Projeto Saúde e Alegria (Alter do Chão do Pará, Brazil)

"*Brazilian Odyssey* by Stephen Murphy offers a sensitive portrait of living conditions through the lens of university visitors and of unsung heroes. In doing so, the author successfully guides the reader through the thickets of this enigmatic country. This book is a compelling read."

—**Stu Sutin, PhD,** clinical professor, University of Pittsburg; lead author, *Strategic Transformation of Higher Education: Challenges and Solutions in a Global Economy,* and several academic articles; former international banker in Brazil

"I've followed the author's works in Rio and São Paulo for years, including his articles in the *Brazil Herald* about life in the hills of Salgueiro neighborhood and his Festa das Crianças for Rio's street kids. *Brazilian Odyssey,* his third book in a series, is based on dozens of interviews with Brazilians of all walks of life. It asks how Brazil can save its tropical rainforests and simultaneously promote the growth of Big Agriculture. The book is timely given current events."

—**Steve Yolen,** co-author, *Brazilian Legend* series (1992); founder and executive editor, *Latin America Daily Post;* UPI correspondent; contributor to several international surveys on Latin America; currently, senior translator of books in Brazil (Rio de Janeiro).

OTHER BOOKS BY STEPHEN E. MURPHY

On the Edge: an Odyssey
Havana Odyssey

BRAZILIAN
ODYSSEY

BRAZILIAN ODYSSEY

STEPHEN E. MURPHY

Odyssey Chapters
Seattle, Washington

bookhouse
PUBLISHING

2950 Newmarket St., Suite 101-358 | Bellingham, WA 98226
www.bookhouserules.com

This is a work of fiction. Names, characters, places, and occurrences
either are the product of the author's imagination or are used in
a fictional manner. Any resemblance to actual persons—living or
dead—as well as businesses, organizations, events, and locales is
coincidental.

Printed in the United States of America

Library of Congress Control Number: 2022912082

ISBN: 978-1-952483-52-3 (Paperback)
ISBN: 978-1-952483-53-0 (eBook)

Odyssey Chapters, P.O. Box 15155, Seattle, WA 98115
www.stephenemurphyauthor.com

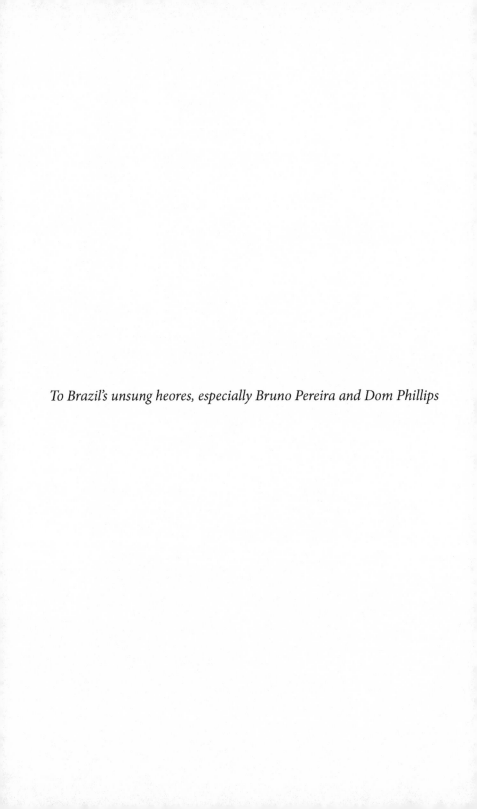

To Brazil's unsung heores, especially Bruno Pereira and Dom Phillips

CONTENTS

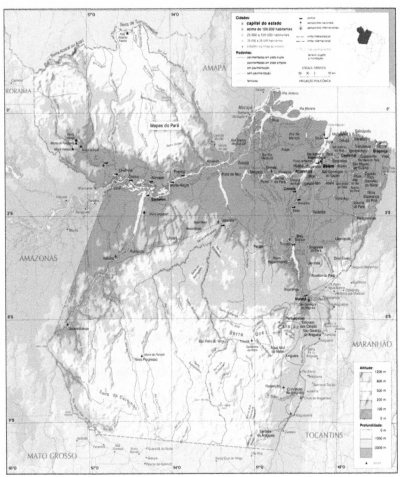

Source: Ms. Camille Bmerguy, Director, Climate Change and Bioeconomy, state of Pará

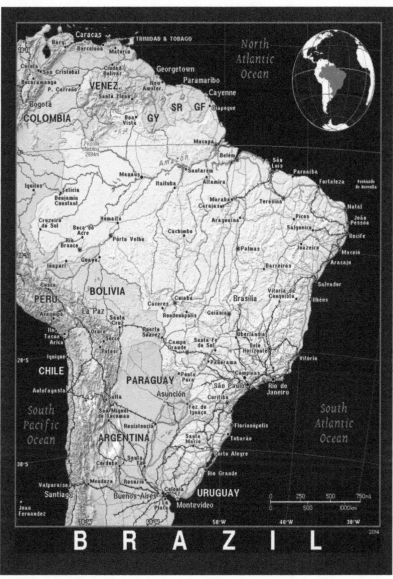

BRAZIL

LIST OF MAIN
CHARACTERS AND
ORGANIZATIONS

ALEXANDRE – *former chief, Federal Police, Manaus, Amazonas, now living near Rio de Janeiro*

ANTÔNIO CARLOS JOBÍM – *composer of "A Felicidade," "Matita Peré," and many bossa nova tunes*

BETO – *son of Jari's boat captain, Monte Dourado, Pará*

BRUNO – *author of books about Rio's militias and o Primeiro Comando do Capital of São Paulo*

CAETANO – *co-founder of NGO Força Comunitária, Alter de Chão, Pará*

CLAUDIO – *professor, Fundação Getulio Vargas, São Paulo, public servant in Rio de Janeiro*

CIMI – *Indigenist Missionary Council, missionaries and Catholic activists helping indigenous people in Central and Northern Brazil*

CUIABÁ – *nickname of astute bodyguard for Luis Carlos*

DANIEL LUDWIG – *founder of the Jarí Project, New York City*

FLAVIO – *federal senator, Rio de Janeiro and Brasilia*

JUNIOR – *son of Luis Carlos, Bogotá, Colombia*

LUCIO – *reporter and professor, Belém do Pará*

LUIS CARLOS – *member of Gulf Clan, Leticia, Colombia*

LUKE SHANNON – *professor, Seattle University*

MARINA – *former minister of the environment, São Paulo*

MATITA PERÉ – *mythical witch from the Amazon appearing at night in the form of a bird*

PADRE JOSÉ – *priest, Salesian Mission, Cuiabá, Mato Grosso*

PAULINO – *assassinated "guardian of the forest," Guajajara nation, Maranhão*

PLINIO – *co-founder of Biophílica, the interior of São Paulo*

PRIMEIRO COMANDO DA CAPITAL – *Brazil's largest crime syndicate, based in São Paulo*

OX BENCH – a bancada do boi, *lobby and paramilitary group representing ranchers*

QUEIROZ – *the "fixer" for a senator, on the move around Brazil*

SERGIO – *president, Grupo Jarí, São Paulo, and Monte Dourado, Pará*

SONIA – *activist for indigenous people, Brasilia*

TATIANA – *Seattle University student, distant cousin of Paulino Guajajara*

TERESA – *founder of NGO to protect wildlife, Cuiabá and São Paulo*

VERA – *social worker, Guarulhos and Paraisópolis, São Paulo*

WERNER – *senior partner, environmental affairs, in Pinheiro Neto law firm, São Paulo*

PROLOGUE

The Jari River near the Amazon
Brazil, August 1981

IT WAS HIS SECOND-TO-LAST NIGHT AT Monte Dourado, a company town carved from the Amazon rainforest. Luke passed a muddy Caterpillar tractor and began walking off the hamburger dinner served at the expat cafeteria. He was heading toward the forest's edge for a glimpse of "the other side." As a twenty-one-year-old college senior, Luke was proud of himself for landing this internship. BankBoston had tasked him to fly all the way from Seattle to inspect Daniel Ludwig's multi-million-dollar tree-to-pulp project. His job was to conduct a feasibility study for the entrepreneur's grandiose plan and to recommend whether to make the loan.

He was quite taken by Ludwig's nerve to create an empire in the middle of the jungle. Luke hoped the billionaire would fare better than Henry Ford had decades ago when he had spent millions to create his rubber enclave in the vast Amazon basin. Still, Luke was impressed and leaned toward approving the loan. It was the era of Brazil's Economic Miracle, and everyone thought big. If

Luke supported Ludwig's brainchild, he'd help open the Amazon to economic development. He stood a bit taller as he approached the tropical woods a football field away.

The supervisor had dispatched a Brazilian worker to serve as his guide and had warned Luke, "Beware of scorpions, boa constrictors, and alligators, Americano. Keep your eyes wide open."

Twenty yards from the forest's edge, the guide received a call on his walkie talkie and then told Luke, "Something's come up. I have to return to headquarters. Just stay in this cleared area, and you should be fine. Don't venture into the woods as this is the hour when predators prowl for dinner."

Luke pressed on. He passed tree stumps and burnt logs and spied a faint trail leading into a tropical arbor. The sun slipped into the horizon, and the sky was turning a darker blue. He walked by some shimmering palms and ventured a few steps inside. Exotic calls came from unseen birds and chattering monkeys. "I'd just like to get a sense of the natural habitat," he told himself, imagining the stories he could tell friends back at the University of Washington.

He took one step, then another and searched the boughs, which swayed before a restless breeze. Luke searched for snakes but couldn't see much in the fading light. Then he heard a weird sawing sound to his right.

As he veered, he glimpsed two yellow eyes observing him from a branch of a *jacarandá* tree ten yards away. He dried his palms on his shorts and peered at a big orange cat, its broad face covered by black spots. The feline swished its tail back and forth, but the rest of its body remained immobile. Then the jaguar blinked its eyes.

Luke tried to swallow, and his breathing came in ragged gulps. Without thinking, he began to hum Jobim's tune, which he'd learned in Portuguese class. He didn't know what else to do and only hoped Brazil's lord of the jungle would sense no threat.

Continuing to murmur the song of lament, Luke stepped slowly backward. He stumbled on a root and tried but failed to catch his fall. He heard a rumble and glimpsed white canines flash.

As he tumbled onto the jungle's floor, his singing stopped.

THE BEGINNING JOURNEY

A Felicidade

Tristeza não tem fim. Felicidade sim.
A felicidade é como a gota
De orvalho numa pétala de flor
Brilha tranquila
Depois de leve oscila
E cai como uma lágrima de amor

Happiness

Sadness has no end. Happiness does.
Happiness is like a drop
Of dew on a flower petal
It shines serenely
Then shakes ever so slightly
And falls as a teardrop of love

—*Tom Jobim and Vinicius de Morais (1958)*

CHAPTER 1

Flying above the Amazon
Overnight from August 8 to August 9, 2021

"PROFESSOR SHANNON, DO YOU CONSIDER YOURSELF a hypocrite?"

Her words ricocheted through Luke's head, arresting any inkling of sleep. From his window, he looked into the abyss. Suddenly, the American Airlines 777 lurched, and lightning cast an eerie pall over the jungle floor. The 470,000-pound Boeing shuddered once more, and passengers began to whimper and then scream.

Shards of light enveloped them, creating skeletal images, which vanished into the mist. Luke gasped at a colossal cumulus on his left, thundering toward the plane. An overhead bin sprang open and showered passengers with sundry carry-ons, and he dodged a laptop and a Target bag, spraying out bottles of shampoo.

He recalled Tatiana's words in class when she reminded him of his past action in this very region. Was this the Amazon's way to exact revenge? He hoped that specters of his past—flora, fauna, and indigenous souls—did not haunt his return to Brazil. As professor of this study mission, he was expected to set a good example.

In the row ahead, another student shook uncontrollably and hung on to his knees. The plane bounced around the airstreams but headed down. Next to him, he heard a passenger pray.

Behind, a rattling sound grew louder, and the forward cabin jerked upward. Luke grabbed the seat in front of him. Acid reflex thrust up from his stomach.

Would this tropical roller coaster ever end?

Across the aisle, Tatiana's head jostled against the window. She opened her coal black eyes and stared directly at him. She shook her head and looked away. Her indigenous roots and quiet presence unsettled Luke, making him curious about her past. Though only five feet four inches tall, her no-nonsense manner commanded attention.

The aircraft surfed the storm currents, rising and falling in jerky rhythm. Slowly, the rattling lessened, and the pilot announced, "We've found some calm at twenty-two thousand feet. Keep your seat belts fastened." Yet from the inky horizon, the storm's tentacles still reached out for them in brilliant form.

Luke released his breath and peered out the portal. Sulphur lights winked through a bank of clouds and disappeared in a flash. He closed his eyes as his mind wandered back forty years to his maiden visit to the Amazon.

* * *

DURING HIS SENIOR YEAR AT THE UNIVERSITY OF WASHINGTON, Luke had secured a plum AIESEC internship with a prestigious bank in Brazil. After a brief stint in São Paulo, he was tasked to evaluate the feasibility for the multi-million-dollar project located near the mouth of the Amazon.

The world's only billionaire in the 1970s, Daniel Ludwig, announced he had acquired 3.6 million hectares, nearly nine million acres, of the rainforest in undeveloped Amapá, having convinced Brazil's military rulers that he would create an integrated tree-to-pulp factory on the Jari River, which would become the cellulose capital of the world. He planned to import a specially designed factory from Japan and thousands of gmelina trees from Southeast Asia. The fast-growing gmelina, he announced, would feed his factory from his immense tree plantation. He would become master of the Amazon as he had in worldwide shipping.

Brazil's military regime supported Ludwig's brainchild in order to develop the area around this tributary to the Amazon, from which flowed more water than any other river on Earth. The American's project would create jobs and secure Brazil's rainforests against foreign intruders, especially from Cuba. After a decade of planning from his New York office, the impresario commissioned two large ship-shaped platforms to be built at the Hiroshima shipyards. As an ensemble, they would become the integrated cellulose factory for his new empire.

The world would hail him as savior of the region, bringing prosperity to the local people. He'd also profit from the rising prices of cellulose and paper. It was a daring undertaking and caught the fancy of the international press.

As a shipping magnate, he decided to float the barges, costing $150 million, across the Indian Ocean, around the Cape of Good Hope, and through the Atlantic's storms. Against long odds, he succeeded and surprised his detractors. The barge-platforms travelled sixteen thousand miles in three months and arrived unscathed at the mouth of the Amazon during its rainy season in 1978.

Two barges floated into specially designed locks, composed of gum wood piles pounded into earth by hundreds of workers.

By closing the locks and pumping water out, the platforms gently settled on the pilings. Ludwig's first part of his grand plan was complete, and he felt prime.

The power-plant barge slipped into different locks downriver and would provide electricity to the new company town, called Monte Dourado. The entrepreneur affirmed that his empire would generate a "mountain of gold" financed by cellulose exports around the world.

Luke showed up a few years later on a muggy ninety-two-degree Fahrenheit day in August. He arrived in a Cessna eight-seater with an American forestry prof from Tennessee. After taking off in Belém do Pará, their plane bounced through stratus clouds over the immense two-hundred-mile-wide estuary. The Cessna wove between squalls and landed under drizzle on a dirt runway three hours later.

"Welcome to our golden mountain. My name is Roberto," offered the short brown greeter with a wide friendly smile. "We'll have to take you to town by boat. A huge *massaranduba* fell overnight and blocked the road. The workers are still sawing through this tree with its big red heart. So we'll have fun plying the Jari instead and see the sights," he shouted and tossed their luggage into a faded green Cherokee.

The driver plowed through a soggy road and parked at a makeshift dock. Waves of turbid water washed over gray planks and swarms of mosquitoes descended on the two gringos.

"This is the Jari, tributary to our River Sea, the name we give the great Amazon. The river is still rising as rains have remained longer this season. Soon, there will be sun," exclaimed Roberto. He tossed the prof's suitcase and Luke's pack to a young teen and introduced his son. "Beto, meet some Americanos here to help make us grow green gold."

They followed the guide and jumped into a twenty-foot, square-sterned boat, powered by a small Honda motor aft. Roberto took station there. The bottom planks were faded green, yellow, and blue, colors of the Brazilian flag. The prof sat amidship on a wooden bench, and Luke and Beto hung onto the bow, dodging small waves.

Roberto plied the river, zigzagging between logs, which sometimes turned out to be *jacarés*, or Brazilian alligators. "Don't put your hands too far outside," he warned, laughing. "They will be bait for the piranhas, my friend."

An hour later under warm rain, they arrived at a dock made of wooden pilings. Luke was drenched. As if on cue, the sun burst out of low-hanging clouds and reflected off rows of manufactured houses. Luke saw towering trees in the distance surrounding the company town.

A tall, thin man, wearing a Panama hat, greeted them: "Welcome to Monte Dourado, professor. And you must be Luke Shannon, our friendly banker. You will find many Americans here who help us build the pulp and paper capital of the world. Sorry about the river ride, but the rainforest has its own rules. Beto will take your baggage to one of our guest homes."

Luke embarked on his whirlwind visit and observed rows of gmelina trees, which had an unusual crooked skew. He visited rice paddies, a surface mine of kaolin, and a power plant downstream. Usually he ate with other Americans—mostly from the South—and listened to them grumble about scorpions, boredom, and unhappy wives.

Two other memories stood out—his visit to the shantytown built across the Jari River and his encounter with a Brazilian jaguar at the forest's edge.

"What do you say, Americano? Would you like to see where we Brazilians go to have fun?" invited Roberto. At dusk they crossed from the west bank, housing the expatriate community, to the other side. By the time the boat made the fifteen-minute trip, night had fallen and humidity rose. Ahead, Luke observed wooden huts on stilts with the river flowing underneath. He heard laughter and samba emanating from a makeshift cabana. This murky villa could be a scene for a James Bond thriller, he thought.

Luke followed his guide up a shaky plank to a boardwalk weaving fifty yards along the riverbank. They pushed through a swinging door to a room twenty by twenty feet, which swayed to the gurgling water. Wisps of smoke hung in the air from hand-rolled stogies of tobacco and marijuana. A half-dozen men with indigenous features sat on benches, and a barman stood expectantly toward the back, surrounded by bottles of a white liquid.

"*Cachaça* is our rustic rum," Roberto explained. "Local distillers leave a few impurities inside to give it an extra kick. My friend makes a tasty version of Brazil's national drink, the *caipirinha*, with lots of lime, some local honey, and a twist of *açaí*. Pedro, two specials for me and my new friend."

They sat on a wooden bench toward the right and heard the wind rustle through the eaves. The rain added its pitter-patter on the tin roof. To their left, a young girl swayed to the sound of Antonio Carlos Jobim. Using his basic Portuguese, Luke translated the words, "Sadness knows no end, but happiness surely does . . ." The girl wore a golden necklace, from which hung fine strands of straw covering her firm bare breasts. Through a straw skirt, her brown legs swayed to the bossa nova tune.

The music transitioned to Jobim's "Matita Perê," based on the Amazon legend of a witch transformed into a bird at night, pestering people for tobacco. The following day the witch would reappear to claim her prize or cast incantations on anyone disrespecting her. The dancer felt the change in tune and traveled many miles away, adrift in her own special world. Luke listened to Jobim's lyrics about a person fleeing the witch's curse, yearning for a better life to no avail. He wondered if the maiden dancer had become the person in that song.

"She is from the Xingú tribe and is our favorite dancer," gushed his guide.

Luke was enthralled and drained his special caipirinha. She looked his way. Luke felt his heart jump as he caught her glance. He didn't want to let it go.

The spell was broken when two tall men with European features entered, gold necklaces jangling around their necks. A man in his thirties and another in his early twenties slowly took in the scene. All conversation stopped.

Roberto whispered, "Take care, my friend. They're from Colombia. They often stop here on their way to Belém."

The younger Colombian stood over six feet tall and focused his intense dark eyes in their direction. "Don't tell me we have a gringo on this side of the river," he exclaimed *en español*. His face wore a smirk, and his older companion nodded in agreement. "Compadre, what are you doing here? Did you lose your way from the company town?"

"*Buenas noches, señor*," Luke answered and continued in Spanish. "I'm just trying to get the lay of the land along the Jari."

"Good answer, gringo. My name is Luis Carlos. I've just arrived from Leticia where three countries share the western source of the Amazon. If you enjoy wild scenes, you should come visit me sometime."

Luke recalled that Colombia, Brazil, and Peru had a common border upriver, seventeen hundred miles to the west. "My name is Luke Shannon, and I am visiting from Seattle," he replied and then added, "Thanks for your offer. Perhaps another time?"

Roberto frowned, but Luke forced a smile and remained seated. The young dancer had slipped out a rear door as Jobim's melody came to its bittersweet end. A heavier air filled the room, even though the breeze whistled through.

Luke dipped his head toward the Colombiano but followed his guide out the door to the rolling boardwalk and pouring rain. He pondered what was really happening in this backwater of the Amazon across from Ludwig's grandiose farm.

* * *

THE IMAGES OF THE COLOMBIANO, THE XINGÚ DANCER, and the jaguar faded away as Luke opened his eyes and refocused on the present.

The flight had stabilized, and he gazed down through the rose-hued mist to endless fields, many planted in circular fashion. An occasional thicket of eucalyptus broke the plains of soybeans, Brazil's top export crop.

The Seattle University's mission was to determine if Brazil's drive to plant acres of soy beyond the Cerrado savanna was destroying forests and native people. Their dean encouraged them to report their findings on return in order to raise the university's profile.

Luke looked across the aisle at Tatiana, her face pressed against the window. She grimaced at the fields below and shot him a quick glance. Involuntarily, her body trembled.

The sun peeked through the clouds to the east as the soybean plantings gave way to Brasilia's outer slums.

In class Tatiana had passionately argued that the world was turning its back on Brazil's unsung heroes battling to save its rainforests and indigenous people. "Instead," she exclaimed, "the land barons cut down our trees and displace my people. All they crave is more land for soybeans to feed China's pigs! We must speak up. We must do something!"

Luke and SU's students were moved by Tatiana's passionate appeal. Now he observed tears spilling down her reddish-brown cheeks.

He wondered what lay ahead for his class, especially Tatiana, in Brazil. Would they be able to accomplish their project in a country ruled by the "Trump of the tropics?" He'd read that the sitting president was supported by large landowners and unofficial militias that played for keeps. Luke hoped they weren't in over their heads.

"*Atenção*," he heard himself say aloud, meaning "beware."

Tatiana turned and bobbed her head in grim reply.

CHAPTER 2

Rua Aristedes Lobo, Belém, Pará
Monday Morning, August 9

L UCIO TURNED THE CORNER AND SAW the reflection of a lean
mulatto keeping pace with him. Humidity began its morning
embrace, so he removed his spectacles to wipe the mist away. Still
hearing footsteps, he turned up Rua Aristedes Lobo and quickened his pace. He barely dodged a homeless man and a swerv-
ing van seeking passengers for the port. Behind, Lucio heard the
man curse and horns blast. A horse-drawn cart's wheel got stuck
in a cobblestone pothole, causing cars and pedestrians to stop in
their tracks. A vintage Mercedes flatbed revved its engines to add
to the tempest.

Using the distraction, Lucio turned down Tiradentes
Street, aiming for the rear door of Riachuelo's store inside the
Boulevard Shopping Center. He'd used the freight entrance
to escape tails in the past. "*Bom dia,* Pedro," he greeted as he
entered the back door.

"*Bom dia,* Professor," said the sturdy guard, who'd been his student in the evening civics class.

As a journalist for fifty years, Lucio had always found time to lecture about the freedom of the press. He stood up straighter and inclined his head.

Weaving through stacks of boxes of all shapes and sizes, Lucio exited the warehouse into the department store's section for women's lingerie. Sales attendants were priming their wares for customers milling around in the mall. The doors were about to open at 10 a.m. Air-conditioning had just kicked in and bathed Lucio with refreshing air. Though a lifelong resident of Belém and accustomed to its humid heat, he appreciated a blast from the A/C.

Lucio wondered how that American academic and his students would react to his tropical hometown, just south of the equator, where temperatures lingered between 75 and 90 degrees Fahrenheit year-round. That insistent professor from Seattle University had pestered him for more than a year, concerning a study mission about big agriculture's effects on Brazil's rainforests. How could Lucio say no, he the defender of his hometown's flora and fauna? Apparently, the prof had a Brazilian student with ties to "guardians of the forest" fighting to save their ancient trees and way of life. Marauders' thirst for land, wood, and gold was unquenchable, he fumed. They kept coming, egged on by the current regime.

He shook his head, recalling so many incidents of this sort, happening over and over again. The authorities offered words of consolation but took little action. In his city of two million souls, the powers that be still maintained sway. If they whispered in the police captain's ear to look the other way, then excuses were made and the culprits not found. However, Lucio would not keep quiet. Throughout his lifetime, he'd raised his voice on the street corner, at city hall, and to the press—to whoever would listen. That included the American prof.

As Lucio was a native son, the authorities hadn't confronted him head-on. Instead, they opted for campaigns of intimidation. They'd sent city inspectors to his residence to fine him for inane violations and had begun whisper campaigns that he was gay. Of late, they'd become more daring, posting threats against him and his daughters on social media. Someone had recently thrown rocks through his window with anonymous notes. They'd also dispatched people to shadow him, like the young man this very morning.

Yet Lucio would not shut up. His cause célèbre was to fight for freedom of the press in his hometown and in his homeland. Otherwise, what was the point getting up every morning?

The store's doors slid open with a whoosh, unleashing a rush of masked shoppers. Lucio snapped out of his reverie and slipped on his hospital mask. Looking at his fellow residents, his journalist side questioned why each one came here today. He sensed anxiety in some eyes and boredom in others. After all, unemployment was sky high and climbing. He wondered how each shopper was getting by.

As Lucio stepped into the mall's inner corridor, he heard gates screeching open to begin another day of commerce. The female attendants, dressed up as best they could, offered pleasant smiles to seniors like him. They always made him feel alive.

"*Bom dia*," wished a girl, attempting to smile. She was wearing a Vivo T-shirt and was charged to entice potential customers to venture inside the cell-phone store. He remembered her from his class as an attentive but shy student. She stood a little over five feet tall and retained the reserved manner of an indigenous maiden. Her eyes were pitch-black, but her skin had the luster of cinnamon. Today, she looked downcast.

"*Tudo bem*, Gabriela?" he inquired in a low voice, using the greeting of "all is well" familiar throughout Brazil. He recalled that her lineage came from the Yanomami tribe in the north, close to the Venezuelan border. Her people had also suffered invading vigilantes, who sought their hardwood, fetching a pretty penny on international markets. Gabriela had a sister who moved to a town in rural Pará a few hours to the south. Her sibling's charge was to organize indigenous women in order to protect their families against outside miners.

"More or less, Professor. Today I received some difficult news," Gabriela mumbled.

Lucio waited for her to continue.

"Do you have time to talk? Though we just opened, I could ask my colleague to stand in for me. The store doesn't get too busy until noon."

Lucio always made himself available to listen to his students. Sometimes he served as a sounding board, other times as a counselor. He always guarded their confidences like the white-browed hawk protecting its grounds over the Amazon. "With pleasure, Gabriela. I'll wait for you at the Boulevard Café just down the mall."

She nodded and turned back to the cellphone shop.

He secured a table just inside the café looking out, where foot traffic was slowly picking up.

Gabriela joined him ten minutes later. She ordered an herbal infusion of *jambú* leaves, said to work as an anesthetic to relieve pain. It also had properties to fight viruses, including Covid-19.

Lucio ordered one as well, hoping it might dissuade the onset of arthritis in his wrists. He maintained his silence so she could speak whenever she felt comfortable.

"Professor, my sister just called from her village, where she's helping organize the Mundurukú women along the Tapajós River.

As you know, they've suffered illegal strip miners, who continue to pollute streams and rivers. They've complained to the local constable, but he never follows up. By treaty, the tribe has the right to use the water for communal needs, including to fish for their daily meal. Now the waters are muddy with traces of mercury, killing fish, wildlife, and people.

"This weekend, several masked men swooped into town early morning and beat my sister and her friend. They were outside on their way to the public restroom. The vigilantes attempted to run them over in their pickup truck and later set fire to the women association's building. They told her, 'If you open your mouths again, we'll be back. And we'll have more fun with you.' They laughed and fled as the fire started raging. All the community woke up to draw water to battle the flames. It took hours to put them out.

"What can we do against such men?" Gabriela muttered, her eyes brimming.

"We must report this incident to the international press. I'll spotlight it in my next edition of *Amazonia Real*. It would be advisable to file a complaint with the Federal Police delegate in town. As the invasion took place on Mundurukú land, the Feds have jurisdiction to enforce the law. What do you think?"

"Let me speak with my sister today, and I'll let you know," she said, deliberately sipping more tea. "Do you think these Federal Police would do something, as the local police always make excuses? We fear the constable is probably paid off by the miners."

"I have a friend in the Federal Police in Belém. Though his boss is a political appointee, my friend is a standup cop. If your sister gives approval, I will speak with him. The Feds usually take complaints seriously and have a history of investigating crime—especially if it occurs on federal land."

The mall clock showed ten forty-five, time for Gabriela to go. As she pushed back her chair and stood up, Lucio did the same.

Gabriela stood on her tippy toes to give Lucio a peck on the cheek. "Many thanks for the tea and for listening to me, Professor. Now I must return to work. Here's my card at Vivo with my WhatsApp number. Let's speak later today. *Muita obrigada.*"

Lucio bent down for her kiss and watched her trudge back to work. He'd make calls when he got home and see what could be done. His friend in Belém also knew Alexandre, the former head of the Federal Police in Manaus, renowned for his integrity. However, when Alexandre had called out the minister of environment for impropriety, Brasilia's politicos had him reassigned. Lucio hoped this standup Fed would not pay too high a price for doing the right thing. Alexandre now was serving in some backwater in the state of Rio de Janeiro. The pols in the nation's capital were a vicious sort, so every federal employee had to watch his or her step.

Lucio would help Gabriela and her sister out. This was his calling in life. He'd continue to uphold the rights of the forgotten and the powerless against the vested interests—be they of the wealthy families, Brasilia, or Chinese hustlers. What else could he do?

Out of the corner of his eye, Lucio saw the same tall mulatto who had tracked him from home.

Gazing at the window display of the Maybelline store on the other side of the corridor, the man turned around and stared at Lucio and then began walking his way.

How would Lucio elude him now?

CHAPTER 3

Barra da Tijuca, Rio de Janeiro
Monday Morning, August 9

"*F*ILHO DA PUTA," FLAVIO FUMED, THROWING the paper-weight at his current assistant. "You're supposed to manage the journalists' drivel and not let them off the hook. Didn't we help fund their favorite escapade to the north and provide them special incentives?"

The young man ducked just in time and heard the quartz figurine shatter against the mahogany wall. Maybe it was time to rethink his current assignment, arranged by his mom. He asked himself if she was having an affair with this political jerk.

His boss's temper rose and fell like a summer storm, even though it was winter in the Southern Hemisphere. The frothy waves of the Atlantic below reflected the turmoil of the Brazilian people. Earlier, he'd passed them shouting and marching in the streets.

"*Senhor*, I did my best to present your father in a favorable light," the assistant whined, "but London journalists have a mind of their own. They asked why the Amazon was still burning and why the president did nothing to prevent ranchers and miners from invading federal land. And that old reporter in Belém, he was still raising cane. The BBC guys listened to him and tuned me out. Unfortunately, the lackey on our payroll offered a weak response. What can I do?"

"You weakling! Tell them that my father supports Brazilian land pioneers and miners grappling to make a living. Our administration does not kowtow to the effete upper classes of São Paulo or the so-called crusaders in the press. All they want to do is spin stories to make themselves look good. All these industrialists want is to suck the blood out of Brazilian workers, make money, and show off their gated mansions in Morumbí. Don't ever forget that these workers are our people! My father—and not the São Paulo capitalists or the fickle press—is their ally in Brasilia.

"Weren't you trained in PR?" Flavio bristled. He couldn't stand this youngster born with a silver spoon in his mouth, but he had promised his mother. Indeed, his mom possessed other assets beside her abundant finances.

His anger unsated, the president's son swept a photo of the new owner's family off the marble table. It broke spectacularly on the pearly floors, sending shards in all directions.

If only he could find competent people, Flavio seethed. He recalled his promise to get her spoiled son a job in PR after she plunked another one hundred thousand Brazilian *reais* into his father's coffers. Wasn't brother Carlos supposed to deal with these journalist types, as well as social media bloggers? This amateur kid was over his head and didn't have a clue how to sway older reporters.

But Carlos had his own issues. One of Trump's burned-out aides had promised Flavio's younger brother his expertise to reach millions of "digital warriors" and to turn the election around like in 2018. Carlos believed in this character's pitch, but Flavio had his doubts. Daddy also hinted that the Russian ambassador had promised hackers to help. The campaign was toying with Telegram to message the voters in 2022. Facebook had begun pushing back. All his siblings wanted to improve his father's standing for reelection—especially now that the press had turned solidly against him. "Fake news" is what he and his family had claimed about these Amazon stories, but Brazilians seemed tired of this American slogan. High unemployment didn't help, but distractions sometimes did the trick.

Flavio frowned at the *Folha de São Paulo*'s recent poll showing his father trailing in next year's election. Brazil's former president, nicknamed Lula, was leading the pack. Brazilians didn't seem to care if Lula had been convicted of corruption or not. After all, everyone knew that politicians had their hand in some type of cookie jar.

Then there was the pandemic, which unsettled Brazilians of all hues. Despite *Papai*'s denial, people had been dying fast earlier this year. Now that infections were declining, why didn't they give him some kind of credit? One health guru opined that at the current rate of inoculation, Brazil would surpass the United States in vaccinations by the end of 2021—quite a turnaround.

But the goody two-shoes press seemed fixated on the burning of the Amazon and exposés about his father. They didn't cotton to Flavio's explanations but listened instead to that prickly reporter in the Amazon and his cadre of worn-out friends. Even Daddy's supporters in the northern militias had asked to get rid of him.

Flavio poured himself another Johnny Walker out of the owner's cannister, enjoying the burning sensation down his throat. The whiskey calmed him as he tried to rearrange his thoughts. He had to remind himself that his people, the working people, were expecting Papai's administration to find jobs for them. He also had to provide them some kind of hope.

On the wall, he noticed a poster of *The Elite Squad*, Padilha's movie about special squads of Rio's police who chased down and eliminated petty thieves. Now these groups worked closely with politicos, gangs, and community sympathizers that the press called "militias." Together, they had provided Papai key support in 2018. Why not again in 2022?

Flavio shook his head and saw a Brasilia newspaper citing his enemies' accusations. They'd whined about his pocketing monthly stipends earmarked for his local Rio staff. But, hey, every pol had little ways to help himself get by. That's why he and others ran for public office. Everyone knew that.

The press called this scandal *rachadinhas*, or the "little cracks," which dribbled public funds to pay for Flavio's pet projects. His family's longtime fixer, Queiroz, had allegedly paid ghost employees and channeled funds to Flavio, friends, and family. His trusted "machine gunner" was in and out of prison, but holding firm.

Now Flavio had to use this inept millennial instead. Well, his mama had oiled Flavio's gears and his family's treasury. As an elected federal senator, it was his right to enjoy all the perks of office.

Flavio cast his eye around this luxury dwelling, facilitated by those little cracks over many years. He'd recently sold this chic condo in Rio's Barra da Tijuca to a friend of a friend. Though the new owner had paid full price, Flavio demanded that he be able to escape here whenever he needed a hideaway. The buyer agreed. After all, Flavio was a big man in Rio and in Brasilia and not to be trifled with.

Everyone recognized that power emanated from the capital. As long as Daddy stayed on top, prestige and influence would flow his family's way. But Papai had to survive calls for impeachment and mobilize his supporters on the streets and from the hustings. If they travelled the democratic route, how was Daddy to prevail in the polls a year away? Somehow, they had to sway public opinion or find another way to retain the levers of power.

Flavio saw his reflection in the gold-plated French mirror and thought he looked disheveled. He had to keep up his appearance. His role in the family circle was to face down congressional critics and the annoying press. Maybe he should reach out to his militia friends again. They knew how to take care of business in 2018, when an irritating councilwoman threatened to out his brother. Perhaps his detractors, especially in the press, would quiet down if something happened to their prima donna.

He glanced out the huge glass windows toward the angry waves, echoing his state of mind. A seagull managed to glide through the air currents above the fray. Like that bird, Flavio needed to navigate Brasilia's headwinds and escape the never-ending pitfalls.

Just then a call came up from the doorman's office. An acquaintance of Queiroz's had just dropped by with a message from his former neighbor. He was the brawn for a local militia.

A plan began forming in Flavio's mind: kill two birds with one stone.

CHAPTER 4

Tom Jobim (Galeão) International Airport, Rio de Janeiro
Monday Morning, August 9

LUKE RAN THE GAUNTLET WITH THE NINE STUDENTS through crowds of visitors, gypsy cabs, and tourist guides. No one held up a Seattle U placard, so he continued outside. Luggage in tow, he searched in vain for their minivan, but saw one with a Cargill sign, several black limousines, and buses from Riotur.

"Professor, I'll see what I can find," proposed Tatiana as rain kept pouring down.

He looked beyond the airport and searched for Christ the Redeemer in the hills. Thick clouds hid this landmark statue overlooking Rio de Janeiro's north and south zones. Luke always took comfort in seeing Cristo and felt uneasy when he couldn't. He hoped its being obscured didn't augur poorly for his study mission. Luke didn't admit to being superstitious but paid attention to Brazilian notions. He shuddered recalling its *macumba* cult, Brazil's form of African voodoo. He'd once attended a séance, which called on netherworld spirits to seek vengeance on the living. The ceremony with drums and incense transformed worshippers to a catatonic state, and its medium uttered bizarre sounds and scary intonations. Luke vowed to never return.

As Luke waited, he recollected that Rio was shaped like a *J* and divided into two zones. Beach districts like Copacabana and Ipanema were located on the hook of the *J* in the South Zone. On the *J*'s stem, worker suburbs stretched for miles to the North Zone and beyond, housing 80 percent of Rio's residents, called *cariocas*. Rugged hills stood high between both zones, separating the more prosperous districts from their poorer counterparts. Cristo stood on top of the tallest mountain, o Corcovado, and could be viewed throughout this metropolis of eleven million souls.

As a young banker, Luke had visited Salgueiro, a favela or shantytown in the North Zone, renowned for its samba. One hot summer, he'd had a fling with an Afro-Brazilian dancer and the time of his life. For Carnaval, he'd even sashayed down Avenida Rio Branco to the incessant beat of Conga drummers and inviting smiles. Everything had seemed possible to that younger Luke. Now he served as an adjunct prof and had to secure transport for this university tour during a pandemic and political uproar.

"Professor, I think I found us all a ride to Copacabana. One of the Riotur buses, chartered for Brazil's Indigenous Association, has extra seats. With a little donation, I think the driver would accommodate us. What do you say?" asked Tatiana, smiling broadly now.

"*Excelente*," shouted Luke, happy that Tati appeared more upbeat. He followed her past the black limos and arrived at the open door of a faded beige Mercedes bus with a sign for APIB, or Brazil's Indigenous People's Association. Luke bargained with the driver and secured a lift to Copacabana for three hundred Brazilian reals, or less than sixty dollars.

They stowed their bags and entered the bus, Luke being the last to board. As he was about to step in, he observed three men dressed in charcoal suits heading toward them. They stopped in front of the black limousine. The first man opened the door for a tall man with wavy, salt-and-pepper hair, speaking staccato Spanish to his cohort. The tall man removed his sunglasses and glanced at Luke, holding his stare an extra second. Then he entered the sleek Mercedes without concern, followed by a companion wearing an ear-piece.

"It can't be," Luke said to himself, "after all these years." He boarded the Riotur bus and sat up front, watching the limo speed out of the airport, a black sedan chasing in its wake.

* * *

LUKE BREATHED A DEEP SIGH OF relief. Their reservations were intact at the Windsor Copacabana, just a block off the famous beach. He made sure the students matched up correctly and gave them the day off until their evening meeting. He had secured a lunch appointment at Maxim's restaurant with a Brazilian author, expert on the so-called militias of Rio.

As an introvert, Luke also needed some time alone just to walk the beach. He recalled his mixed experiences with hotels. On his last university visit to Havana, Luke had suffered an interrogation at the airport and missed his ride to Hotel Nacional. Once at the hotel, he had found his reservation cancelled, and he had had to fend for himself. The experience had set off a series of cascading events, which placed his mission and safety at risk. Now, he was a persona non grata in Cuba and couldn't return without suffering another inquisition. Involuntarily, he shook his head and pushed out of mind the harrowing escape during a tropical storm. At least he had discovered his long-lost son, bred of passion thirty years ago.

Luke turned the corner toward the beach and wondered what he'd find in this country where he'd worked years ago. Their current project to evaluate the impact of Big Ag on deforestation was high profile and would likely make waves. He had read that Brazil's administration paid little notice to the destruction of its rainforests. The current president was quoted as saying, "We encourage poor miners, loggers, and farmers to seek their fortune in our vast Amazon. We need jobs, not NGOs, in Brazil."

He stumbled in a pothole on the mosaic sidewalk, where loose stones were cast about, and took care to step around a homeless man sleeping on a cardboard mat, a thin shawl covering his head. On the one-way street, Luke forgot to look both ways before crossing and barely avoided a pizza delivery cyclist speeding the wrong way. He reminded himself that he was no longer in Seattle and had to be constantly vigilant to survive the anarchy of Rio's streets.

As Luke reached Avenida Atlântica, he breathed in the salt air. He turned his face toward the faint glow of sun, struggling through late-morning clouds. As much as he would have liked to go swimming, the waves crashing high along the three-mile-long beach told him otherwise. This being winter, the waters came from the colder currents of Antarctica. Maybe another time.

All of sudden, sirens blared as motorcycle policemen zoomed up the seaside boulevard, preceding a five-car motorcade heading north toward downtown. "Son of a bitch," he heard someone shout. The president of Brazil stood up to wave through the limousine's open roof. Brazilian flags flew on the front bumpers, and a few pedestrians waved back. Others shook their fists and shouted expletives.

"And there's his corrupt son by his side," blurted the waiter outside of Maxim's restaurant on Atlântica. "He's never satisfied and always wants more. For years, I've seen him drink the Scotch of others until he was barely upright. Somebody else always picks up the tab—including this café when he decides to walk away."

Luke meandered toward the Fort of Copacabana, which adjoins Ipanema beach to the south. He was heartened that most people were masked up and tried to give each other distance as they strolled or jogged along the beachside walk. Often, their dogs had different ideas, not keen on social distancing.

He passed Posto 3, or the third Petrobras gas station. *Cariocas*, the locals, often note the posts to remember their place on Copa's beach. Luke walked to Posto 4 and looked up the street ending on the Hill of the Goats. He'd briefly lived there as a young bachelor; his red-room fiestas were the talk of the town. That was then. Now, he observed himself off a storefront window, more gray than brown sprinkled through his thinning hair

The beach clock showed twelve fifty. It was time to meet Brazil's famous crime writer for lunch. Luke felt mist in the air and remembered that cariocas did not like gray or rainy weather. They often stayed indoors until the sun reappeared. He hoped his guest would show.

As he arrived at Maxim's, the sun poked through the rumbling clouds. The beach clock read 13:05. Luke found a seat toward the back of the covered area on the mosaic sidewalk, its plastic tarp rustling in the breeze. Thanks to WhatsApp, a friend of a friend had introduced Luke to Bruno. Though from São Paulo, the writer was in town to promote his recent book regarding paramilitary militias taking charge of several Rio neighborhoods, especially in the North Zone.

A thin man sporting black-rimmed glasses and stringy, gray hair peered tentatively inside the tarp. Luke stood up, saying, "Tudo bem?" They exchanged loose hugs—the typical greeting in Brazil—and went to the corner table to share small talk. When the waiter arrived, they ordered freshly squeezed orange juice and grilled Brazilian sole, accompanied by a tasty mix of broccoli, rice, garlic, and olive oil.

Luke learned that Bruno had earned his PhD from the University of São Paulo, researching organized crime in his hometown. As a student, he was fascinated by groups that justified the use of violence to rid society of anti-social elements and to restore order. He reminded Luke that death squads had been active in Rio and São Paulo since the 1980s to remove "bad elements" from society. With drugs offering more money and power, such squads had expanded their horizons. They'd become more sophisticated and made alliances with military police, politicians, and even the sitting president of the republic.

"Police and military sympathizers loved the sound of 'law and order,'" Bruno said, "and rallied around Bolsonaro's candidacy. The irony is that many of these groups flout the law to secure more territory and money-making ventures. In many neighborhoods, they strike deals with community leaders and even Pentecostal pastors to consolidate power. Whenever they need muscle, they call upon off-duty police in nearby precincts to enforce their version of law and order. Residents learn to toe the line. Such militias now take charge of districts throughout Rio's North Zone and even in trendy municipalities like Búzios and Angra dos Reis."

"Do these groups have international connections?" asked Luke. "At the airport, I recognized someone who used to deal drugs between Colombia and Brazil's Amazon years ago."

Bruno lowered his voice. "Yes, they do. The largest crime syndicate, based in São Paulo, is called the PCC, or Primeiro Comando da Capital. It has representatives in Paraguay, Bolivia, Colombia, and Venezuela. I've heard it's about to establish a beachhead in Italy to better access European markets.

"The PCC began years ago in São Paulo's prisons, causing inmate riots at the behest of leaders on the outside. They control Paulista prisons and pick and choose inmates for their soldiers in the field. They also maintain many accountants, attorneys, and politicos on their payroll and remain the most powerful crime group in Brazil. They deal in anything that makes them money—legal or not—such as pilfered Amazon hardwood, gold, or soybeans. More recently, they've been buying hospitals, hotels, and plantations to launder illicit gains. They do not abide fools or opposition from any quarter.

"Rio's militias and a smaller syndicate, Comando Vermelho, pale by comparison. I've written about the PCC and how it's expanding in Brazil and abroad. You don't want to cross paths with them. They take no prisoners, eliminating anyone or anything that gets in their way. They don't give a damn about negative PR. They only care about the size of their bank accounts and the sound of US dollars being tallied by counting machines."

Bruno's iPhone buzzed, and he took the call, repeating "*sim*" three times. "It's been a pleasure, Professor Shannon. It's time to begin my show and tell with local bloggers and telecasters. Even though I'm from São Paulo, I hope they don't mind if I speak about the growing militias in Rio de Janeiro."

Luke reminded himself of the historical rivalry between Brazil's two largest cities.

The writer paused and warned, "Take special care during your study mission and avoid any allies of the PCC."

Luke gave the writer a loose hug and saw him enter a black Volvo waiting in front of the restaurant. The car did a U-turn on Avenida Atlântica and sped north toward downtown.

The sun disappeared into a bank of clouds, and Luke sat down again at his table. The waiter asked if he'd like anything else.

Taking a moment to collect his thoughts, Luke decided to order Brazil's national drink, the *caipirinha*, made from rough rum, key lime juice, and sugar over ice. The tropical cocktail was all he could think of to calm his jangling nerves.

CHAPTER 5

Paraisópolis, São Paulo
Tuesday Midday, August 10

VERA STOOD FIVE FEET TALL WITH CURLY BLACK HAIR framing a round face, taut with fear. A local dealer had just grabbed her by the shoulder and pushed her inside this mud-and-stick hut in the middle of São Paulo's largest favela, numbering 180,000 souls. "The boss man wants to have a word with you.".

The woman didn't reply but peeked out of the window to a hodgepodge of makeshift casitas of wood, brick, and tin, climbing the hill toward the chic neighborhood of Morumbí. She heard sewer water gushing down gutters outdoors and closed her eyes to meditate and pray.

"Did you hear what I said?" the man over six foot tall exclaimed, a gold chain with a Star of David swaying around his massive neck. Though Afro-Brazilian as well, his eyes emanated no light and did not waver. He stared directly at Vera and pulled out a .45 caliber pistol from his waistband. A body lay immobile across the threshold of the back door. Apparently, the boss had accused him of being a snitch and shot him on the spot.

Vera opened her eyes and shuddered, fearing the young man was dead. She spied a vulture circling overhead and wished she had wings to fly away.

"Senhor, I am a social worker and do my best to protect children and women from violence. They take me into confidence so I may provide them medical help from trauma or injuries. I am their link between families and community services. If I become an informer, why would anyone believe in my word anymore? How could I do my duty as social worker and fulfill my destiny to serve our people?"

"Stop this talk about your social work! And destiny—what *merda!* It may end today if you don't answer my question. Who else did you see in that home that harbored this snitch for the military police? I have no time for this." He waved his pistol before her face.

Vera forced herself to swallow. "Senhor, I am not a snitch but a social worker and rely on people's trust. I let the judiciary system run its course and do not interfere. My responsibility is to provide health services to battered women, children, and families so they survive these hard times. I cannot be party to anyone's death."

"But you wouldn't have to do the act. That's the job for my boys here," the boss man retorted, grazing her damp cheek with the cold revolver.

She cringed. After a few seconds, Vera murmured, "Senhor, if I were to give you his name, I would be an accomplice to murder and would be more guilty than the person pulling the trigger. I cannot do that. Kill me if you must, senhor, but I cannot denounce anyone who confides in me. If my calling is to die right now, I am at peace with the Lord."

The boss frowned but slowly turned away. If only he could find brave militiamen like this pint-sized social worker, he mused. He stepped over the body and exited this ramshackle hut. "Watch her," he shouted over his shoulder.

His two henchmen shared a baffled look, wondering what to do with this squat woman, still quivering before them.

Hours passed. Finally, the shorter of the two men received a text and took Vera roughly by the arm. They left the hut and wound their way down a dirt path, past residents who looked the other way. The neighborhood grew quiet as the three descended the favela to the paved street a hundred yards below.

Putting her on a packed bus, the shorter fellow commanded, "Don't come back," patting his revolver under a loose-fitting shirt. He lingered as the bus pulled out into late afternoon traffic to begin its climb toward the exotic world of Morumbí.

Vera gazed out the window to mansions surrounded by high walls, lush tress, and roving guards. She wondered what it'd be like to live in one of these compounds, compared to her humble kitchenette. She'd enjoy the respite for a while. But after a few days, without her work on behalf of São Paulo's invisible women, what would be her purpose in life? She followed in the footsteps of her mother and father to serve people of her community. So, too, did most of her living siblings.

Her old Samsung buzzed, indicating a new message via WhatsApp. The American prof had landed safely in Rio with his students and wanted to get together. He had spoken with Vera about visiting her green initiatives in the favela. She had agreed but had suggested interviewing some of the battered mothers and children who had turned their lives around in Paraisópolis. But after today's confrontation, should she dare bring them here?

The bus driver downshifted to skirt a crash between a pickup truck and a delivery motorcycle for Rodeio, a trendy Brazilian BBQ. An ER attendant was applying a tourniquet around the young cyclist's leg. Blood gushed out onto the damp pavement. Vera proclaimed aloud, "Thank God, he's alive," and other passengers gave a thumb's up. The bus continued past the accident through the worker suburbs as Vera nodded off.

She awoke just in time for her stop at Guarulhos and tramped home in the gathering gloom. Overhead, planes flew to land at São Paulo's international airport. Vera was at wits' end and needed a hug. As a professional thoroughly dedicated to her work, she had avoided marital ties. Her family, her community, and her faith kept her going. In moments like this, she tried not to ask herself if her commitment to help battered women and children was worth the sacrifice. Right now, she just wanted to embrace some human being and to be consoled.

An older lady of the project, wearing a homemade mask, said a quick "Good evening" but moved away before Vera could touch her shoulder. Weighed down by today's events, Vera felt loneliness creeping into hidden crevices. In the dark, she held the railing to ascend the many stairs to her third-floor flat. The hallway light was still out, but she saw no one loitering in the shadows.

The social worker took several deep breaths and pushed the squeaking door open. Vera stumbled on a loose tile, searching for the light. On entering the drab studio, she felt something fuzzy rub her leg, reminding her how much she yearned for a human touch. She really needed a hug.

CHAPTER 6

Copacabana, Rio de Janeiro, en route to the Northwestern Suburbs
Wednesday Morning, August 11

THE MINIVAN, WHICH LUKE HAD ARRANGED ONLINE, showed up a half-hour late. The driver took the scenic route past Sugar Loaf on Botafogo Bay, through downtown Rio, and up Avenida Presidente Vargas past miles of workers' suburbs in the north. Due to their late start, the traffic moved slowly out of town. The driver swung onto BR 101, the highway going to Rio's West Zone, where militias controlled vast swaths of this suburb of over three hundred thousand.

As they exited to Campo Grande, they passed a checkpoint with a pair of military police holding semi-automatic weapons. The driver knew the MPs, who waved the minivan on, and entered the Brahma-Antarctica brewery, their first destination. At the company's entrance, another armed guard lifted the barrier and pointed to a parking space under eucalyptus trees. Luke met the corporate PR man, whose white beard and potbelly reminded Luke of Santa Claus.

They toured the brewery and heard a pitch from Santa about

how the firm was using green methods of brewing, recycling water and growing hops with organic fertilizer. He also showed off the eucalyptus grove and smiled proudly to his audience—especially to Tatiana.

The highlight of the visit was to tip a few *cervejas* at the corporate bar, putting everyone in a better mood.

The PR guy did not directly answer Luke's question about police checkpoints or local militias. Instead, he evasively said, "You can never have too much security."

Luke thanked him and proceeded to the minivan, whose driver was chatting with the guard. They reversed course down BR 101 and drove through the tunnel under Corcovado, returning to Rio's ritzy South Zone

On arrival to their second destination, Luke asked the driver to return in two hours' time. He and Tatiana guided the class through the main gate of Rio's Botanical Garden, a 338-acre park featuring seven thousand species of tropical plants, birds, and animals. They learned that early specimens were collected by the Catholic Church on this land and later enhanced by the arrival of Portugal's fleeing royal family in 1808. To protect Brazil from Napoleon, they set up a gunpowder factory but also accepted exotic plants from visiting Portuguese captains. Dom João VI encouraged the importation of species from Africa and the West Indies and became a strong advocate for this botanical preserve. The plantation evolved into a public garden for Rio's residents in 1822, the year Brazil declared its independence from Portugal.

The group gazed up at the Corcovado hill as the right arm of Christ the Redeemer was breaking through the clouds. Luke felt more at peace. He led the class through the Avenue of the Palms, bordered by hundreds of royal palms. A half-mile inside, they arrived at a cast-iron fountain spurting water. A sign stated that UNESCO had designated the gardens as a biosphere reserve in 1992 and Brazil had identified Jardim Botânico as its unique national heritage.

They approached the Fountain of the Muses, whose four figures represented music, art, poetry, and science. On its far side, Luke spied a man walking back and forth. Of medium height, the man had a shock of black hair and trimmed black beard that contrasted with an elegant gray goatee. Hidden behind sunglasses, the man had the air of a Hollywood producer and not a federal policeman. He betrayed his trade by looking constantly over his shoulder and, with his hands at the ready, awaited his contact under a thicket of bamboo trees.

"Alexandre?" Luke inquired.

The man inclined his head. "Professor Shannon, tudo bem?" he responded, the suggestion of a smile on his lips.

"All is well. Thank you for taking the time to meet, despite the restrictions placed on you. After our WhatsApp chat, it's great to meet you in person," Luke exclaimed, offering his hand.

They shook and shared a loose hug.

"Let me speak briefly with my class, and then let's take a walk around the garden," Luke said. He returned to the fountain and asked Tatiana to continue the garden tour with her classmates and to meet back in an hour. He had previously mentioned that he'd scheduled a private meeting with a confidential informant about the forces at play in the Amazon. Tatiana guided the class toward the mountains and smiled coyly at Luke's visitor before moving on.

Luke paused and let his informant lead the way from the arbored avenue to a footpath through the forest. A friend at

Thomson Reuters had connected Luke with Alexandre, the former chief of the Federal Police of Manaus in the Amazon region. The Policia Federal was well regarded and well paid, considered *la crème de la crème* of Brazil's law enforcement. Its men and women were often compared to the American FBI for their diligence and integrity.

The two walked in silence for several minutes, hearing the birdsong of the Brazilian *sabiá*. Luke loved the luxurious air, scented by wild orchids and exotic bromeliads. At a crossroads, his guide aimed toward an obscure greenhouse, examining the surroundings with care.

"Thank you for taking time to meet in person, and please call me Lucas," Luke said. "Your story piqued my interest as you were in charge of the largest seizure of illegal lumber in the Amazon. Though you applied current law, why did authorities disapprove your actions? My class and I are trying to understand agribusiness's influence on deforestation in Brazil. Your insights are welcome."

"Lucas, it's been a difficult year for us in law enforcement. Brasilia has turned a blind eye to illegal loggers, miners and land grabbers on federal and indigenous lands. As you're aware, the former minister of environment, Ricardo Salles, was denounced by the agricultural attaché of the US embassy for trafficking illegally sourced hardwood. How can we apply federal regulations if federal ministers flout the law? I called Salles out, and the minister of justice had me reassigned to a small town outside of Rio. Some have called my predicament a political form of house arrest. They're letting me complete my doctorate in criminal justice in order to keep me quiet. They permitted me to come to Rio today since a colleague wanted me to examine a case involving pirated hardwood."

They walked around a pond with huge water lily pads shaded by several tall Brazilwood trees, native to the Atlantic Forest. A few people were watching fish jump as vultures flew hungrily overhead. "Alexandre, I heard that you and a friend composed "SOS Amazônia," a song about pirated Amazon hardwood. Is it true that it will be featured at the COP26 conference in Glasgow, Scotland? Congratulations on your composition and for standing up for the rainforests. The powers that be don't seem to be succeeding in keeping you too quiet."

The policeman smiled. "We do what we can, my new friend, and yes, "SOS Amazônia" will be heralded at the environmental conference, though it's doubtful the president and his handlers will sing along. Let me share a few verses with you:

> Burns are illegal. Are synonyms of ignorance.
> Destroy all nature. End this violence!
> The whole world accompanies this ignorance up close.
> We are turning green areas into useless deserts.

"Wow, Alexandre. You are truly a Renaissance man. Maybe you should consider doing a documentary about your story and your music. You'd be a sure hit, even though the minister of justice may not enjoy the lyrics.

"What more can you tell me about current events in the Amazon? We've read reports from the National Institute for Space Research that this is a record year of deforestation with so many trees being cut down all over Brazil."

"Lucas, have you heard about the Ox Bench? The *bancada do boi* is a powerful lobby of ranchers and land barons raising cattle and soybeans and acquiring land wherever they can. They cut down acres of old-growth trees during my tenure in the Amazon for pastureland and, more recently, to plant cash crops. Several have struck deals with the PCC, Brazil's powerful crime syndicate, to harvest hardwood, falsify certification documents, and export to European and American buyers. If only we could find a way to track the hardwood's DNA.

"Minister Salles was involved in this trade but got caught. Thanks to international criticism from governments and NGOs, he had to resign. Brazil's free press also exposed his malfeasance. But the minister of justice did Salles's dirty work and dismissed me from my post in Manaus. I'd served in the Amazon region for years.

"Still, shifty groups and the Ox Bench keep pushing northward into the Amazon basin—especially into the state of Pará. They usually pay off some *posseiros*, who've possessed the land for years and survive by subsistence farming. The Ox Bench's MO is to harvest the valuable hardwood and sell it to illegal brokers who arrange the paperwork for shipment abroad. Afterwards, they burn down the remaining forest and turn it into pasture for cattle or fields for soy.

"Under this administration, its PR machine proclaims that soybean plantations create jobs. They don't admit to the destruction of tropical forests and small farmers' and nut-gatherers' livelihoods. The big boys often fake documents to occupy federal and indigenous lands in order to create larger holdings. Laws don't deter them as long as their political pals provide cover.

"At least, these tropical species of fauna and flora are safe in Rio's botanical gardens," Alexandre concluded, still searching the woods.

A toucan observed them over its large orange beak, and capuchin monkeys whistled to one other on branches of the stately *jacarandá*.

Luke followed him onto another trail leading back to the fountain. They passed through a swarm of pink dragonflies, mesmerized by the sound of their vibrating wings. He marveled how well this former head of Manaus's Federal Police knew his way around Rio's immense park. Perhaps this was his favored venue for clandestine encounters.

Through boughs of a Brazil nut tree, the Fountain of the Muses came into view, giving Alexandre pause.

Tatiana had gathered the students on the fountain's far side, while two Military Police were circling slowly in company with an older, stout man. The plainclothesman scanned the plaza area and pedestrians strolling by.

"Lucas, thank you for hearing me out. It's time for me to go. Let's keep in touch via WhatsApp. Tudo bem?"

Alexandre gave him a loose hug, reversed his course, and quickened his pace. Luke heard him humming his song of protest as the federal policeman disappeared into a low-ceilinged greenhouse shrouded by coconut palms.

Turning around, Luke saw the plainclothesman enter the same trail he was on. Luke slowed his footsteps but came face-to-face with the heavy-set man whose standout feature was his bulbous nose. A question was forming on the cop's lips.

What was Luke going to do?

CHAPTER 7

Rio de Janeiro Botanical Gardens
Wednesday Afternoon, August 11

THEY STARED AT EACH OTHER FOR SEVERAL SECONDS. Luke wiped his palms on the Levi jeans. Since he didn't know what was going on, he kept his cool and stayed quiet.

The plainclothesman ventured, "Tudo bem, my friend? Enjoying a stroll through the woods?"

"Yes, the Botanical Gardens are beautiful, and my class and I have appreciated its peace and quiet," Luke affirmed, waving to Tatiana who had caught his eye.

The plainclothesman turned around and saw her and the students approaching. A few other tourists were nearby snapping shots of the Fountain of Muses. The plainclothesman continued, "You didn't happen to notice a man dressed in a suit during your walk, did you? I thought I saw him on this path a little while ago."

"There was another group of people around the lily pond. Maybe he was with them," Luke said, relieved to see Tatiana come forward and give him a kiss on each cheek,

"Tudo bem, professor?" she said, looking quizzically at Luke and the other man.

"So, you are a professor, then," interjected the heavy-set man, checking out Tatiana and the students around her.

"Yes, we are from Seattle University on a study mission, senhor. Is there anything else I can help you with?" Luke said, hoping to spring free.

"Let me take a look at your passport, professor. It's just a formality but required of all visitors to Brazil."

Luke handed it over without words. The two military police had joined them, resting their hands on their holsters.

The plainclothesman returned it, saying, "That will be all," shaking his head.

Tatiana took Luke by the arm and strolled past the two MPs, who ogled her with pleasure. She smiled and walked toward the park entrance, the class following behind. Luke didn't look back and kept breathing deeply.

He also fretted about his students' safety and their mission in Brazil.

* * *

THAT EVENING, LUKE RECEIVED AN INVITE from a friend whom he'd met in Rio years ago. An entrepreneurial sort, John had founded a business school in São Paulo and supervised virtual courses in business with Portuguese-speaking countries in Africa. The American expat had married a lovely carioca who lived in a fancy apartment in Barra da Tijuca. John spent four days in São Paulo to run his school but left every Thursday afternoon by air shuttle for weekends in Rio. He had invited Luke's class to the Paissandú Athletic Club and three of his students as well. "I have a surprise visitor and mutual friend who may join us," he told Luke with an air of mystery.

The club was tucked away behind Leblon and Ipanema, near the shimmering Freitas Lagoon. On arrival, Luke and his class marveled at the sight of Christ the Redeemer, highlighted by a crescent moon.

John was at the club's entrance and greeted Luke warmly, giving him a tight hug, typical of longstanding friends. His mystery guest was Luke's friend who had helped secure his internship with BankBoston years ago. "Professor Claudio, tudo bem? How are you juggling your classwork in São Paulo and government responsibilities in Rio?"

"Not easily," Claudio replied, giving his American friend a tight hug. He'd just left his downtown office and removed his tie for the festive occasion, but he still wore a friendly smile. Though now in a public position, he retained the inquisitive look of his professorial background. As a Paulista, his schedule was the reverse of John's, spending Friday through Monday morning in São Paulo, where he lectured at the prestigious Fundação Getulio Vargas business school. He was known as a student's friend. Claudio and John were both frequent flyers of the Rio-São Paulo-Rio air shuttle and sometimes crossed paths.

John sported black-framed glasses and curly if unruly hair. He wore a Caribbean-style guayabera but radiated scholarly airs. He guided Luke, Claudio, and Seattle U's students through the courtyard's swaying palms and over the footbridge of the curvy pool.

"I hope a *feijoada* dinner is acceptable to you," John said to Luke. "Brazil's national dish is served every Wednesday and Saturday for lunch, but the club kept some just for us tonight. Your students should have plenty to eat. They've set up a buffet on the terrace. How does that sound?"

"Tudo bem," affirmed Luke enthusiastically. Over a liquid lunch at the brewery, they had only munched on cocktail sandwiches. With the aroma of black beans, pork, and garlic hanging in the air, the students ravenously eyed the buffet. Luke's stomach rumbled in expectation.

The group climbed the sandstone steps to the club's patio, crickets chirping from the gardens. John introduced his three students, and Luke asked their Seattle U counterparts to share a little about themselves. They all ordered Brazil's national libation, the *caipirinha*, encouraging them to speak. Claudio, Luke, and John shared the ups and downs in their own lives, as well as challenges in the classroom.

As the sole Brazilian in Seattle U's ranks, Tatiana offered a mini-lecture about *feijoada*: "This dish evolved in Brazil's northeast region, where slaves worked in the sugarcane fields. To survive, they received scraps of pork from the owners' table, including ears, tails, ribs, and feet. They added garlic, indigenous spices, and black beans, serving it over rice with a side of collard greens. It proved so tasty that the plantation owners asked them to bring the dish inside their manors. It became popular throughout the Northeast, including my home state of Maranhão. Brazilians from southern states like Minas Gerais, Rio, and São Paulo sampled it and loved the zesty concoction. That's how feijoada has become Brazil's national dish."

When the second round of caipirinhas arrived, their conversations rose to a feverish pitch. Attracted by the feijoada's aroma, the students squirmed in their seats. In unison, they rose to serve themselves from the abundant buffet, mounding beans, rice, and all cuts of pork onto their plates. Many went back for second and third helpings. Their hunger satisfied, they began chatting with one another about their future lives, plans, and dreams.

Luke noticed one of John's students looking downcast, not participating in the give-and-take. When the student rose to get dessert, Luke joined him in line. "Tudo bem, Mauro?"

"More or less, professor," he mumbled, not meeting Luke's eye.

"Is there anything I can do to help?" Luke asked, trying to understand the young man's pain.

"I heard your students talk about their job prospects in America. After I graduate next year, what am I to do in Brazil? Unemployment is high and corruption too. I'm from a family in the North Zone with no silver spoon." He paused and murmured, "Professor, I'm sorry to dampen your spirits on this occasion, but that's how I feel. If you find a way for me to work in America, that would give hope. Here, I only feel melancholy."

Mauro left his dessert on the table and turned away from Luke. Excusing himself from the other profs and fellow students, he escaped through the club's back door.

His heart in his mouth, Luke asked himself what he could do for this tormented young man. He also sensed intense emotions boiling just beneath Brazil's tropical façade.

CHAPTER 8

Belém en route to Santarém
Thursday Afternoon, August 12

Lucio accepted a ride by the captain of the ferry boat, departing from Belém's Maritime Terminal. His friend had reserved a first-class cabin on the fourth deck for him. As a younger man, Lucio didn't mind hanging his hammock on the lower decks, but on this trip, he wanted to stay away from the hubbub of tourists, adventurers, and spies.

He hoped his detractors would not pursue him on board. Lucio wanted simply to disappear. Since his daughters had left for Rio to visit friends, he was home alone. Though he'd battled the oligarchy for years, the struggle was wearing on him. Since unknown men treaded on his heels in Belém, days along the Amazon should give him respite. He was looking forward to staying at a friend's guesthouse near Santarém for a pastoral R & R.

So far, he had not crossed paths again with his shadow, who had followed him Monday to the shopping mall.

* * *

When the young man sauntered toward him at the Boulevard Café, Lucio decided to stay put in his chair, waiting to see what would happen next. He felt relatively safe in this public place and knew the manager on duty. Lucio noticed the man did not approach cautiously like a policeman. Rather, he did what Americans would call the ghetto walk, swaying back and forth. He wore an "I Love New York" T-shirt and earbuds, bobbing his head to a musical beat. Lucio guessed his age at around twenty-five and didn't consider him a professional. Still, an amateur could do him harm.

His shadow gave Lucio a surreptitious glance and went inside to order a *cafezinho*. He returned with his little coffee and slumped into a seat two tables away. After fussing with the spoon as he stirred more sugar into the small cup, he peered up at Lucio, who kept his stare. The young man looked away and began humming a song blasting from his earbuds. After a minute, he gave Lucio a questioning glance and mumbled, "You're making important people angry."

"Are you talking to me, young man?" inquired Lucio.

"Ah, yes. You're the old reporter, right?" A moment of doubt spread across his lean face.

"Old I am, and reporting is my profession. Are you a student of journalism, and did you come to interview me?"

The young man burst out laughing and slapped his knee.

Just then, Lucio's cell phone buzzed, indicating a message had arrived on WhatsApp. He saw it came from that persistent American prof. An idea came to him.

"Excuse me, young man."

Feigning speaking on the phone, Lucio made up a conversation with the Seattle U professor, saying "tudo bem" several times. He continued, "You want a photo of where I am seated now? That's fine by me. Let me take one with my new friend, who's followed me to the Boulevard Shopping Mall." Lucio abruptly turned his iPhone around, snapped a few shots of his shadow, and continued talking with himself. "Professor, did you receive the photo yet? Wonderful! Let me ask the man his name." Lucio prepared to question the tall mulatto but instead saw him bolt upright, knocking the table over and coffee cup to the floor.

The young man looked confused and angry. He blurted, "Watch yourself, old man. You've pissed off too many people in town."

Customers in the café peered at the scene, and a middle-age man rose from his seat.

Lucio's shadow spun around and walked away from the café without a second glance.

Messaged delivered.

* * *

FEELING SOMEWHAT SAFE AT THE FERRY TERMINAL, Lucio pushed the Panama hat down over his forehead and clipped on dark glasses. Standing back in the long maritime terminal until most passengers had boarded the *Amazonas,* he didn't want to run into any old-timers or police informants who might recognize him.

Lucio showed his first-class ticket to the porter who waved him to the second deck, above the noise of cars and trucks boarding. A few tourists attempted to hang their hammocks in the open-air, third-class section while batting away the pesky mosquitos. Some local workers chuckled at the gringos' expense. Lucio almost went to their rescue but not today. He wanted to remain incognito, so he scampered up to the third deck and passed through local passengers in the second-class section. They hung their hammocks with dexterity and visited the cafeteria for a little coffee. Though this level was sheltered by closed windows, the sputtering A/C tendered only lukewarm air.

Climbing to the fourth deck and the first-class section, Lucio saw a middle-aged couple whom he vaguely recognized. Lucio slipped quickly inside to avoid any conversation. Pleased that his cabin had a flush toilet and a portal looking out, he folded down his bunk, shut his eyes, and took his afternoon siesta.

The reporter awoke to a shifting deck and dimming light. He washed his face and put his small carryon bag in the tiny closet. Wearing his hat, he entered the vacant passageway and climbed the ladder to the open-air deck. Lucio felt the ferryboat turn to port and noticed the darkened island of Marajó to starboard. Here, the Pará River would mix with streams and tributaries of the Amazon, creating the Strait of Breves. He hoped the captain had followed local tradition and tossed an offering to the river's spirits to guarantee safe passage

Lucio decided to stay on the deck until the riverboat landed at its first stop, the community of Macapá. He overheard a couple of fishermen trading stories about their recent catches. They all gazed out at the strait and the setting sun.

"My son caught this huge *pirarucú* weighing more than two hundred pounds and attempted to lug it on his shoulders. Even after he called another fisherman, they barely hauled the monster ashore. It yielded them several reais and steaks to take home for dinner. My son's prize measured over six feet, but I've seen bigger boys exceeding ten feet.

"The pirarucú is one of the largest fish in the world. It is difficult to hook and more difficult to land. My son used hundred-pound carbon test line and a huge fly to attract its attention. He's caught smaller ones of four feet long chasing schools of fish on the surface. For the big boy, he had to go upriver from Monte Alegre and cast his fly into their out-of-the-way pools. Luckily, those illegal miners hadn't polluted that water yet," he confided.

"Further up the Amazon, we may see some of the monster fish surface. It needs to come up for air every twenty minutes or so. I wish I'd brought my son's steel rod with me."

Lucio recalled that the pirarucu, or the giant Arapaima, belong to a carnivorous, air-breathing fish group of pre-historic age. The big fish crush its prey with a large tongue studded with sharp teeth. It seeks out oxygen-poor waters to feed off smaller fish, which became torpid and slow. During the dry season, the fish build up large fat reserves, needed for parental duties to come. Because of its red scales, indigenous tribes named it "pirarucú" meaning "red fish." It has a peculiar profile, with a long and narrow front body, a flat rear, and a rounded tail.

He had enjoyed many a pirarucú barbeque with residents along the Amazon. On special occasions, riverine villages offered savory dishes highlighting this traditional fish. He'd attended festivals celebrating the town's anniversary or saint's day. In others, he'd commemorated the arrival of the dry season and the end of floods. "Why not?" thought Lucio. A fiesta to raise the villagers' spirits was always welcome.

Once, he watched native cooks use the pirarucú's razor-sharp tongues to grate chicory roots used in a spicy stew. Licking his lips, he almost smelled the aroma of the fish simmering in a large pot with sweet potatoes, coconut milk, and palm oil. A touch of lime, cilantro, and *malagueta* pepper gave the dish an extraordinary flavor.

The fishermen kept praising the pirarucú and how it provided protein in the family diet. In the fading light, they spied a miner swirling water in a pan seeking some kind of ore from a bubbling stream. The taller man asked, "What will happen to our fish if the authorities continue to look the other way? These illegal miners, or *garimpeiros*, still dump mercury into our creeks. What will become of our big fish, which have sustained us for generations? We have to protect our companions in the River Sea. They need our help. There may come a time that we'll have to battle these invading miners."

Lucio inclined his head and was about to join the fishermen's conversation. Instead, he squinted at a heavy-set man who slipped through an emergency access to the top deck. Lucio had seen him before in a Belém precinct of the civil police. Two years ago, he and a colleague had interrogated this detective about his ties to plantation owners taking land from squatters. They suspected that some police pushed out the *posseiros* so the big boys could plant soybeans on their land. This cop was also accused of organizing assassinations of indigenous leaders who fought against invaders. Lucio's sources said the detective had recently constructed a four-thousand-square-foot mansion in a prime neighborhood. Police sources called him "a bad apple." Another BBC journalist affirmed, "He's owned by the vested interests. Beware."

Yet here he was on this riverboat, scanning the travelers on deck.

Lucio pulled his Panama hat further down, even though light was fading, and walked purposefully toward the hatch leading down to the first-class section. He didn't want to cross paths with this dirty cop ever again.

Suddenly, the man turned around and aimed toward the same exit, looking right and left.

Lucio hastened his stride. This trip was supposed to be a

break from cops and snoops; he was tired of playing this game of cat and mouse. He had to reach the safety of his stateroom, or else he'd be toast.

A voice behind him exclaimed, "Don't I know you from Belém?"

CHAPTER 9

The Jockey Club, Rio de Janeiro
Friday Afternoon, August 13

THE TWO MEN REGARDED EACH OTHER and cautiously entered the special dining room overlooking the race track. They both stood six feet two inches tall. The older man wore a Savile Row light-wool suit and a striped rep silk tie over a white shirt showing cufflinks of the Colombian flag. His black hair was streaked with gray, and his complexion suggested Mediterranean roots.

The younger man appeared restless and wore a navy-blue sports coat over a beige Tommy Hilfiger polo shirt. His rosy face glowed from a day on the links at the nearby Gávea Golf Club. Checking himself in a mirror's reflection, he thought he had put on more weight. Flavio cleared his throat and thought he should take command of this meeting.

He was saved by a knock on the mahogany door by a family confidant who had set up this tête-à-tête. "Queiroz, tudo bem? It's been too long. I'm so glad you were able to get us together today. Please make the introductions," Flavio said, giving his assistant a tight hug.

Flavio had known Queiroz for decades. His fixer had loyally served his family in many capacities. Since the congressional inquiry about the "little cracks" of payoffs, Queiroz had been in and out of prison. He proved to be a standup friend and stone-walled the investigators. Flavio had asked his father to apply pressure through the minister of justice to release Queiroz.

"Senhor Flavio, it is my pleasure to present a friend of a friend, Dom Luis, who is also a member of the Jockey Club. In fact, I believe one of his yearlings is going to race today. Thank you for sponsoring our get-together, senhor," Queiroz said, approaching the Colombiano tentatively before giving him a loose hug.

"My pleasure, senhores," the older man returned, approaching Flavio to offer a handshake and loose hug. Luis's second cousin had met Queiroz several years ago when the militias had tried to ship gold and hardwood through the Amazon to European ports. The senator's fix-it man had ties to Rio's militias, the Red Command, and the now-deceased northern crime family. Queiroz had once asked his cousin Otoniel to arrange fake documents to ship contraband from the Manaus Free Trade Zone.

Otoniel's greed and hot temper, however, riled up local Customs inspectors, who tipped off the Federal Police. The Feds busted Otoniel and gained acclaim. As the head of Colombia's Gulf Clan, known for violence and drug trafficking to Europe, Otoniel was a major prize. Brazil and Colombia's ministers of justice patted themselves on their backs and crowed about their successful war on crime. Now his cousin was languishing in a Brazilian jail, awaiting extradition. His destination was where no Colombian ever wanted to set foot, inside a federal court in the United States.

"Shall we order lunch before the race begins?" asked Luis, leading them to a table for three overlooking the downs. The dishware bore the Jockey Club logo, and the glasses were crystal. An elegant chandelier hung overhead. They sat in red-upholstered chairs and gazed at trainers walking the yearlings around the track. Luis pressed a button under the table, and a waiter in a white, starched jacket entered through a side door, two bodyguards standing outside.

Flavio ordered a double Johnny Walker on the rocks, and Queiroz followed suit. Luis asked for a Campari and tonic with a twist of lime. They engaged in small talk about the weather and soccer. When their drinks arrived, they toasted "chin-chin," the Brazilian version of cheers.

The waiter took their orders, with Flavio and Queiroz opting for rare chateaubriand "with lots of blood" and Luis a filet of *badejo* sea bass with capers in butter sauce.

When their meals arrived, all three dodged the underlying reason for their rendezvous. Flavio and Queiroz also ordered Spanish Grenache to accompany their rare steaks, eating and drinking with relish.

Into the conversational void, the luncheon's host recounted his affair with horses. "When I was a young boy, I was tasked to feed and care for these noble beasts. It was love at first sight. We understood each other without need of words. Horses were my safe zone during tumultuous times in my family and my country. As an adolescent, I rode yearlings and raced bareback on the plains of Colombia. Like Brazil's former president João Batista Figueiredo, I often prefer the company of horses to men. We know where we stand. With homo sapiens, it's never easy to read their minds. Agreed?"

Queiroz sucked in his cheeks and looked at his boss for guidance.

After a moment, Flavio responded, "Yes. The minds of politicians I deal with are always a work in progress. It's like peeling an onion through many layers to discover what lies at its core. Once I uncover what the pol desires—prestige, power, or money—I try to accommodate. But I always keep my eyes and ears open. Their public views can change without notice. To survive, I must cultivate informants inside and out of government and keep abreast of what's lurking under their pronouncements."

"Well said, Senhor Flavio."

They waited for the waiter to clear the plates and ordered coconut flan all around.

When dessert arrived, Luis inquired, "Senhor Queiroz, how may I be of service to you and your friend?"

"Senhor Luis, thank you for hosting us here at the Jockey Club. I wish your yearling well this afternoon." Queiroz sported a two-day's stubble and forced a smile. Into the silence, he continued: "As you're aware, our ties with the northern family have taken a hit this last year. We thought the removal of the Policia Federal's chief in Manaus would let us have a freer hand, especially in the export of hardwood. But our rivals in São Paulo are pushing their weight around. It's now difficult for us to make shipments from the Amazon basin. You know that area well. We thought you may have ideas to help us out."

"Understood, Senhor Queiroz. What do you have in mind for my associates, and what should they expect for this accommodation?" replied Luis, looking intently at both men.

Flavio shifted in his seat, nodding at his associate to respond.

Queiroz played with his napkin. "Senhor Luis, we have patriotic lumbermen who need transport from outlying areas where they harvest hardwood. Even though the Feds' presence has been cut back, São Paulo's PCC is filling the void. We need help in logistics and understand you have access to a fleet of Cessnas. We'd be willing to share the profits with you. On our investment, we expect double or triple returns. We could also provide political cover. We have friends with some *policia civil* in Pará. Tudo bem?"

Interrupting the silence were Flavio's cell phone and the club's announcement of the horses approaching the gate. Flavio excused himself and retreated to the corner.

Luis viewed the jockeys mount their yearlings and stood up to witness the start. After a couple of minutes, the bell rang, and eight horses galloped around the track for one and a quarter miles. Luis shouted, "*Ándale*," and raised his fist. He cheered as his horse, Belleza, placed second in the afternoon event. Pleased, Luis smiled broadly and patted Queiroz on the back.

Flavio returned. "Thank you, Senhor Luis. After speaking with your associates, please let Queiroz know what cooperation your group could provide. Unfortunately, Brasilia is calling and I must attend to the people's business.

"It's been a pleasure. Let's have our cafezinho another time. Perhaps, if we come to an understanding?"

"Very well, senhores. Let me accompany you out, so you don't get lost in the Jockey's corridors," said Luis. Just then, the club's audio system played Tom Jobim's famous tune, "Matita Perê," making the Colombian cock his head. His guests looked a bit annoyed, so he quietly led them through the back hallways and through the club's main entrance. They shook hands and exchanged loose hugs. The two Brazilians walked out to the turnabout and entered a black Volvo, which swept them away.

Luis Carlos, followed by his bodyguards, peered at the bronze statue of Linneo de Paula Machado, godfather of Brazilian horse racing. Linneo, like Luis, possessed a passion for thoroughbreds. That was why Luis had become a member in Rio's traditional jockey club and socialized in its VIP lounges. This was his comfort zone in the Marvelous City.

He ambled back to the club's entrance as aficionados were leaving the afternoon competition. Luis wanted to congratulate the jockey and the trainer, as well as to nuzzle Belleza, for their stirring performances.

Before reentering, he noticed a man his age approaching Linneo's statue. He was leading a group of young people and pointing toward the bronze sculpture. Luis appreciated the man's enthusiasm and took another glance. He had the appearance of an Americano and, though older now, had the manner of someone Luis had met years ago. Luis never forgot a face and thought they had once crossed paths at that bar along the Jari River. At the time, in his early twenties, he was just learning the ropes from his older cousin. Luis looked back on pleasant memories, especially with the seductive native dancer, who had swayed to Jobim's bossa nova. Maybe it was the same man.

If so, what was he doing at the Jockey Club, and who was that gorgeous woman by his side?

CHAPTER 10

Rio de Janeiro, en route to São Paulo
Saturday Afternoon, August 14

Thankfully, Tatiana knew her way around the Novo
Rio terminal with its dozens of bus lanes for destinations all
over Brazil. She had negotiated with the travel agency next to their
Copacabana hotel a special discount for ten seats with reclining
beds on the Expresso do Sul's 1230 bus. Tatiana had arranged a fee
of twenty dollars for each passenger, not a bad price for this 260-
mile trip to the industrial capital of Brazil.

Luke was happy to observe passengers masked up and concluded that Brazil's community health system deserved a lot of
credit. Despite early denials from the presidential palace about the
need to vaccinate, Brazilians had sought the Covid-19 shot whenever available. Initially, only Sinovac was on the market. More
recently, however, state health authorities had imported the Pfizer
and AstraZeneca's vaccines, making them available to health cen-
ters in their respective states.

Friends told him that Pfizer had offered to sell Brazil forty million doses in 2020 but had refused to pay a gratuity for each shot

to some entity offshore. As the story went, the Chinese and Indian firms had agreed to do so. The Chinese had delivered the vaccine formula, working with São Paulo's Butantã's Institute, but the Indian firm had not. As there was still more demand than supply for any vaccine, wealthier Brazilians often traveled to Miami for a "medical" holiday, including shopping and nightlife in South Beach.

Tatiana led them through the throngs and arrived at the thirty-fourth lane for Expresso do Sul bus to São Paulo. The conductor opened the sleek Mercedes doors and started scanning their tickets. They looked across the platform at another bus, which had seen better days. It was boarding a more diverse public with cages of birds and large bundles, its destination for Maranhão in Brazil's Northeast. Luke happily entered their sleeper bus, whose A/C was blasting for the six-hour trip. Tatiana had arranged Luke's seat to be up front, away from the students in the back. Luke appreciated her thoughtfulness, as she was aware of his habit to take an afternoon siesta.

A middle-age woman sat next to him, and wished him "Good afternoon." Luke returned her greeting. As her cell phone went off, she began instructing someone how to feed her poodle while she was away in São Paulo. Luke tuned her out as the Expresso pulled out of the terminal.

Luke noticed a few tugboats and many Petrobras oil tankers anchored in Guanabara Bay. They passed worker suburbs in the North Zone and continued through the lowlands of Rio de Janeiro. The Baixada Fluminese was a hodgepodge of makeshift structures, where workers migrated to build affordable dwellings. Now, these suburbs, like Duque de Caxias and Nova Iguaçú, had become sprawling cities, with municipal governments and militias vying for power. Their bustling interurban population numbered over two million anxious souls.

He smiled at the daily scenes of kids kicking soccer balls in vacant lots and merchants selling housewares, birds, fruits, produce, and meat in open-air markets. Horse-drawn carriages bumped along cobblestone alleys, and turkey vultures soared in currents overhead. Daily life continued on.

The Expresso do Sul accelerated and veered onto Brazil's Route 116, or the Via Dutra. Named after President Eurico Dutra, the toll road became Brazil's first super-highway seventy years ago. It connected Brazil's two main cities, Rio de Janeiro and São Paulo, and was the lifeline to spur economic growth along the corridor. It remained the arterial for truckers, buses, and private vehicles between the two metropoles and supported towns and cities in populous southeastern Brazil.

The bus's motion and the woman's conversation lulled Luke to sleep, and he began dreaming of Tatiana and the Colombian man. She was teaching the Colombiano how to dance the samba and laughed at his stiff attempts. The musical beat changed to bossa nova and brought them together cheek to cheek. Luke was viewing the scene from inside a glass cage suspended overhead. He detected a sly look on the Colombiano's face and tapped the pane to warn his student. Tatiana did not look up but continued dancing without concern. Their images appeared distorted to Luke as in a carnival mirror. Luke pounded all the harder on the glass but to no avail. A smokescreen descended and covered the couple below. All Luke could see was his reflection off the glass.

He woke up with a start, his head bumping against the window. Looking outside, the bus rumbled past green fields and rolling hills, shrouded by low-lying fog. Once again, he shook his head, upset that the Colombiano had penetrated his dream.

The impromptu meeting outside the Jockey Club was the

great surprise so far this trip. He learned that Luis Carlos owned thoroughbreds and enjoyed horse racing, but Luke questioned if that was his real game in 2021. Dressed in an elegant suit and shadowed by bodyguards, the Colombian had certainly moved up in the world. Luke vaguely recalled him hanging out in that rough bar along the Jari River and the Xingú maiden dancing to Jobim's tunes. He fingered the card in his pocket and noticed that it listed two addresses: one in Belém do Pará and another in Leticia, Colombia. "Thoroughbred" was printed on top, along with a horsehead logo.

Tatiana seemed quite taken by him. She also had accepted his card and gave him a kiss on each cheek, typical among good friends in Rio de Janeiro. That Tatiana had entered Luke's dream with the Colombian jolted the professor. He turned around to check and saw his prized student turning under a blanket. Her classmates were also catching a few winks, as was the woman next to him.

The bus slowed when a sign for Aparecida, São Paulo, came into view. Luke saw the winding Paraiba River and recalled the story of the three fishermen in 1717. The town leader had dispatched them to procure the community's meal from the river in honor of the visiting governor. The men cast their nets for over an hour but secured nothing but minnows. One fisherman invoked the name of Our Lady of the Immaculate Conception, praying that God would grant them a good catch.

They flung their nets again and one dragged up a headless statue. Another salvaged a darken head and put it aside. He played out the net a final time and pulled in a multitude of fish. Together they praised the Virgin for her benevolence. They cleaned the statue and the head and joined the parts together. They were shocked to see that it was a black version of Our Lady of the Immaculate Conception. Something special had just happened.

For years following the discovery, admirers and pilgrims came from all over, especially Afro-Brazilians, to offer prayers to the black Madonna. Veneration of the Aparecida Virgin (Appearing Virgin) gained more followers as many miracles were attributed to her name. A respected family built a chapel to encase the statue in the eighteenth century. It was later enshrined in the local basilica. The town was renamed Aparecida in 1928 to honor Brazil's patron saint, Our Lady of Aparecida.

Luke was astonished at the size of the new basilica, which could hold up to forty-five thousand persons. It was designed by a famous architect in the form of a Greek cross. Only St. Peter's Basilica in the Vatican was larger.

When Brazil's Pentecostal churches grew rapidly in the 1970s and 1980s, the image of the black Madonna became a source of conflict between Catholics and Protestants. One zealot of a Protestant sect removed the image from its stand and ran out of the basilica with it under his arms. Chased by attendants, the statue fell and broke into pieces. Local artisans painstakingly reassembled the statue and restored the black Madonna to the altar. The image of the Aparecida Virgin had since become a cause célèbre between Catholics, protecting their traditional faith, and the growing Evangelical movement in Brazil.

Since this was an unscheduled stop, Luke wondered if the driver had decided to show off the famous cathedral to tourists on board. As the bus approached the basilica's entrance and its immense parking lot, a guard flagged it down. After some words through the window, the driver opened the door to permit a slim, middle-aged man to enter. The driver didn't seem perturbed and spoke briefly with the new passenger. They both turned to search the back of the bus.

Tatiana rose from her chaise and approached the front, touching Luke on his shoulder as she passed by.

What on earth was going on now?

CHAPTER 11

Aparecida to São Paulo
Saturday Evening, August 14

TATIANA PRESSED HER NOSE TO THE WINDOW as the glow grew
larger. The bus had just passed through São José dos Campos,
where Brazil's aerospace industry and space research agency are
housed. She turned away from the window and became absorbed
in conversation with the mysterious visitor from Aparecida. She
had secured the man's WhatsApp number from a relative in her
home state of Maranhão and made contact with him while boarding the bus in Rio.

The man was a representative of the Indigenous Missionary
Council, a grassroots organization to support indigenous people
and to help them survive encroachments by invaders throughout
the Amazon basin. As the tribes had worked with this Catholic
group, known by its acronym CIMI, for fifty years, they had a part-
nership of trust and respect. Despite its shoestring budget, CIMI
and the tribes battled illegal miners, woodcutters, and ranchers,
egged on by the current administration. The press was their strategic friend.

A missionary of sorts, the man had been visiting a priest in Aparecida when Tatiana had reached him by Zap, the name Brazilians used for WhatsApp. Thanks to the simpatico Catholic driver and the helpful parking attendant, the man was able to catch a ride on this bus heading to the big city. Since the CIMI rep worked with thirteen thousand members of the Guajajara nation, it was providential to meet Tatiana with the same tribal roots.

She peppered him with questions about her relatives and how her people were faring against the onslaught of outsiders, often armed. Her eyes brimmed as he shared news of death and misery in the villages. When he recounted the events leading to Paulinho Guajajara's assassination by vigilantes two years ago, Tatiana turned away. Paulinho was her distant cousin and renowned as the tribe's guardian of the forest.

Even though her classmates didn't speak Portuguese, the two kept their voices low. Other passengers on the bus might have ties to big landowners who did not want CIMI anywhere near their plantations. They did not appreciate the missionaries publicly protesting abuses of indigenous and worker rights. The Ox Bench's strategy was to acquire land when no one was looking, clear it, and plant soybeans as quietly as possible. They didn't want any do-gooder raising a ruckus or attracting the nosy press. The missionary gave Tatiana his card with his Zap number and wrote the number of her cousin.

"*Muito obrigada,*" she thanked him, touching him on his shoulder.

The sign for Guarulhos International Airport flashed by. The missionary told her he planned to stay with a friend in this workers' suburb outside São Paulo. The friendly driver had agreed to drop him off near the airport.

Tatiana pushed the stop button, and the bus slowed and halted under a pedestrian bridge. The visitor and Tatiana got up, exchanged two kisses, and bid each other a warm goodbye. The mystery man thanked the driver and disappeared into the evening fog, typical of winter in São Paulo. Meanwhile, jet engines roared overhead, preparing to land at this metropole's primary airport.

The lights grew brighter as the Expresso do Sul drove through worker boroughs and makeshift favelas, approaching the city's North Zone. Fighting through early evening traffic, the driver arrived at the Tietê terminal, which sprawled for blocks. It was the largest bus complex in Latin America. After New York's Port Authority, Tietê was the second largest terminus in the world. Thousands of people milling around in this huge station made Tatiana catch her breath.

The last time she visited South America's largest city had been five years ago, when a distant cousin had gotten married to a middle-class Paulista man. The wedding reception had taken place in the chic Pinheiros Club in the city's South Zone with much hoopla and live entertainment. Her cousin had seemed happy, but Tatiana hadn't fit in. She had hardly known anyone and hadn't liked the way the well-heeled guests had looked down on her. Very few people of color had been in attendance.

Tatiana had also been astounded by the never-ending sea of vehicles and lights in this megalopolis of twenty-two million. The streets were clogged with all makes of cars, trucks, buses, motorcycles, and scooters in pell-mell motion. She had witnessed accidents, often involving motor bikers, which snarled traffic for miles. Though drivers fumed, this was São Paulo. Getting stuck in traffic was commonplace, especially when it rained.

After five days in the big city, the decibel levels had overwhelmed Tatiana, so she had departed early to her adopted town in the Pacific Northwest. At the age of thirteen, coming from a quiet village in Brazil to Seattle had been a big step for her. São Paulo was three times the size of the whole state of Washington and much, much louder.

Now Tatiana shivered at the thought of returning to Brazil's "city that never sleeps." She tried to boost her courage for what lay ahead.

* * *

HER MOTHER HAD CALLED TATIANA "THE NEGOTIATOR," as she was the first of the twins to leave her womb in robust health. As a child, she managed to secure food for the family with her steady look at more prosperous villagers. Tatiana had to negotiate to stay alive. Shortly after turning eight years old, Tati, as she was called by the tribe, lost her mom to undiagnosed breast cancer. She bore her grief silently, but her siblings wailed day and night. Fortunately, Tati had endeared herself to another neighbor who adopted her as a "child of creation," a frequent relationship among humble, indigenous communities.

Tati's brother and twin sister were sent elsewhere in the Guajajara nation. Her older brother later disappeared chasing a get-rich-quick scheme in the North. Later, her twin died from a stream's poisoned water, caused by an illegal miner's runoff. Thanks to Tati's adopted mother, the girl went to a school set up by CIMI missionaries. She learned to read and write in the thatch-roofed classroom but usually stayed quiet in class. Nevertheless, when she spoke up, students listened. The teacher considered her the brightest pupil in the community.

Yet, misery haunted Tatiana. When a storm broke, a flash flood washed her adoptive mother and her thatched hut away. At age eleven, Tati lost the second *mamai* of her young life. Again, she grieved quietly. Though the villagers offered sympathy, Tati knew she had to fend for herself.

Trapped in town during that tropical storm, an American missionary learned of Tati's predicament and was moved. He had met her before in class and admired her spark of life. Speaking with the village elder, the missionary offered to become responsible for Tati in the United States. After several days of discussion, the chief agreed, and CIMI's attorney volunteered to navigate the bureaucracy of the ministry of justice. A bishop intervened, and a year of negotiations ensued. At last, CIMI secured the ministry's imprimatur for Tati to exit Brazil.

Another eight months transpired dealing with US immigration officials in Brasilia, who reluctantly granted her a tourist visa valid for ten years. The missionary's sister, a middle school teacher in Issaquah, a suburb east of Seattle, agreed to become Tati's official sponsor. At the age of thirteen, Tatiana took her first flight by airplane, five time zones to the west. Trembling, she landed at SeaTac airport on a rainy day in March.

In her new country, Tatiana was dumbfounded at the fast pace of life, the many cars on paved roads, and the abundance of everything in supermarkets. It was her first time to shop in any big store. Her American mother taught English and learned a little Portuguese online in order to communicate with her. She praised Tatiana as a quick learner. With the school's permission, the woman took her Brazilian daughter to her language arts class. Once in school, Tati picked up English fast. She joined the pupils on fieldtrips, including a visit to the Cascade Mountains. It was the first time Tatiana had ever seen or touched snow. She was thrilled and screamed for joy as the snowflakes melted in her palm.

Yet Tatiana's favorite pastime was to sit by the Issaquah Creek and listen to the rushing water, the rustle of the willow trees, and the robin's song. She learned that "Issaquah" in indigenous tongue means "the sound of birds" and felt a special bond.

At Issaquah High School, she played soccer, participated in class discussions, and blossomed. She graduated with honors. On her eighteenth birthday, she became a US citizen, thanks to the efforts of a local congresswoman. At her American mom's urging, Tatiana applied to Seattle University. Her poignant story and passionate spirit won her a four-year scholarship to the Jesuit university. There, she continued playing soccer and excelled academically.

For her summer break, Tatiana requested to join Professor Shannon's study mission to Brazil and received acceptance. She listened carefully to each student and got to know them as individuals. Her colleagues complimented Tatiana for her seriousness and can-do attitude, not to mention her stunning if exotic good looks. They also admired her fiery spirit and elected Tatiana as their group leader.

At the age of twenty-three, she was returning to the largest city in South America, but not without trepidation.

* * *

BEFORE ARRIVING AT TIETÊ'S TERMINAL, Tatiana had used her Uber app to secure a minivan for the nine students and Professor Shannon. She led them through the bustling crowds and boarded the van without incident. An hour later, they wound through traffic and arrived at the Estanplaza Paulista hotel in São Paulo's Garden district. The neighborhood was known for its fancy hotels, sleek condominiums, and chic restaurants. They checked in and agreed to meet in the lobby at nine o'clock to go out to dinner. Two students had intestinal issues, and another couple decided to stay in to "catch up" with one another.

Tatiana and her Filipino roommate, Grace, went down to the lobby and found Professor Shannon and two male students talking soccer and another coed looking bored. Luke had made reservations for them at Rascal, a popular, all-you-can-eat trattoria just three blocks away. Tatiana enjoyed walking outdoors but bundled up to keep warm from the city's notorious winter fog. On their walk to the restaurant, they passed many swank high-rises protected by steel gates and roving guards. A few low-rise art galleries and doctor's offices were sprinkled among the towers, representing a bygone era of stately homes.

"Look, there's Starbucks," exclaimed Grace, pointing out young people drinking hot chocolate on the patio of a former colonial residence.

The group arrived at Rascal and waited outside in the line. Luke entered and talked to the hostess, who confirmed his reservation but asked them to wait. After twenty minutes, they entered the huge, well-lit eatery with hundreds of diners under a thirty-foot ceiling of glazed glass and cast-iron grating. The maître d' seated them at a table covered by a white tablecloth and not far from the fifty-dish antipasto and salad bar.

Luke ordered an Argentine Malbec to celebrate their arrival. They all toasted chin-chin to a successful visit in São Paulo.

Tatiana and the hungry students rose in unison to visit the cold buffet. They loaded their plates with hearts of palm, serrano ham, Italian salami, and many Brazilian salads and greens. Tatiana told the class that Japanese immigrants had brought their gardening skills to Brazil after the First World War, growing produce, like leafy and cruciferous vegetables. Bok choy, broccoli, and arugula subsequently graced Brazilians' diets and improved their health. She mentioned that Japanese parents pushed their sons and daughters to study hard in order to move up the social ladder. Nisei Brazilians now occupied executive positions in corporations, schools, and government, numbering almost two million in metro São Paulo.

Continuing to fill their plates, Tatiana and the students migrated next to the hot buffet counter where Italian chefs in white aprons and tall white hats pan-fried varieties of cannelloni, cappelletti, raviolis, and penne and then drizzled them with distinctive, savory sauces. The fragrance of garlic and olive oil enticed them to return again and again. They ended their feast at the dessert table with tempting sweets like coconut custard from Bahia, whipped avocado with Kahlua liquor, and *brigadeiro*, a traditional Brazilian truffle made with condensed milk and cocoa, rolled in chocolate sprinkles. A cholesterol fest indeed!

Luke paid the bill of $180, and Tatiana and the students thanked him heartily. Everyone was slow to rise from the table and reluctantly left the warmth of the nearby fireplace. They wound their way out of Rascal into a misty night as the clock showed 23:45. The line into the restaurant had grown longer and went around the block. Paulistas were accustomed to dine late into the early morning hours.

As Tatiana was feeling a little tipsy, one of the guys held her arm to keep her moving past the Starbucks and the InterContinental Hotel. Despite the effects of the wine, Tatiana's internal radar still scanned the surroundings. She didn't like what she saw just twenty yards ahead. A group of five teenagers had crossed Alameda Santos, aiming straight for them. Tatiana spied a narrow, cobblestone street sloping down behind the hotel. She shouted, "Everyone, turn here now."

Her companions finally caught on to what was happening and saw the teen gang closing in. They followed Tatiana, hurrying down the hill, trusting that their hotel was at the bottom of this alley.

Close behind them, they heard footsteps pick up and begin running down the slippery street. São Paulo's fog enveloped them in pursuit.

CHAPTER 12

Estanplaza Paulista, São Paulo
Sunday Morning, August 15

"T UDO BEM, PROFESSOR?" GREETED TATIANA. She was seated in the hotel's dining area, where a country breakfast was set up for guests. The patio was surrounded by a tropical garden with two rufus-bellied thrushes jumping from branch to branch in search of food.

Recalling last night's escapade, Luke was unsure how to reply to her.

They'd made it to the hotel's entrance after midnight. Fortunately, the guard had just opened the automatic door to go out for a smoke. He had been almost bowled over by the fleeing gringos rushing in. The guard had stared at the teen gang, which had just turned the corner on Alameda Jaú. Thinking quickly, the guard had touched his right side as if he were pulling out a pistol.

The impromptu thieves had stopped abruptly in the middle of the avenue. After a second, the leader had spat out "*Mixou!*" (attempt failed, in street talk). The gang had reversed course and hustled up the narrow alley, disappearing into the morning mist.

Luke and the students had arrived gasping for air and walked around the lobby to settle down. He had thanked the guard for his timely appearance and Tatiana for her warning. Luke and his students had looked anxiously over their shoulders through the glass door making sure the gang was really gone. Although the two male students had toyed with the idea of going out on the town, they had had second thoughts and joined the others, heading up to their rooms, calling it a night.

It had taken Luke more than an hour to regain calm in order to try to get some sleep. He had tossed and turned in the early morning hours, escaping dreams of turmoil and pursuit.

"More or less, Tatiana," he belatedly answered, concern flickering across his face. Involuntarily, he shook his head but sat down with her and Grace and ordered chamomile tea to soothe his stomach. He didn't know what else to say and didn't want to dwell on last night's crazy scene. Instead, he invited them to the country brunch spread out on three large counters. Rather than bacon and eggs, he opted for Brazilian papaya and rustic oatmeal but just picked at his food. Tatiana loaded up on fresh guava, pineapple, and jackfruit, which had arrived from northern Brazil.

To fill the silence, Luke said, "I was thinking of going to the eleven o'clock Mass at São Luis Gonzaga on Avenida Paulista. I thought a little prayer might do me good. If you'd like to join me, a cab could take us there. Afterwards, we could walk back and see the artisans' fair along this main avenue. They close the thoroughfare every Sunday so that Paulista families can take leisurely strolls without the noise of cars. It is a safe venue and the civil police are always present," he added, trying to sound confident.

Just then, the sun broke through the clouds. Rays of light showered the garden, making the thrushes chirp louder. The birdsong made them smile, and Tatiana told her roommate that the rufus-belled thrush was the national bird of Brazil. In a lighter mood, the two Catholic students agreed to join Luke for the late morning Mass. As they were leaving the dining room, two male students arrived looking bleary-eyed. They begged off going to church and got double-espressos instead.

Luke hired a Yellow Cab at the stand outside and arrived with Tatiana and Grace at the neo-classical chapel minutes before eleven o'clock. Luke mentioned that Saint Luis Gonzaga was born in Italy and had a special history for assisting suffering youth. He volunteered to help children and their families battle Rome's typhus epidemic in the late sixteenth century. His commitment to give care, despite the risk, resulted in Luis succumbing to the disease at twenty-three years old. The Catholic Church recognized his dedication and sacrifice by naming him the patron saint of youth and students.

Wearing masks like the rest of the congregation, they entered and sat toward the back of the rectangular church. Luke meditated on Luis's life and gazed at the saint's statue, encased atop the marble chancel, The church was mostly full with older ladies and families with children. A few tourists took photos of the marble altar under a pale-blue dome, A mosaic rendition of Jesus and the Virgin Mary graced the walls on either side of St. Luis Gonzaga's full-body sculpture. Behind the saint's statue, a golden light gave the chapel an ethereal feel.

The altar boys began the procession, walking deliberately and holding the crucifix and candles high. Next came the deacon, casting incense from the censer on both sides of the main aisle and over the altar. The priest entered last, offering blessings on the congregation.

As best as they could, Luke and Grace participated in the Mass *em portugues* but uttered the Lord's Prayer and the Nicene Creed in quiet English. Tatiana responded consistently in Portuguese and smiled kindly at Luke for his attempts.

Luke felt at peace. Whenever he travelled to cities around Brazil and the Americas, he appreciated the quiet inside a church. Today's pomp of the High Mass helped clear his head. He asked the Lord to forgive his pride and to guide him and his class safely in its study mission.

After taking Communion and receiving the priest's blessing, the congregation followed the procession out the door. Luke saw an attractive, middle-aged woman, whom he thought he'd met years ago. It was during his stint at the Bank of Boston, and she was at a local bank in São Paulo. He even remembered her first name. "Teresa, is that you?" he inquired, removing his mask.

The lady, dressed in a dark-blue pantsuit, looked over her shoulder and then smiled. "Luke Shannon, what are you doing in my city without a word? It's so nice to see you again. I still recognize you, which means you've kept yourself in reasonable shape," she replied and approached to give him an air-kiss on each cheek.

"Teresa, let me present you to two students from Seattle University, Tatiana and Grace. We're on a study mission to Brazil. Ladies, Teresa and I knew each other when we were bankers a few years back," he declared, smiling broadly.

Tatiana approached and gave her two kisses, and Grace extended her hand.

Teresa took her hand but then gave her two kisses as well. "It's a real pleasure, Luke, Tatiana, and Grace. What are you planning to do now? If you're free, may I invite you for tea at the nearby

Cultura Bookstore? It has a pleasant café upstairs, and we could catch up after all this time. And I'd like to learn more about your study mission."

Luke and the students agreed, as they didn't have to join the rest of the class until six that evening.

Teresa led them across the divided six-lane avenue without motor vehicles. Though barely two miles long, Avenida Paulista was adorned with high-rises, including many banks, museums, and even a huge McDonald's. It was the go-to place for demonstrations and celebrations and attracted residents and tourists of all walks of life and dress. The Paulistas were enjoying their Sunday stroll under sunshine and unusual serenity. Still, Luke had to keep an eye out for cyclists who didn't always stay in the bike lane. Most pedestrians were masked up, but the cyclists and skateboarders rode around without.

When they reached the Conjunto Nacional at the corner of Rua Augusta, Teresa explained that this was São Paulo's first multi-purpose high-rise commercial center, completed in 1958. The circular staircases inside led them past boutiques, restaurants, barber shops, and a large cinema complex. Offices and apartments were located on the upper floors, and a neon sign with "Ford" graced its rooftop at night. She guided them to the multi-level bookstore that would have put Seattle's Barnes & Noble to shame. On the mezzanine, they sat at a corner table overlooking rows of books and magazines from all over the world. Luke and the students ordered espresso, and Teresa green tea, engaging in small talk.

After they'd consumed their beverages, Luke and Teresa excused themselves so they could catch up on personal news. Tatiana and Grace decided to check out the bookshop, including its CD section, featuring Brazil's most famous artists.

Teresa had married the CEO of a prominent bank and was an empty nester. Her children had graduated from prestigious local universities and had begun their lives outside. Now, she dedicated much time to protecting the Pantanal wetlands around Cuiabá, Mato Grosso. She was heartbroken over recent fires destroying some mangroves and many animals. "Global warming has struck Brazil," she lamented. "It's no longer just a gringo thing.

"We are strapped with those mafiosos in Brasilia for another year, who deny there is a problem with deforestation. Let's hope those of us striving to save our environment can survive. They don't care a whit about the damage done to trees or animals, let alone the people that depend on rainforests, savannas, or clean rivers. We'd better get rid of this gang in 2022, or Brazil's rainforests and institutions will be in greater peril.

"And what about you, Luke? I see no wedding band on your finger. *Que passa?*"

Luke looked down at his hands and then back at his rediscovered friend. She had an elegant coiffure and raven hair, with streaks of gray shimmering underneath. A large diamond shone brightly on her left hand. "Indeed, Teresa. I've suffered from what psychologists may call 'arrested development' as I was out and about for many years. Last year, I returned to Cuba in search of my ex-lover whom I'd met in Washington, DC. Tragically, Ana Maria had died in a car accident the month before I arrived. I only could put flowers on her grave. May she rest in peace," he said, as Teresa touched his arm.

"However, I discovered that she gifted us a son, born of passion thirty years ago. His name is Lucas, and he lives with me in Seattle. His paintings have gained a following stateside. He is slowly adapting to our faster pace of life. The first six months, though, were

85

really rough. Lucas grew up in a rural village and got used to a pastoral life in Cuba. Seattle was a shock to him. He still takes long walks along our lakes and rivers whenever he's stressed out.

"I've recently joined Rotary and have met a delightful lady my age. She lost her husband to cancer several years ago but seems willing to try again. We've been seeing each other and enjoy each other's company. Having lived solo for so many years, it's difficult for me to open up. Trying to think or act as a couple is a constant challenge for me. Any words to the wise?" Luke asked, taking heart from Teresa's look of empathy.

"Just breathe deeply, Luke, and keep your Irish temper under control. Don't forget the big dates, like her birthday and your anniversary. Remember to always shower her with flowers. We always like flowers," she counseled, touching his arm again.

"Are you still swimming?" Teresa asked. "I remember you going out beyond the surf in Guarujá, giving us a worry. I still swim three times a week in the club's Olympic pool to keep both body and spirit in shape."

"We still have that in common, Teresa. During the pandemic, I began swimming year-round at our local Sammamish and Pine Lakes. I get occasional applause and some catcalls from visitors and fisherman," he confessed.

The two students returned with sacksful of CDs. Tatiana showed off two Marilia de Mendonça albums, whose poignant songs struck a deep chord with her. Grace got some classic bossa nova tunes by Tom Jobim.

Teresa and Luke got up from the table, and the four left the bookstore, returning to Avenida Paulista, still under brilliant sunshine. Luke and the students told Teresa about their mission to find out how big agriculture affects the country's diminishing forests—especially the increased soybean plantings in Brazil's savanna and lower Amazon regions.

"Yes, in Cuiabá, where my family maintains a greenbelt and animal refuge, we're surrounded by huge plantations of soy. If you'd like to visit, you may find the contrast interesting between the natural wetlands and the encroaching fields of grain. We support a jaguar and parrot preserve, called Onçafari, which you may enjoy."

They arrived at the outdoor artisan fair, exhibiting dozens of paintings, sculptures, and jewelry throughout the two-block Trianon Park. Jostling with tourists, they checked out the artwork on the sidewalk, and Tatiana tried on necklaces made of aquamarine. Luke recalled that Brazil was renowned for its variety of semi-precious stones.

Teresa took a call and then returned. "Luke, let me give you my card with my WhatsApp number, as well as the phone of our animal refuge in Cuiabá. If your group would like to visit, please be my guests. In a few minutes, my family is going to pick me just below the Art Museum of São Paulo.

"Tatiana and Grace, it's been wonderful meeting you. I hope you have a productive and safe trip in Brazil. Do take care and keep up the good work. Luke, you treat them well, my friend. Please call me before you leave town," she implored, giving Luke a hug and two kisses. She kissed Tatiana and Grace, smiled, and gave a wave. Weaving through the cyclists and skateboarders, she reached the cantilevered museum building on the other side.

On the sidewalk underneath the museum's second floor, two groups were gathering and raising their voices. Some younger men and women were waving placards and shouting, "Down with Bolsonaro!" Across from them, soldier-looking types, screamed, "Viva Bolsonaro," and looked ready to pick a fight.

Milling nearby, Luke observed the ringleader of last night's gang with more teens. He feared they were searching for other victims to strike. "Ladies, try not to look across the street. We don't want to attract their attention. It's time for us to leave," Luke said. He took them each by the arm, navigating through the artists' stands and a Bahian street-kitchen. Luke breathed in the enticing aroma of fried *acarajé* cooked in African palm oil and saw the woman in white fill the fried chickpea pastry with *vatapá*, a puree of coconut, peanuts, and pink shrimp. Luke resisted the temptation to stop and willed himself and the students into Trianon Park.

Hopefully, the tree boughs of the old-growth Atlantic Forest would shield them from the thieves. He heard the chattering of green parakeets and saw single men wandering around looking for trouble.

All he wanted was to make it to the other side.

CHAPTER 13

Monte Alegre to Santarém via Riverboat
Monday Afternoon, August 16

LUCIO WOULD HAVE ENJOYED VISITING THAT quaint community of adobe homes with a lively artist colony. But no way
did he want to run into that cop again in that isolated place with
no means of escape. It was an unusual port to stop at, but maybe
the cop was dealing drugs or receiving payoffs from the local constable. Who knows?

Fortunately, Lucio had escaped him on the observation deck
by slipping down the ladder to his first-class cabin and locking
the door. He heard footsteps pound down after him. Holding his
breath, he didn't answer the knock and saw the handle turn. But
the deadbolt did its job. Lucio relaxed a bit when he heard the cop
thumping on other doors further down. After a woman's scream,
"What do you want with me?" he didn't hear anything more, except
the hatch closing.

Afterwards, Lucio texted his friendly captain, Pedro, who visited him in his room. Feeling relieved the cop was berthed on
another deck, Lucio decided to hunker down inside the cabin. The

captain kindly had a waiter bring him meals from the cafeteria and offered a bottle of cachaça to drown any regrets. Lucio would have enjoyed ambling on the ferryboat's deck and contemplating the vibrant life along the Amazon. Another time.

For now, Lucio had brought a book along about life in an Israeli kibbutz. He had fantasized about creating one in the Amazon for environmental students and sought out NGOs to sponsor his brainchild. No one took his idea too seriously; even the Israelis had excused themselves from consideration. If only his fellow citizens had more law and less disorder in their veins, he mused.

Viewing Brazil's national flag of green, yellow, and blue out his portal, Lucio wondered who had come up with the slogan "Order and Progress" inscribed over the blue universe in its center. Alas, he concluded, it expressed his fellow citizens' aspirations if not their current predicament of nationwide unrest.

As promised to his student Gabriela, Lucio had almost finished writing up the story about the miners' invasion of the Mundurukú village. The international press often monitored his blogs, so they could pass on Amazon news to foreign audiences. He planned to post the story in Santarém.

He had also telephoned the honest cop at the Policia Federal to report the incursion. The policeman did not answer his WhatsApp and was probably chasing bad guys in the wilds upriver. Cell phone service was iffy at best along the river and nonexistent inside the rainforest. Instead, Lucio finished the conclusion of his blog, saved it, and would send out on arrival.

The engines slowed, and he looked out his portal at Monte Alegre, the last stop before Santarém. He saw the shady detective disembark and meet another heavy-set man on the dock. "What are they up to?" he wondered but wouldn't dare show his face. Instead, Lucio turned away, leaned back on his bunk, and took a nap.

He was jerked awake when the ferryboat's engines went into reverse, causing the decks to reverberate. The boat bumped against the wharf and ground lethargically to a stop. Lucio looked outside and saw many boats plying the river. He finished repacking his carry-on and tossed water on his face. Detecting more creases and more strands of grizzled, white hair, he concluded that he could use a haircut.

Knock, knock, knock.

Through the peephole, Lucio eyed the captain again. Though only five feet six inches tall, Pedro appeared lean and wily. A life-long resident along the Amazon, he knew the River Sea's twists and turns and often hired out to the rich and famous for pleasure cruises on their yachts. His bronzed skin and high cheekbones suggested native roots, and his eyes said "don't mess with me." Lucio felt fortunate to call him a friend.

"How are you, Pedro?" he inquired enthusiastically, opening the door and giving the captain a tight hug.

"Tudo bem, Lucio. The coast is clear. That policeman disembarked at Monte Alegre, and no one suspicious came on board. Most of the passengers have already headed off, and the cars and trucks are offloading as we speak. The mates are cleaning up and will remain on board. Could I invite you to a caipirinha to celebrate our successful cruise? We didn't hit any logs, alligators, or pirarucú, and no one fell overboard. So I count this as a successful trip," said the captain in a pleasant manner.

"How kind of you, Pedro. Let me see if my friend from the community group has arrived. He was going to meet me on the dock and take me to his village of Alter de Chão. Have you visited it in your travels? But before going, I'd enjoy having a quick drink for the road."

"Sounds good, Lucio. But recently, the Tapajós River has suffered runoff from the illegal miners, muddying its pristine waters. Let's hope they haven't affected your friend's community," he said, his eyes flaring. He led Lucio to the lower deck where the last vehicles were driving off.

The wharf abounded with vendors of fruits, vegetables, and tourist mementos, as well as fishermen exhibiting the varied catches of the day. One explained how he'd lifted his trophy pirarucú on his back to carry it ashore. His tourist audience stood rapt in attention, open-mouthed at the seven-foot fish hung alongside the five-foot-seven riverman.

"*Salve*, my friend!" (Be saved) greeted a mustached man. "Welcome to Santarém. What does our star reporter think of our bustling city?" He had curly gray hair under a white ball cap with Sport Club Corinthians Paulista's signature anchor logo printed in red and black. His long gray striped shirt broadcast "*Da flora, Nossa Catinha*" (Out of the flora, comes our little pet). His eyes smiled, and he gave Lucio a tight hug.

"The waterfront sure looks busier now than during my last visit. I also see more freighters in port picking up soy," moaned Lucio, pointing out grain elevators across the bay, loading a ship flying the Chinese flag. A tug was standing a hundred yards offshore to guide it to the flowing river, heading east.

"Yes, a lot has changed since you came last. The Ox Bench is pushing its weight around, demanding more grain elevators and berths for larger ships," the man replied, shaking his head. He smiled and extended his hand to Lucio's companion. "And who is your friend? I am Caetano at your service."

"I call myself Pedro and am the captain of *Amazonas*. We just landed and would like to celebrate our safe arrival with a little white lightning. Would you care to join us?" the captain invited, meeting the other's hand and giving a loose hug.

Caetano agreed and led them along the Tapajós River to a squat brick building, painted red with "Botequim" in large gold letters on a black overhead sign. The grate was open, and the one-room bar was sandwiched between a home under construction and a white stucco store called Lindo Ceu (Beautiful Sky).

Inside stood a few fishermen, tossing down straight cachaça with a beer chaser. They greeted, "Good afternoon," to the visitors, who responded in kind.

Caetano ordered a bottle of a locally distilled version, made from the local *açaí* fruit. The brew had an earthy taste, a cross of blackberries and unsweetened chocolate. In the corner at a standup table, the three men took double shots with a twist of lime while overhead a fan moved the humid air and mosquitos around.

The bartender suggested *ovos rotos* (broken eggs) to accompany their drinks. The subtle aroma of the dish's cilantro and oregano made the men's stomachs growl. The sweet potato fries with chopped peppers and chorizo, smothered with running eggs on top, hit the spot. They finished the bottle, scraped the pan-friend dish, and were about to order another when Caetano's cell rang.

He listened and replied, "I'll be there within the hour." Caetano hung up and let out a long breath. "Friends, the civil police have visited our community again and asked for me. I must return to keep them at bay. Some consider me a thorn in the sides of the soy growers and land developers, who often pay them tips. I can't pay in reais but have to pay in kindness and by being present. Would you like to stay, Lucio, or accompany me to Alter de Chão?"

"Captain, would you excuse me if I don't join you for another round?" asked the reporter, who left a twenty-real bill on the table.

"No problem, Lucio. I'll catch up with the fishermen to hear their latest stories of the river. Go with God, my friends."

They gave each other tight hugs, and Lucio followed his guide out the open grate.

The two men walked a couple of blocks and climbed into Caetano's little Fiat, which looked like it'd seen many ups and downs. He drove through town and swung onto the asphalt road. As he accelerated to one hundred kilometers an hour, the small sedan began to vibrate. Caetano just smiled and continued past the savanna with spindly trees and yellowed grass, coming to a patch scarred brown. After a few miles, they passed a sea of green soybeans and a tractor tilling another field.

"This is where we had the wildfire two years ago. A few bad elements in the civil police accused volunteer firemen and me of setting it. Can you imagine that? Life is still difficult for us green groups in the North. Still, we do what we can to protect the rainforests and to keep the land grabbers away," Caetano groaned.

"This August is especially dry along the Amazon," he continued. "With hectares of burned trees, meteorologists predict our region will reap what it sows—higher temperatures and more fires. Those allied to the soy growers, miners, and loggers say global warming is a foreign idea. Yet we all are suffering in Santarém and the rest of Brazil as well. Let's hope no one casts a cigarette into this tinder box."

They passed through an entrance with Força Comunitária on a sign under an arbor of coconut palms and Brazil nut trees. A half-mile in stood the community center where two blue-and-white policia civil cars were parked. A crowd of angry villagers surrounded them, raising their voices. They all turned to see Caetano arrive in his dusty Fiat.

Two men wearing yellow T-shirts with a red triangle and an upside-down triangle inside were waving their hands.

"Not again," Caetano murmured. He parked and walked evenly to the policemen dressed in blue. "Gentlemen, how may I help you?"

"There is a complaint against these men by the new owners of the land next to your compound. We came here to interrogate them but waited until you arrived. They were trespassing on the new owner's land last night, when he was clearing its undergrowth. Can you shed light on their actions as we're aware that you work with them?" the taller of the two cops inquired.

"Gentlemen, when did that land sell? It has been the property of the state of Pará for decades. As to these men, they are volunteer firemen, who give their all to protect us from wildfires, especially during the dry season. I've just returned after two days in Santarém. I wasn't aware of this new owner or of his clearing the savanna. He should have at least informed us and the volunteer fireman in order to monitor. We certainly don't want to repeat the fires of 2019, do we? These men acted properly when someone spotted the flames. Could you introduce me to the new owner so we can resolve this situation?" Caetano kept his voice on an even keel.

"Hmm, I'm not sure that's possible. The new owner is from Cuiabá, in Mato Grosso. As you've helped our families secure Covid vaccinations, we'll report back to our superiors that it was a misunderstanding. I'll ask who is the foreman so you two can meet and work out procedures for clearing brush. Tudo bem?"

Caetano concurred and shook the taller policeman's hand. He watched them return to their blue-and-white VW sedan. The policeman and woman in the other vehicle followed their lead out of the community's gates.

"My friends, let me present you to a dear friend from Belém who reports on environmental issues. He'll be staying with us for a few days. Lucio, here are our loyal villagers, the backbone of our community, and two brave firefighters," Caetano exclaimed.

Lucio and Caetano spent the next hour talking with the town members, who smiled, told jokes and stories, and gave the visitor tight hugs. A bottle of sugarcane cachaça appeared, adding to the merriment. After they'd squeezed the last drop, villagers waved goodbyes and wandered back to their huts, no worse for wear.

Lucio followed his host to a tropical bungalow under a thatched roof with a view of the Tapajós River. They looked out the window toward the entrance and detected a wisp of dust or smoke lingering on the horizon. Caetano made another call to make sure another fire wasn't burning. He showed the reporter to his room with a river view as the sun declined over the forest. Lucio thanked him but skipped dinner, feeling a little tipsy.

What he really yearned for was peace, quiet, and rest.

* * *

LUCIO'S EYES BURNED, AND AN ACRID SMELL penetrated his nostrils. He coughed again. Then he heard a boom and felt a shock wave. He looked outside the window to the dirt street and saw his host's wife's beloved Fiat going up in flames. Caetano was outdoors directing his neighbors to form a human chain to pass buckets of water from the community well. Hand to hand, they passed an assortment of containers to slowly douse the fire. Thankfully, his car's tank had been on empty, or the gas explosion would have been much worse.

Lucio joined the brigade outside in the bucket line, but Caetano's wife's quaint car would be no more. What a way to begin his vacation in the village, which TripAdvisor had heralded as the "Caribbean in the Amazon."

What was going on in this land acclaimed for its tropical serenity and laid-back life style?

CHAPTER 14

Ibirapuera Park, São Paulo
Tuesday Noon, August 17

LUKE AND THE STUDENTS ARRIVED MIDDAY at the 390-acre park, considered São Paulo's greenbelt and lungs for its twenty-two million residents. Located in the South Zone, Ibirapuera was on a par with Mexico City's Chapultepec and New York City's Central Parks in size and space. Luke led the class through the main entrance, a noontime thoroughfare. On the benches, a lunchtime crowd had brought box lunches to ogle joggers, cyclists, and skaters doing figure eights. His destination was the Plaza of Peace to get together with Vera, the social worker from Paraisópolis.

Last night, she had texted Luke that it would be unsafe for the students to visit her health clinic tucked away in the favela's hills. Recently, the drug lords had made life difficult and threatened her safety. She was sorry they couldn't view the women's new urban garden but promised to bring photos. Vera suggested meeting in São Paulo's first metropolitan park to find solace from the urban scene. She also confessed that she needed a break.

Luke stopped by the popcorn man, who was doing a brisk business. He treated all his class for only ten reais and then led them to the connecting ponds where they watched the swans gliding in stately order while ducks scurried after bread tossed by passersby. Luke stopped to admire couples holding hands on the sloping banks and another duo in full embrace under an ipê tree, abloom in pink. Tatiana looked longingly at the kissing pair, as did Luke, mesmerized by romance in the air.

He entered a vast meadow with the sign reading *Praça da Paz*. He was expecting a different kind of plaza but began searching for a large rubber fig tree, Vera's point of rendezvous. Tatiana pointed out a huge tree, from whose branches dozens of roots cascaded down, similar to a banyan. "This must be the spot," Luke said looking around the green. He observed a Brazilian candle plant in a nearby garden with a bevy of blue-backed hummingbirds supping its nectar.

Through another thicket of blooming ipê, Luke heard human voices rising and falling. Across the glen, a small group emerged, led by a five-foot dynamo, gesticulating to a taller woman of color. A reporter with a Band TV microphone was interviewing the taller woman dressed in a pink pantsuit and commanding attention. A cameraman was recording the conversation, and a small, youngish crowd followed, some carrying signs with Greenpeace Now.

The shorter woman caught Luke's eye and shouted, "Luke, is that you? At last, we can meet in person." She left the entourage and almost ran to them under the rubber fig tree. Her smile was wide, and her brown skin glistened under the winter sun. Luke had chatted with Vera twice by WhatsApp and was impressed by her bundle of energy. They gave each other tight hugs and kisses on each cheek and then took a few moments to size each other up.

"Vera, how wonderful to meet you in this beautiful park" Luke responded *em português* and then switched to English. "Class, this is Vera, the woman I spoke about. Regrettably, we can't visit her community center where she partnered with medical students to bring help to São Paulo's poor during the pandemic. She had to navigate threats from gangs and indifference by city officials. But Vera prevailed. She's a fighter for the public good! Please introduce yourselves and offer any Portuguese words you may recall."

Each student gave his or her name and major, usually ending the short discourse with "tudo bem?"

Tatiana was the last to speak and introduced herself *em português*. She stated that she was from the Guajajara tribe in Northeast Brazil and had been adopted by a CIMI missionary's sister, living in Seattle, Washington. Part of their study mission, she explained, was to determine the impact of big agriculture on Brazil's rainforests and indigenous people. "Vera, I am also seeking justice for my people," she exclaimed, attracting the attention of the svelte woman, who joined them around the tree, trailed by the cameraman.

"Luke and students from Seattle University, let me present you to the Honorable Marina, Brazil's leading environmentalist. Tatiana is from the Guajajara tribe of Maranhão and is part of a study mission from Seattle University. She is seeking justice for her people and for the rainforests that house them. You two may have a lot in common. Maybe you could join forces. What do you think?" asked Vera, brimming with excitement.

Luke recalled Marina's story of being born to a family who tapped rubber for a living in remote Acre in Brazil's western corner with Peru. Orphaned at sixteen, she found her way to the state's capital. Nuns took pity and invited her to live with them in their convent, where she received a Catholic education. Marina was the first of her family to learn how to read and write. Later, she worked as a maid for room and board and completed her degree in history at the state university when twenty-six.

In 1994, she was the first rubber-tapper ever elected to Brazil's Senate and caught the fancy of Brazil's Labor Party. When Lula was elected president, he tapped her for his environment minister. During her term, Marina slowed deforestation in the tropical forests and encouraged sustainable development in the savanna regions. She often presented at world forums on the environment. Like Vera in her community, Marina was also known as a crusader for women's rights around Brazil.

Marina stepped forward and gave Tatiana two kisses and a tight hug. "Sister, let us get to know one another. If you wouldn't mind, I'd like you to share what you just told us with the reporter. I want him and the Brazilian people to realize that our campaign is not a minor issue. To protect our forests and vulnerable people and to pursue social justice are our common causes around the world."

The reporter and cameraman turned their attention to Tatiana, who proceeded to recount what happened to her and her family in the tribal village years ago. No one remained dry-eyed. She reminded them how her distant cousin, Paulino, had paid the ultimate price as the guardian of the forest for the Guajajara people in 2019. "They still have not caught the assassins of the protector of our trees and our people. All they've offered are lame excuses and unfilled promises. Thanks to Professor Shannon, our study mission plans to visit Brasilia and meet with elected representatives. I plan to raise this case with them and with whoever will listen to me. We have waited too long," she declared, tears flowing down her cinnamon cheeks.

"We demand justice. Please help me," Tatiana cried out, looking directly into the camera lens. Through her anguish, she was speaking to the Brazilian people.

Luke came alongside her and held her tight, saying defiantly, "We plan to fulfill our study mission, come what may."

The video and mike man, recorded it all.

Later in the day, Luke discovered the TV duo were able to convince their editor to place the interview on the national evening news.

The consequences of the reporter's story would play out in unexpected ways.

CHAPTER 15

Setor de Mansões, Dom Bosco, Brasilia
Wednesday Morning, August 18

FLAVIO PACED AROUND HIS VAST OFFICE to calm himself. He was also acclimating to his immense new manor, which he had purchased in a sweetheart deal from a friendly broker. The press asked how he could purchase a million-dollar plus mansion with so little income. Yet they ignored the reality that elected officials, like himself, played by different rules, accessing special financing unavailable to most Brazilians. These were the perks of office. Surely, even reporters knew that.

He was planning to meet his Brasilia press assistant, who had alerted him to two stories that piqued his father's interest. One concerned that troublesome journalist from Belém; the other was about new arrivals from the United States. Flavio had even received a call from the embassy's chargé d'affaires about the university's study mission.

The first story showed that white-haired reporter, almost shouting at TV Globo after his friend's car was firebombed at the NGO's center in Alter de Chão. This Lucio claimed that authorities had harassed its residents and turned a blind eye to illegal logging and burnings on federal land. He also got the foreign press riled up, which considered him one of their own. The journalist claimed the current administration had created havoc in the Amazon for not enforcing federal law and damaging indigenous people.

The second story was aired on Band TV, which often favored the administration's views regarding big agriculture. It came from São Paulo, where the tele-reporters were interviewing that environment minister has-been. They then latched onto a lively Brazilian-American student visiting from the States. Apparently, she had ties to a tribe in Maranhão and demanded justice for the killing of her cousin, Paulino Guajajara, two years ago. She and her pushy gringo prof planned to come to Brasilia to challenge Brazil's Congress and the ministry of justice to take action. Her poignant story had even upset Flavio's wife last night, who had pestered him as well.

Why did he have to get bogged down in these petty matters? Yet papai had asked him to take care of this as Daddy had other political battles now. So take care of it Flavio would. Which reminded him that he hadn't heard from Queiroz since last week's meeting with the Colombiano. Had they found a way to move the hardwood through the Amazon and to export it with legal paperwork to foreign buyers? If so, it would yield a nice commission and offer more "little cracks" of income for family and friends down the road.

He heard a rap on the door, followed by his *mayordomo*'s voice, "Senhor Flavio, the press assistant has arrived."

"Tudo bem," he sighed. He then shut the automated shutters, sheltering him from nosy reporters with listening devices. The realtor had told Flavio that the anodized aluminum frames offered greater protection against outside snoopers, as well as the tropical heat. He stepped behind his mahogany desk, provided by a friend who manufactured hardwood and leather furniture in the Manaus Free Trade Zone. Plopping down on the black leather swivel chair and rewinding the TV tapes, Flavio commanded, "Enter."

A thin, pallid man somewhere in his forties entered with tentative steps, his half-moon glasses drifting down his long nose. He reminded Flavio of a weasel with specs. At least he followed orders, unlike his younger version back in Rio. One of the press corps had asked if he was the senator's bookkeeper, as his appearance suggested that of a rundown accountant. But the assistant's job was not to face the press; that was Flavio's fiefdom. As long as the fellow got the facts and stories right, Flavio couldn't care less how he looked.

"So, Pedro, what do you recommend we do about these two news items? They paint us poorly in the international and local press. There are so many Indian-lovers nowadays that we have to find a way to deflect such criticism. Even the word 'genocide' is being tossed around to describe some administration policies. Daddy doesn't like that."

His assistant stood before the huge mahogany desk and wiped his palms on the plastic folder full of newspaper clippings from around Brazil. "Umm, we could invite that Brazilian student and American professor to meet with you or one of your allies in Congress," Pedro suggested in a monotone voice. "As to old Lucio up North, no one has found a way to silence him. He's always been a loose cannon with local authorities. He seems to have a death wish, always battling with your allies up there. Yet the foreign press adores him."

Flavio's eyes flashed, and he felt his temper rise. That Belém reporter—what was Queiroz doing about him? He wanted to hit someone or something. Stifling his instinct, Flavio knew he had to exercise self-control. There were so many eyes and ears around here, including hidden spies. Whom could he trust but his family? Though competent, his assistant's nondescript manner also irritated Flavio. He was so boring that he often made Flavio's eyes glaze over and his mind drift.

"Fine, get some pols from the Big Center to meet with her and that prof when they arrive in Brasilia. Wine them and dine them and try to discover what their agenda is in Brazil. She looked pretty sexy on TV last night and might respond to being catered to. But don't invite her relative to the get-together, or we'll have a real firestorm on our hands. Call the Band TV reporter and find out when she and that prof come to town. Get the rundown on that pair of troublemakers.

"As to that worn-out reporter up North, I've got another idea. One that does not involve wining and dining. For that, I'll need you to reach Queiroz as soon as possible. Do you know where he is?"

"I'll find out, Senhor Flavio. He's a hard man to pin down, and there's still a warrant out for his arrest. Let me call around. He usually responds to texts, but he takes his own sweet time," Pedro droned. He saw Flavio's eyes flash again and thought it best to retreat before another eruption. "I'll leave these press clippings for you here. Will that be all, senhor?"

Flavio grabbed the tennis ball and squeezed it harder and harder to help him decompress. Finally, he replied, "Yes, but find Queiroz."

After the assistant left, Flavio worked the phones for an hour, promising to do this or that for his allies in the Big Center, or *Centrão*, as it was known in Brasilia. It was an apt name as the only thing these pols cared about was lining their personal coffers.

If constituents got something in the process, so much the better, as long as the Big Center got the lion's share. That's how it worked in the halls of Congress, and Flavio knew how to play the game quite well.

One of the clippings in the folder was background on Paulino Guajajara's assassination on November 1, 2019. It included a copy of Greenpeace's obituary, along with that fearsome photo of him as the guardian of the forest. It showed a stocky reddish-brown man with black war paint on his face, shoulders, and bare chest. His black eyes were slits of anger, the right eye slightly larger than the left. An orange amulet hung around his broad chest, and his thick lips were turned down at the corners. Flavio would not have wanted to face him anywhere.

Fortunately, five loggers had made sure of that. Enlisted by Flavio's allies in the North, they had invaded Guajajara lands late at night, hunting Paulino to earn their bounty. That guardian had proven very bad for business. Apparently, the loggers had heard some movement and trekked deeper into the forest. They had waited in the underbrush, and when they had seen two men enter a clearing, they had shot Paulino and his companion at close range. Paulino had lain riddled with bullets, dead at twenty-six years. Laércio had managed to escape through the thick woods, bleeding from wounds in his arm and back. He had barely survived.

Still, from the first aid station, his tribesman had raised the alarm to the international press, which had wired news of this high-profile assassination around the world. Paulino was the forty-second member of the tribe to have been murdered in recent years. The Catholic Indigenous Missionary Council divulged over 160 incursions into indigenous lands the year of Paulino's death and decried the lack of law and order.

Flavio didn't like CIMI but vaguely remembered the incident a couple years ago. As the pandemic had grabbed the headlines this past year, interest in the Indian killings had begun to wane. The press was now raising other issues, like deforestation, which caused Brazil's trading partners in Europe and North America to fret. With the arrival of someone from the States with indigenous roots and a gringo prof decrying the loss of trees, the story would have legs.

The Brazilian student said she wanted to raise her cousin's image from the dead. She demanded justice. That prof wanted to find connections between Brazil's big agriculture and deforestation. Together they could light a flame under both stories.

Flavio would do what he had to do to prevent that from happening. He'd have to handle these visitors with care. Papai did not want to get blindsided again by incidents about "genocide" of native people. Flavio dreaded being shamed by his father in the family circle. And if that reporter from Belém were to join forces with these two do-gooders, it'd be all hell to pay.

Just then, Flavio got a text from his assistant. Queiroz was last seen up North and ready to comply.

CHAPTER 16

São Paulo en route to Brasilia
Wednesday Afternoon, August 18

LUKE WAS SHEPHERDING HIS FLOCK through São Paulo's crowded municipal airport, called Congonhas, named after its eponymous viscount who served as São Paulo's provincial president following Brazil's independence in 1822. It was the favored venue for commuters travelling to and from Rio, Belo Horizonte, and Brasilia, conveniently located in the city's South Zone.

Taking a moment, Luke admired the urban architecture of its circular hall, surrounded by marble pillars and mosaic scenes, hardly noticed by the other passengers bustling across its checkerboard floor. His class grabbed handcarts for their baggage and followed him to the GOL Airline counter. They jostled with well-dressed political types, wheeling and dealing to board the full flight.

Luke had received a call from the Band TV reporter, asking if he'd seen the story. Yes, he had, and Luke thanked him for airing the interview, telling the reporter their flight number and ETA in Brasilia.

The ten in his group all showed their vaccination cards and passports at the check-in counter and wound their way through security on the second floor. The flight took off a few minutes after four o'clock and banked to the northeast, affording everyone a panoramic view. Luke and the students marveled at the never-ending high-rise apartment buildings as far as the eye could see. But they frowned at the bumper-to-bumper traffic on arterials and bridges crossing the Tietê River as it snaked its way through South America's largest city.

Having gotten seats together, they compared notes about their lunch meeting earlier with the prestigious attorneys from Pinheiro Neto.

* * *

THE STUDENTS LEARNED THAT BRAZIL HAD SOME of the most stringent environmental laws in the world, which were mostly cast aside by the current administration. The senior law partner, Werner, affirmed that the firm did pro bono work for NGOs battling deforestation but needed moral support from abroad.

Werner highlighted other private groups acting on their own, buying or receiving land as a tax write-off and creating projects of sustainable development. Brazilian law required that 20 percent of any land used for agriculture be reserved for natural habitat, permitting 80 percent to be planted with cash crops like soja. Such laws, however, were not strictly enforced as the Ox Bench pushed deeper into the savannas and the rainforests.

After the attorney's presentation, Werner invited the students upstairs to the law firm's salon. Like many other firms, Pinheiro Neto had closed its dining room during the pandemic but agreed to host a privately catered meal. Luke and students enjoyed a tasty lunch of Brazilian sea bass, called *badejo*, over rice pilaf with fresh asparagus from the interior of São Paulo. They learned that the badejo were also declining in numbers due to the warming of the Atlantic Ocean. Luke commiserated with his hosts as sockeye salmon faced rising temperatures in the Pacific Ocean, causing an uneven supply of his hometown staple. He presented Werner with a box of smoked king salmon from Alaska, which elicited a gracious smile.

Over a tasty custard for dessert, Werner introduced two representatives from private land management firms to present their cases. The first to speak was Plinio, who confessed his youthful idealism to save Brazil's rainforests. In 2007, he joined forces with Dr. Claudio, a respected professor of agriculture, and founded Biofílica. Their modus operandi was to encourage land donations by like-minded Brazilians, including green firms like Natura SA and its executives.

Besides earning profits using sustainable agricultural techniques, their firm also garnered carbon credits by generating more oxygen and less CO_2 by planting more trees. There was an active Brazilian market for such credits, as corporations sought to lessen their emissions footprint. Biofilica became a mover and shaker in this growing space and received visitors from around the world.

Through donations and partnering with green-oriented farmers, CEOs, and NGOs, Biofilica had assembled millions of acres of land in Brazil's savannas and tropical forests. Its focus on sustainable development caught the eye of the local press, as well as publicly traded firms. France's Carrefour, with a large supermarket presence in Brazil, recently announced it too would create a reforestation entity. Even Bolsonaro had given lip service to private initiatives as it provided his administration positive reviews.

The next presenter was Sergio, the current CEO of Grupo Jari, a producer of paper and packaging. A compact man with friendly eyes, he was soft-spoken but direct: "The remains of Daniel Ludwig's project had withered from neglect for decades. It was on the verge of bankruptcy, despite the millions invested in the seventies. We spoke with our community leaders who offered their support. Taking a deep breath, our management group acquired the project from receivership in 2000. We began replanting eucalyptus and encouraged local residents to grow manioc, beans and vegetables and to harvest indigenous Brazil nuts and fruits like açaí.

"Little by little, we began to grow again. Thanks to worker input, we repaired and returned the cellulose plant to operation. Recently, we found a special niche to manufacture special wrappings for hamburgers and hot dogs. Before taking this action, we listened to the workers at the factory. We now operate as a community venture, each of us taking care of the other. The young men no longer move away and now they live along the Jari River. They have opportunity to grow and raise their families in their native land.

"For twenty years, we've struggled but insisted on using sustainable methods to grow all crops. Like Plinio's firm, we are raising more trees, generating more oxygen, and creating carbon credits. By selling these credits to corporations, we generate income and remind them to lower their environmental footprint. We believe that our Jari community has turned the corner and is profitable in a financial as well as human sense.

"What do you think, students of Seattle U?"

The students reacted with enthusiasm as Sergio handed out some of the new hot dog wrappers. They promised to tell Sergio's and Plinio's stories to the world.

* * *

NOW ON THE PLANE, LUKE TASKED THE STUDENTS to investigate whether other firms and NGOs like The Nature Conservancy were entering this promising field of sustainable land management. "This could prove a viable alternative to the current slash-and-burn approach of the Ox Bench," he affirmed.

"In Brasilia, let's find out if any elected representatives are working to support such endeavors. If so, we can highlight their and Pinheiro Neto's efforts in our study report and in our conversations with the press."

The Boeing 737 banked slowly north but shuddered from a crosswind sweeping up from the savanna. Besides feeling the turbulence, Luke observed swirls of dust on the horizon. Everyone remembered the electrical storm over the Amazon so returned to their seats and fastened their belts. As the sun was setting, the plane began its wobbly descent. Two planes lit up to starboard, aiming for the runway ahead. Juscelino Kubitschek International crept closer, and its lights flashed along its landing strip.

The airport was named after Brazil's visionary president who founded Brasilia in 1960. Kubitschek's action to relocate the capital from Rio to Brazil's interior was fiercely criticized as a "pipedream" and caused galloping inflation at the time. Today, the former president must be pleased that the capital city had grown to almost five million souls.

Luke pointed out two illuminated parallel towers, bordered by an upward facing disk on the right side and a smaller, disk facing downward on the left. "This is Oscar Niemeyer's masterpiece, designed by Brazil's most famous architect. The National Congress buildings reflect an international style and symbolized Brazil's coming of age. Its team included designers of the UN Plaza and the who's who of architecture. We plan to visit the Chamber of Deputies and the Senate during our stay."

Suddenly, the 737 bounced onto the tarmac, the crosswind still lashing its side. It braked and slowly turned toward the airport, its two sleek terminals connected by a long pedestrian causeway. As the plane neared the gate, Luke spied a TV cameraman waiting in the arrivals area along with two men dressed in suits.

"Get ready for the unexpected," Luke counseled the students. "And welcome to Brasilia."

After Luke disembarked, a Band TV reporter approached him. "Professor Shannon?"

Luke had met the TV-radio group's owner, Johnny, during his Bank of Boston days and thought this could be his way to welcome the study mission to Brazil's capital city.

The local reporters had received a heads-up from their Paulista counterparts and wanted a brief interview for the late evening news. Luke and Tatiana answered questions about their study mission. He emphasized their interest in speaking with elected representatives about actions to protect Brazil's rainforests and indigenous people. After ten minutes, the reporters thanked them and left.

The two men in suits, a tall thin man and his short, robust companion, advanced toward Luke and Tatiana. They reminded Luke of a modern-day version of Don Quixote and Sancho Panza.

The tall thin man, wearing half-moon glasses, introduced himself as Pedro, the press assistant to an undisclosed Brazilian senator. His shorter colleague mumbled his name as João, but to Luke, "Sancho" seemed a more apt moniker. The press assistant inquired where Luke and the students were staying and if he could invite them all to dinner. Luke replied that they were staying at the

Mercure Brasilia Lider hotel in the northern commercial zone and thanked him for his thoughtful offer.

"Students, these gentlemen are from a Brazilian senator's office and would like to invite us to dinner tonight. What do you say?" asked Luke.

They roared their approval, with the male students asking, "Can we have steak?"

The taller man replied, "Tudo bem," but did not smile.

The students' enthusiasm to eat was a constant source of admiration to their prof. As coached by Tatiana, the students gave a thumbs up as their sign of approval. She had instructed them not to use the American OK sign, as it had a sexual connotation in Brazil and throughout Latin America.

Luke arranged to meet the two men at the main entrance to the Brasilia Shopping Center at 8:30 p.m., a five-minute walk from their hotel. After thanking the visitors, he shook hands and exchanged loose hugs. Tatiana and Grace gave each man an air kiss, but didn't elicit much reaction from either. The other students gave another thumbs up and headed to baggage claim. Tatiana began working her iPhone to make sure the Uber van would be outside.

They found their GOL flight bin and collected their bags from the carrousel, stacking them high on carts. With no lost luggage, they passed laid-back cabbies seeking riders. Though not as bustling as São Paulo's airport, there were many taxis, limos, and vans awaiting passengers from the full flight. Tatiana led the group confidently to the white Uber Kombi and asked the driver to head north to the hotel.

Luke explained how Brasilia was planned to look like an airplane, with wings extending north and south from the fuselage, which housed most government buildings. He reminded them that they intended to visit the twin towers of the deputies and senators, as well as the presidential palace.

Assuming a professorial tone, he continued his lecture: "Remember that Brasilia was designed in an era when air travel was becoming more popular. The wings have commercial and housing areas numbered by quadrants and blocks; our hotel is at the beginning of the northern commercial zone. Oscar Niemeyer and his international team wanted to create a new urban concept in Brasilia. Its configuration as an airplane symbolized Brazil as a country taking off.

"The move of the capital from Rio de Janeiro was harshly criticized at the time. Yet President Kubitschek wanted to develop the country's hinterland and open it to farmers and adventurers seeking livelihoods beyond the crowded coasts. Decades later, millions of acres of savanna have been irrigated, ploughed, and planted with soja. These landowners have also become extremely rich and powerful. They have created the bancada do boi, the Ox Bench, to lobby politicians in Brasilia and in state legislatures nationwide.

"Today, Brazil rivals the United States as the top exporter of soy to the world. Our charge is to discover ways to conduct sustainable agriculture and to preserve the declining tropical forests. Plinio's and Sergio's approaches may be the answer, but let's see what the pols have to say."

They arrived at their French budget lodge within a half-hour and marveled that few traffic lights marred their trip. The taillights of cars served that purpose, pointed out Luke, with stop-and-go traffic along the main roadway. After checking in and freshening up, they returned to the lobby at eight o'clock. They wandered toward the shopping mall, surrounded by high-rise hotels but fewer trees than in São Paulo's Garden neighborhood.

Luke's delegation arrived at the Brasilia Shopping Mall at eight thirty and found Pedro and João in their same suits, looking weary. "Good evening, gentlemen. Again, thank you for inviting us out tonight. Does either of you speak English? Only Tatiana and I converse in Portuguese." Pedro replied in broken English, "How are you, my friends?" but João just shook his head. Leading them upstairs to the food court, the press assistant stopped at the Companhia do Churrasco, proclaiming, "Here's your beef steak, Brazilian style." The guys responded with glee and asked for *picanha*, a special cut from the top rump, a mainstay in Brazilian barbeque. Luke, Tatiana, and Grace looked next door at the Divina Fogão and selected a typical casserole with yellow rice, beans, cilantro, and cuts of pork. The press assistant dithered but finally picked *canja*, a special chicken soup, to help his digestion. Sancho happily arrived with three Big Macs and fries. Caipirinhas were ordered all around.

Luke and Tatiana sat down with the two assistants and explained their study mission. Luke reiterated that they sought to understand the connection between big agriculture and rising deforestation.

Pedro wore a frown when Luke mentioned the Ox Bench. "A bancada do boi has many friends in Brasilia and is allied to powerful interests. Its members might not look favorably at your mission, so do take care."

Sancho just nodded but ravaged his burgers.

Pedro's cell rang, and he excused himself from the table. Five minutes later, he returned to advise that he had to leave early in order to speak with his boss. "Thank you for meeting, Professor Shannon and Tatiana. We'll be in touch."

They rose and just shook hands. The lean assistant gave a half-hearted wave to the other students, who replied with a thumbs up.

His companion reluctantly trailed him out of the food court toward the escalator. Sancho looked back longingly at the Cacau Show boutique, exhibiting dozens of chocolate truffles, candies, and cakes.

Luke scratched his head and looked at Tatiana, who also wore a puzzled look. "I wonder what that twosome has in mind for us tomorrow," he said. "We should reach out to our other contacts. Your Guajajara relative paints a high profile here and abroad. It's time to give her a call.

"It's time to roll the dice."

THE ENDING JOURNEY

Matita Peré

No Jardim das rosas
De sonho e medo
No clarão das águas
No deserto negro
Lá, quero ver você
Lerê, lará
Você me pegar

Matita Peré

In the garden of roses
Of dream and dread
In the brightness of the waters
In the black desert
There, I want to see you
Here, *lará*
Catch me if you can

—*Tom Jobim (1973)*

CHAPTER 17

En route to the Articulation of Indigenous People of Brazil, Brasilia
Thursday Morning, August 19

TATIANA DIDN'T EVEN HAVE TO MAKE THE CALL.
The assistant to the president of the Articulação dos Povos Indigenas do Brasil telephoned early to invite her to APIB's headquarters that very morning. They had observed Tatiana's interview from São Paulo and yesterday's news story on Brasilia's local TV. Impressed with her passionate appeal for justice, they wanted to cooperate with her study mission. That Tatiana was of the same tribe as the association's leader added importance and urgency of getting together.

They agreed to meet at eleven thirty at APIB's office in the Northern Wing, not far from the University of Brasilia. Tatiana felt her body tingle in excitement. She would finally meet someone of her Guajajara nation, who had fought publicly for indigenous rights around the world. She did a little dance around her bedroom in exaltation.

Tatiana tracked down Professor Shannon, who had just finished his swim in the pool. She found him with a towel around his shoulders, dripping in the hall. For a middle-aged prof, he didn't look half bad. "Professor Shannon, they just called me from APIB to meet the president. Isn't that great? They saw our TV interview about Seattle University's mission and want to work together to raise the profile of indigenous people," she exclaimed, giving Luke a spontaneous kiss on his damp cheek.

"That's wonderful, Tatiana. Congratulations. I believe that divine providence has intervened in your behalf. By the way, I also received a call this morning from that senator's assistant who had dinner with us. He wants me to meet him again at an undisclosed location later this afternoon. This is getting too cloak-and-dagger for me. Doesn't this sound bizarre to you?" Luke asked.

"Very strange, Professor. I wonder what senator he works for, as most politicos want their names known far and wide. And what is the rest of the class going to do?" she inquired, glancing over him again.

"I plan to take your colleagues on a tour of the senate and congressional buildings which we viewed last night. It's too bad the senator's assistant didn't invite us to his boss's office. We'll probably have to grab lunch afterwards in the congressional cafeteria—probably not as elegant as where you'll be dining. Let's meet at the end of the day and compare notes. Get ready for more adventures," Luke said, giving her a wet kiss.

Tatiana returned the favor and strolled back to her room, excitement building about the day ahead. She began swaying to a bossa nova tune she'd heard on the radio. Imagine, she thought, Jobim and Vinicius were writing these songs well before I was even born. Yet, "Matita Perê" touched a chord deep inside her, and she uploaded the whole album onto her iPhone.

She entered her room as the hotel phone began ringing. She ran to answer it. "*Alô*, this is Tatiana speaking. . . . *Bom dia, Dona Sonia.* What a pleasure. Yes, I look forward to meeting you very much. . . . Thank you, but I don't want to inconvenience you. You are so busy with many responsibilities. . . . Are you sure you don't mind? . . . Yes, I can be ready by ten thirty. . . . Wonderful. *Obrigada e até logo.*"

Tatiana put the receiver down as quietly as she could, despite her bubbling emotions. This orphaned young student had just been invited by the most renowned person in the Guajajara tribe to take a ride in her car for a private tête-a-tête. Imagine, the most famous indigenous woman in all Brazil would be coming by to pick her up in an hour's time.

Doing another little jig around the room to a rhythm known only to her, Tatiana swept around and around as if she were dancing with the mysterious person recounted in Jobim's song. Tears streamed down her cheeks as she raised her voice, "*Obrigada, Meu Senhor! Obrigada, Guajajara!*" thanking the Lord and her nation for this precious moment in time.

Just then a sunray touched her balcony, and a rufous-bellied thrush, which she called a *sabiá laranjeira*, lighted on a bough of the ficus tree. She slowed her dance and walked softly toward the open sliding door, letting her blouse and beach wrap drop to the floor, still humming the bossa nova tune. The thrush cocked its head but did not fly away. They stared at each other for seconds, an eternity for Tatiana. Then this Indian maiden slowly swung around, almost purring, as she headed to the shower.

Reveling under the torrents streaming over her youthful figure, Tatiana was transported back to the waterfall of her native village. Her young life flashed back, from her pueblo to Seattle and now in Brasilia. Would this be the day she would embrace her destiny?

Tatiana dressed in a white blouse bordered in gold and wore a small Quileute Indian totem around her neck. Her mid-length skirt was straw-colored, and she wore leather sandals on her small feet. Checking herself in the mirror, she decided on no makeup. She looked better without. Pushing her black hair to one side, Tatiana took a deep breath and left the room. Looking back toward the ficus tree, she saw no thrush but heard its song nearby.

She walked down three flights of stairs and ran into Grace in the lobby. She told her roommate the great news.

Grace gave her a high five. "You look great, Tati. That small totem from La Push, Washington, looks well on you. Have a wonderful time with your tribal leader, and let's catch up tonight. The rest of us don't have as exciting a program. We plan to take a tour of the twin towers of Congress and the National Cathedral." Grace gave Tati a tight hug and two kisses. Seeing a black Volvo drive up to the hotel's entrance, Grace raised an eyebrow and bid, "Good luck."

The car's back door swung open, and a brown arm waved Tatiana in.

Tatiana entered with her mask on and met Sonia, a stout woman of similar color across the seat from her. Over her long black hair, the APIB leader wore a white headband patterned in red diamonds bordered in black and a red amulet around her neck. Her eyes were lively with a hint of mischief, and her mouth was covered by a homemade mask. Sonia told her Caucasian driver to head for the twin towers.

"Sister, welcome to Brasilia. How wonderful to meet a fellow tribeswoman from the United States. You must have a fascinating story but also one of pain, like most Guajajara people. Is this your first time to the capital? Let's take a quick tour around the Planalto so you can get a sense of how it's laid out. Then, we'll visit the Memorial of the Indigenous People, where the tribes' histories and artifacts are on display. Thousands visit from all over the world. Sadly, their stories have not been updated under the current administration, nor do they reflect current events hurting our people," Sonia said, her black eyes aflame in anger.

While driving by the twin towers and the Alvorada presidential palace, Tatiana shared her past, recounting how she had lost two mothers as a young girl. She highlighted the generosity of a CIMI missionary, whose sister took her into her home in the Pacific Northwest. Recalling her first journey to the States, Tatiana exclaimed, "They have so much stuff; I was overwhelmed. Everyone always seems to be in a hurry. But America gave me the opportunity to get my education and to spread my wings."

Sonia listened attentively and consoled Tatiana with words and her touch. Tatiana was a bit put off by the interruption of constant texts, which the APIB president received and made in the midst of her story. Sonia excused herself by saying that she would be part of a delegation to the Glasgow's environmental conference, COP26, to take place in November. "As we often have more chiefs than Indians when at a big confab like this, I have to massage many egos. It's important to hear them out and keep everyone in the family happy," she declared.

She had been invited to speak at COP26 to address attendees about the circumstances and suffering of Brazil's indigenous people under an administration that did not enforce the law. "They have set the vigilantes loose on us in the North. Illegal pan miners, loggers, and land grabbers come and go as they please.

Remember that the bancada do boi is our enemy," Sonia blazed, her eyes becoming two slits of obsidian.

They travelled west to the Buriti Plaza and passed the Memorial JK, the final resting place of Brazil's twenty-first president. The mausoleum was also designed by Niemeyer to honor Brasilia's founder and was highlighted by a unique twenty-five-foot tower with a life-size figure of Kubitschek on top, surrounded by a molded concrete scythe.

Sonia pointed out the Indigenous People's Memorial across the avenue and had the driver park in her reserved spot. They stopped at a spiral-shaped building announcing O Memorial dos Povos Indígenas. Exiting the car, they held down their skirts, though Tatiana enjoyed the breeze. The closer she approached the entrance, the more her heart accelerated. She was at last returning to the shrine of her bloodline and her tribal past.

They followed the curves up the long red ramp and entered the circular museum. Sonia had called ahead, and the guard whisked them through the turnstile before a student group from São Paulo. The two women passed a bronze rendition of a warrior wearing armbands and a chief's headdress with a spear. The statue made Tatiana recall her own village elder many years ago. Though not as strong as the depicted tribesman, her village chief wore a similar headdress. What she remembered most was that he always kept his head erect. He was the rock of her community and respected by all for his wisdom.

Tatiana listened to her companion identify artifacts of numerous tribes, including shaman vestments of straw, woven baskets of geometric design, clay pottery, and circular headdresses of feathers. Her guide pointed out the display of the Guajajaras, showing a ring-shaped headdress with blue and orange-brown feathers sprouting outward, with touches of white on the extremities. "These colors represent the sky and the earth of our nation," Sonia confided. "The white on the feather tips shows the white water of rapids coursing down, before the miners invaded our lands and dirtied our rivers," she complained. Some of the Paulista students were listening, a few shaking their heads.

Tatiana then turned and looked toward the round courtyard outside. She was startled at the array of tree stumps that encircled wooden shafts of various sizes and lengths rising from the ground. She didn't know why, but the simple remembrance of shorn trees provoked tears again. In her mind, Tatiana imagined these shafts as hands grasping upward, seeking freedom from oppression.

Sonia came alongside and shared the moment of silence, letting the indigenous sculpture carved from trees speak to each woman in different ways. Then she said, "This is a special place, Tatiana. I have chosen it as the site for another interview with the press later this afternoon. I thought this might be the time and the place to demand justice for our slain tribesman. November will mark the two-year anniversary of Paulino's death. We cannot let his sacrifice pass unnoticed.

"Let us adjourn for a quick lunch. We can work out what each of us should say in order to maximize our impact before the cameras. Remember there are many organizations here and abroad, including in America, that care deeply for indigenous rights. Our aim is to reach out to our allies and to stimulate support. We cannot let Paulino die in vain. He was the guardian of our forest, slain by evil men. We can no longer remain silent. This will be our big day. Are you ready to raise a battle cry like the Guajajaras of yore?"

"I believe so, Dona Sonia. The so-called law enforcement is sweeping his memory away and not searching for his killers. What injustice! If such a crime had been committed against a member of the Ox Bench, the response would have been swift and harsh. Yet in my cousin's case, the authorities continue to make excuses, hoping we'll forget about Paulino. I, for one, will not. Yes, let us stand up to these oppressors," affirmed Tatiana, clenching her fists and wanting to shout out loud.

"*Falou*," replied the APIB president. "Well said, my sister in arms. You are the warrior our people need." She let out a cry, which startled the thrush outside and the tourists in the museum. Sonia raised her right fist high. "Onward," she exclaimed. She led Tatiana past the surprised guards in a determined manner. The students opened their ranks to let them pass.

The indigenous pair left the memorial and embraced the dazzling sun. The breeze off the savanna fanned Tatiana's face, aglow in expectation.

CHAPTER 18

The Senate Chambers, Brasilia
Late Friday Morning, August 20

FLAVIO FUSSED AND FUMED, TRYING TO WALK OFF HIS ANGER. His quixotic assistant had all the excuses of the world and had failed to keep the two Indian women apart. Instead, he had wined and dined all the students and had a one-off chat with that belligerent prof, but to what end? Where could he find competent people to defend Papai and his family against such accusations?

Brasilia was a nest of vipers, and Flavio looked forward to flying back to Rio later today. The steppes were a dismal place. Why JK had this vision to move the capital here away from the Marvelous City was beyond his comprehension.

Yet this was where he had to work the corridors of power. Flavio didn't mind coddling the egos of the pols of the Big Center so they would abide Papai's will. A selfish bunch, but that was the nature of the beast. How should he deal with this latest tempest, and would o Centrão slither away like a slug in the rain? In his frustration, Flavio squeezed the macumba doll with Lula's head on top. His dull assistant had gifted him this dummy, showing some moxie and a sense of humor. Or maybe it was his assistant's gift for self-protection in order to keep his boss from exploding at him.

He crushed the doll's head again and stuck another pin in its back, hoping his adversary would feel the pain. His assistant revealed that a *santeiro* of the dark cults had put a special hex on it at a midnight session. Hopefully, Flavio's ire would penetrate the former president and debilitate his body and spirit so he would stumble and fall in 2022's election. He so wanted Papai to be victorious and show his enemies in Brasilia, São Paulo, and the press who was boss. His family would overcome and reign supreme.

However, how should Flavio deal with this latest allegation, whose reports were laid neatly in the press folder? He had also seen snippets of the two Guajajara women's interviews this morning on "Bom Dia, Brasil" and on TV Record's newscast. Even the latter network, owned by that evangelical pastor, was raising the issue of the unsolved murder. Why would it be concerned about some lackey who called himself the "guardian of the forest"? Then again, it's possible their so-called bishop was planting churches among the Indians, trying to rake in their reais. The bishop always favored cash flow. But his TV network had supported Flavio's father's election last time around. Hopefully, it would again.

The bottom line was that the worst scenario had played out. Flavio had warned his assistant not to let the women's meeting happen. Yet, that Guajajara student from America had linked up with that distasteful APIB chieftain and decried the government for "genocide." They claimed that agents of the Federal Police and Environmental Institute were being hamstrung by edicts from Brasilia and that the federal laws protecting indigenous lands were flouted by invading miners, loggers, and cattle ranchers. These entrepreneurs were only trying to make a living, for heaven's sake. Flavio squeezed the doll's head again harder and tried to collect his thoughts.

Looking out the window of his seventeenth-floor suite in Annex One of the Senate Building, Flavio detected a storm brewing on the horizon. He didn't want to be caught in some weird tempest, however unlikely in August. With the recent drought and unstable weather punishing Brazil this year, he couldn't take the chance. As Daddy was out of town, Flavio didn't feel obliged to respond to these Indian allegations in Brasilia. In fact, he'd do so from Rio de Janeiro with its more uplifting views than those on this barren desert.

Flavio called his assistant and asked her to get him on the next flight out of town. As he didn't want to be hounded by reporters, he'd get picked him up in the Congressional garage. "Tell Pedro to join me downstairs in a half-hour and to bring some sandwiches. There's no time for lunch as I'd like to be in Rio before sunset. Also, get me the WhatsApp number of TV Record's political reporter. Advise his assistant that I'd like to offer him an exclusive interview later today when I arrive. . . . Yes, it's about the allegations made by that APIB duo. That will be all for now. *Obrigado.*"

The grandfather clock showed twelve fifteen, so with luck, he could get on the two o'clock flight to Rio. If necessary, he'd pull rank to guarantee his reservation. Flavio did not want to cross paths with those two Indians on a warpath against Papai. That would be the show of shows for the news types, coveting discord and dissent.

Flavio picked up his travel bag and stuffed the news clippings, along with Lula's dummy, inside. To others, he didn't want to telegraph his secret weapon against Daddy's opponent. They'd find out soon enough.

Without looking back, Flavio left his grandiose office. His secretary printed out the GOL flight reservation and wished him a good weekend. He returned the greeting and waved to the staff. Thoughtfully, one of them had already called the private elevator reserved only for senators to whisk him to the underground garage. He enjoyed the perks of being a federal senator.

Flavio nodded to the young elevator operator, closed his eyes, and thought about what he'd say to the TV reporter later in the day.

* * *

TONIGHT, WOULD BE LUKE'S FINAL DINNER with all the students. Everyone would be heading back to Seattle tomorrow night, except himself, Tatiana, and maybe Grace. His plan was to take a side trip to the Pantanal near Cuiabá, stay with Teresa's friends in the wildlife refuge, and visit a priest working with indigenous people. Afterwards, he'd head up north to meet with the elusive journalist, who texted him earlier from Santarém.

Tatiana's interview had created a furor in the press, forcing Luke to deal with the aftermath. As Tatiana was Brazilian, critics hadn't railed about gringo interference into national affairs. The APIB head was a favorite of the journalists, so they didn't mind her occasional outbursts. However, a local reporter snidely asked Tatiana about the purpose of the so-called study mission and what students from Seattle wanted to accomplish.

"We are connecting the dots between Big Ag and deforestation," she affirmed, "and seeking ways to protect the woodlands and my people from land invaders."

The reporter didn't ask another question after that.

Band TV had just finished its interview with Luke, who echoed his students' words. He added that he was working with another prof at the University of Brasilia to join forces. The reporter gave a thumbs up and left.

Then, Luke got another nasty call. In no uncertain terms, the press assistant said his boss was very disappointed and disturbed by the professor's "aggressive tone." The Ox Bench was unhappy and was not known to take criticism lying down. "*Atenção*," the thin man cautioned again, telling him to beware.

To clear his head, Luke decided to take a quick swim. He climbed up the backstairs to the rooftop pool and glimpsed the sun fading into clouds on the western horizon. He also heard the prattle of parakeets from a large ficus tree and wondered what they were chattering about. Looking around the high-rises surrounding the Mercure hotel, he wondered what it'd be like living in Brasilia. Under Bush I, Luke had spent three years in Washington, DC, as Worldnet TV's director and enjoyed the excitement of the capital city. However, he tired of the full-court press of the Beltway lobbyists, who were always seeking a favor or an edge. He feared Brasilia would have a similar feel and was glad he was just a visitor.

Luke dove in the twenty-meter pool and did the breast stroke under water until he reached the other side. Then, he turned and completed several laps of the backstroke and the American crawl. He finished with a flourish of butterfly strokes and almost bounded out of the pool when he was done. Feeling refreshed, he wiped himself down and bid farewell to the parakeets calling out while colors of orange and red lit up the horizon.

As Luke was walking down to his room, he felt the vibration of his T-Mobile cell. Fortunately, a friend had shamed him into ditching his flip-top phone last year in favor of a Galaxy Android. He confessed that he enjoyed hanging onto his oldies and goodies, which provided comfort in a topsy turvy world. He still wore his faded Seattle U T-shirt of twenty years, holes and all.

During this visit, however, he had discovered that Brazilians hardly responded to emails but did via WhatsApp. So, he begrudgingly looked at the message on his smart phone, hoping another reporter was not calling him out.

The text was from his friend Vera of Paraisópolis, who just arrived to attend a conference for community organizers. She wanted to get together tonight and asked if she could bring a friend from the NGO, No Extinction, whose aim was to save Brazil's jaguars. In São Paulo, Teresa had mentioned that all animals of the savanna, wetlands, and forests were at great risk. Wildfires caused by a very dry season had forced birds, reptiles, and animals to flee. Additionally, illegal loggers and cattlemen continued to push northward into unoccupied lands, burning unharvested woodlands and any animals caught inside.

Luke texted Vera back, inviting them to stop by his hotel at eight o'clock to share pizza and beer with him and the students during their last-night celebration. He then called Tatiana to order pizza for a dozen of them in the Mercure's petite dining room.

At the appointed hour, he found Grace, Tatiana, and two of the guys talking about her interview on morning TV. They had just seen another newsclip by a federal senator who had called them "know nothings" on TV Record. "You sure set the media world on fire, Tatiana," affirmed her roommate, giving her another high five.

The group turned toward the hotel entrance and saw a beige Fiat pull up. Out popped Vera, beaming and lighting up the night. Luke walked briskly toward her and gave two kisses and a long hug. This five-foot dynamo always energized him. A tall, slender woman followed, her luxurious blond hair dancing with every step.

"Luke, let me present you to Fernanda, whom we just call the Gaucha as she's originally from Rio Grande do Sul. Her task is to save the jaguars and animal refugees from the savanna and wetlands."

Luke gave the fair-skinned woman two air kisses and introduced her to the students, who were still straggling down. They chatted briefly and saw Don Giovanni's van arrive with boxes of pizzas, exuding aromas of garlic, oregano, and olive oil. Luke tipped the delivery boy and directed everyone to the long table in the adjacent dining room.

The hotel's waitress tried to take individual drink orders but the guys shouted for "*cerveja*." The tall Brahma Pilsner beer was ordered round, as well as a few bottles of Brahma Malzbier, preferred by the women visitors. Conversation slowed down as everyone tore into the pizzas, featuring Brazil's version of margherita as well as the mozzarella, Parma ham, and Kalamata combos. Their favorite was the *tri-colore* pesto pizza, ringed with *funghi* and exhibiting the three colors of the Italian flag. As cerveza loosened their tongues, the decibel level rose dramatically. The pizzas quickly disappeared.

Nevertheless, short Vera and her taller companion raised their voices above the din. They began to recount their crusade to save panthers from last year's fire around Cuiabá. "We had to jerry-rig several pickup trucks to install makeshift bamboo cages for the fleeing animals. The zoo trainers attracted the wary jaguars by the scent of meat hanging inside each pen. At first, the lord of the jungle approached cautiously but then scampered up the ramp into the enclosure. They opted for the odor of meat rather than the smoke rising from the forest. A mother entered with her cub as the blaze began to claim the woods. We were able to save six jaguars, but imagine the others consumed in flames," Vera exclaimed, the students rapt in attention.

Suddenly, two broad-shouldered men wearing cowboy hats entered the hotel lobby, shouting to the clerk, "Where are the gringos?" The young attendant behind the counter gasped but no word escaped. The taller cowboy looked toward the room where Seattle U's fiesta was taking place and charged inside, saying, "So, you want to tangle with the Ox Bench, do you? Well, I have news for you. My fellow ranchers have arranged a homespun present for you talkative ones, the old gringo prof and his Indian helper," he slurred.

His shorter version stomped in with two boxes of off-putting stench and dumped one on Luke's plate and the other on top of Tatiana's pizza.

"*Come merda*," said the tall cowboy. "We're tired of eating your shit on TV. So we brought you dessert, courtesy of bancada do boi. Consider this our last warning. If you cross us again, we will come not with cow dung but something much worse." He stared at Luke, his eyes smoldering. Luke stayed seated but kept the rancher's gaze, which irritated him even more.

The shorter cowboy, anticipating his companion's eruption, pulled him ever so lightly away.

Perspiration started creeping down the students' faces as the room temperature rose apace.

The cowboys wheeled around, knocked over a table, and left everyone in stunned silence.

CHAPTER 19

L UIS CARLOS AWOKE WITH SUN STREAMING through partially drawn curtains overlooking a tropical forest and the Piray River. The residents of this city of two million were moving about below. Trying to recall the previous evening's one-night stand, he believed that the mestizo woman had been vouchsafed by a friend of a friend. She proved to be pleasant company and claimed to have studied at college. However, she didn't spend the night. Since his divorce, no one ever spent the night with him. Luis jealously guarded his privacy, preferring it over companionship with unknown women, however beautiful or sexually charged they might be.

Santa Cruz de la Sierra was a hidden gem, just east of the Andean Mountains where the rainforests sprouted up, sweeping through Bolivia's lowlands toward the immensity of the Amazon basin. Yet Brazil remained his chosen turf, even though he was born in Colombia.

This city of Bolivia's eastern plains featured an entrepreneurial spirit and the enthusiasm of the tropics, livelier than the two dull capitals of La Paz and Sucre high in the Andes. Thankfully Luis didn't have to do business up there, where they chewed coca leaves to ward off altitude sickness and a boring life. Founded in the 1500s, Santa Cruz reminded him a bit of Cali, though less hot and humid. He had always managed to cut favorable deals here, be they in hardwood, horses, or cocaine. His associates always treated him like royalty—quite different from what he received in his violent homeland or the double entendre in Brazil.

According to his associate of old cocaine money of the seventies, Santa Cruz was the fastest growing city in the Americas. The city was planned around concentric circles, with downtown being circle one. Developers were now pushing out to circle number ten, with many nouveau riche buying up condos to hide illicit gains. The community had the smell of fast money, where Ben Franklin was king.

Luis showered and asked room service for Santa Cruz's typical *majadito* breakfast, consisting of rice, beef jerky, fried plantains, chopped onions, and tomatoes. Its origin dated back to the pre-Columbian era when rice, grains, meat, plantains, and cassava served as staples among native people. The hotel served it with eggs sunny-side up and chimichurri sauce. The Colombian licked his lips in expectation.

Gazing out the window, he noticed some *tajibo* saplings, their yellow flowers budding early under the winter sun. The woman last night had announced that the "city of rings" would be transformed these coming weeks, abloom in yellow and rose of the tajibo and jacarandá trees. Despite cooler temperatures, lovers left their homes to promenade under the sea of color, their romantic spirits rising above the verdant plains. She had confessed how a young man had once knelt down before her under the yellow blossoms. He had offered her a plain wooden ring, proposing matrimony, and she had said yes. Tragically, it was not to be. Her fiancé was killed by a rival gang, like so many other young men in her hometown.

The woman's story led Luis back to his own violent youth, when he had made his first kill, egged on by his cousin now en route to an American jail. Though he tried so hard to close that door of reminiscence, it was difficult to keep it shut. When least expected, some story, song, or incident would barge through his consciousness and try to pull him down into the black hole of his past.

Involuntarily, he shook his head and entered the bathroom to shave. More creases ran along his forehead and flaccid skin drooped along his neck. Like the tajibo trees and all earthly creation, Luis was part of the natural cycle of life. He could control many things and exercise power over people, horses, and countries to do his will. Yet he could not hold back the ticking clock. He shook his head again and nicked himself with the razor. "*Caramba!*" Luis exclaimed aloud, angry with himself for going down memory lane. What purpose did it serve? Such brooding often led him to question his reason for being on earth.

Regarding himself more closely, wasn't he a success by contemporary standards? He had ranches in his homeland and horses stabled in Rio, São Paulo, and Cundinamarca. His fleet of Cessnas could deliver merchandise throughout the Amazon basin, including Peru, Brazil, his homeland, and Santa Cruz de la Sierra. He had fathered two children with his divorced wife, even though relations weren't close. At least he had left offspring in the world to carry on the family name, honoring his father's request. "Caramba," Luis shouted again at the mirror.

The knock outside shook him back to the present, away from his twisted past. Putting the Glock into his bathrobe pocket, he cracked the door, keeping the latch engaged, and then let the waiter enter with the abundant Bolivian breakfast. By the resonance of his Spanish, Luis concluded that he was a fellow Colombiano. He tipped him with a crisp Ben. The young man effusively thanked him, saying "*muchas gracias*" over and over. The older Colombian replied, "*De nada*, but keep your eyes posted if any countryman shows up in the hotel, OK?" The waiter said he would and left singing Shakira's latest tune.

The aroma of the majadito settled Luis down, spiking his hunger following last night's escapade. He poured himself a large cup of espresso, even though the beans came from Brazil. Juan Valdez coffee of his homeland was still the best. The Colombian devoured Santa Cruz's typical meal. Contemplating the blooming trees and the people wandering through the park, he shook off self-doubts lurking and let out a prolonged sigh.

Luis removed the nine-millimeter automatic from his pocket, with which he always travelled in Bolivia, Peru, and the hinterland of Brazil. Only in Rio and São Paulo did he "travel light" when his bodyguards shadowed him. In Santa Cruz, no way would he go without his G-18, which had once before saved his bacon. Even though his local associates treated him well, he could never let down his guard. Someone always carried a grudge or was consumed by greed. He had to pay attention, even though he did his utmost to treat friends and foes with respect. Who knew if some upstart had put a secret bounty on his head? There was always someone who wanted more. Death could easily find Luis Carlos, as it had countless others in his family tree.

Caramba, what a life, indeed!

Just then he heard the buzz of his iPhone grumbling on the nightstand near his king-sized bed. Outside the sun shone overhead, so the text was likely from an associate inviting him to wine and dine over churrasco at his vast hacienda on Circle Five. The rancher's interests were usually horses and hardwood, though he had dabbled in white stuff to get his start—who hadn't in Bolivia? The cattleman of similar age had proven a reliable customer and supplier for more than twenty years. He had earned his creds.

Luis looked down at his Apple iPhone 13 Pro Max and saw it vibrate again, as the clock showed twelve thirty. He picked it up and viewed the first message from Queiroz. The fixer had been pestering him since their lunch to open a new route to export illegally cut mahogany through Manaus and beyond. Luis was of mixed mind whether to accommodate the Brazilian's request as he didn't want to diss the Primeiro Comando da Capital. The Colombian cartel had maintained a correct but infrequent commercial relationship with São Paulo's powerful syndicate. The PCC was an unforgiving lot and was expanding throughout the continent and across the Atlantic. Luis must carefully ponder his move.

Queiroz inquired if Luis was planning to visit Cuiabá this week, as a fancy thoroughbred was up for auction. How could Luis Carlos resist? He was always on the lookout for prized equestrian mounts, especially in Brazil, where he could race them in either of the two Jockey Clubs where he was member. The Colombian might be able to fit in a quick trip to this riverine city, favored by Brazilian and Bolivian smugglers. However, he'd have to give Queiroz an answer regarding the uppity senator's request. He'd think of some way to ship their wood under the radar so as not to anger the PCC. Why not give it a try and garner a friend in Brasilia?

The earlier text was from an unregistered number beginning with a 206 area code from the States. Intrigued, Luis opened it up and found a simple question, "Tudo bem?" Underneath was a photo of that attractive student with indigenous roots whom he'd met outside of Rio's Jockey Club the previous week. When she had given him two kisses on the cheek that afternoon, her touch and fragrance had set him off. He desired to see her again. Maybe he'd reconsider his rule and have more than just a fling with her. She had a mature yet foxy presence.

His breathing ratcheted up a notch and excitement displaced the dread which had hounded him this morning. New energy flowed inside him. Without a second thought, Luis texted her back, "*Tudo bem, e você?* Where are you now on your study mission?"

Only a minute passed before the answer arrived: "Heading to Cuiabá. And you?"

Luis Carlos broke out a brandy from the minibar, splashed it in his espresso, and drank it down in one gulp. He decided to take one more chance. He certainly wasn't getting any younger, and he always embraced new challenges. Why not? he asked himself. Luis sent off his reply.

And altered the course of his life.

CHAPTER 20

The Salesian Mission, Cuiabá, Mato Grosso
Early Sunday Evening, August 22

THE PLANE FROM BRASILIA LANDED LATE, but Luke and Tatiana found an airport cabbie who knew where the Salesian mission and school were located. The air was deadly still, and the humidity enveloped Luke when he disembarked from the Bandeirante jet. He didn't want to imagine what the heat would be like in the summer on this river port. Its winter felt warmer than most Seattle summers.

Reading his guidebook, he discovered that Cuiabá was founded in 1719 by adventurers and miners panning for gold. The Salesians arrived in the following century to offer education to the Portuguese and indigenous people. A local tribe named the town after the Cuiabá River, which meant "arrow-fishing," its chief pastime before the miners showed up. Luke told the cabbie that he looked forward to tasting the town's fresh-water favorite, the golden *dourado*. The driver cautioned to make sure that the fish were caught upstream, away from the recent runoffs from the soybean farms.

Luke looked over at Tatiana, who was squirming in her seat. After the incident with the two cowboys dumping dung on their pizza, she was really down. They had popped her balloon of being a TV celebrity and a Guajajara warrior demanding justice for her people. The Ox Bench warning had sent a chill through her. She had asked Luke how she could stand up to such rough men. He had tried to console her by saying that the bancada do boi wasn't the only force in Brazil. Their study group had identified several others battling to preserve Brazil's rainforests, indigenous people, and fragile democracy. Luke credited Tatiana for keeping her cool.

This afternoon, however, a switch had clicked on inside her. She appeared more upbeat and began querying him about Cuiabá. Tatiana didn't admit to a friend or family member in this old colonial town but talked about "meeting new people" and seeing the Patanal animal refuge. Luke scratched his head and confessed his inability to read the swings of this young woman's moods.

After the dinner incident, Grace decided to return to Seattle with the rest of the students Saturday night. Luke accompanied them to Brasilia's international airport and detected relief on many faces. The students would fly on American Airlines over the Amazon again, landing early morning in Miami to clear Customs. After several hours' layover, they'd take the long flight back to Seattle, ending a twenty-hour marathon. They promised to work on the study report and their recommendations to Seattle University and the Sierra Club, agreeing to get together just after Labor Day.

Before leaving to attend her conference, Vera had mentioned that her brother was a padre helping the Salesian mission in Cuiabá. If they didn't mind sleeping on native mats, the priest had invited them to overnight in the rectory's humble room. Luke and Tatiana had agreed. Vera would be joining them Monday and planned to visit indigenous villages and worker communities supported by the mission outside of town. She'd also expressed interest in seeing the refuge that gathered animals from last year's fire. The driver skirted the Cuiabá River, which looked low in its banks. "There's been a drought in western Brazil, and we've had to ration water. The world and the weather have turned upside down, but the cost of living keeps rising. What is a working man supposed to do?" he complained. The cabbie bumped over the cobblestones until he entered a paved road, arriving at a colonial building with an upstairs sign of Colégio Salesiano São Gonçalo. A red *S* resembling a lightning bolt spliced through a blue circle on a white background. He turned around and asked, "Is this where you want to go, Professor? The school closed at six o'clock."

Luke peered at the large two-story school, painted beige with white trim around its Roman style arched windows. A faint street light blinked from the corner, but no illumination appeared inside. Above the shut wrought-iron entrance, five tiles in raised relief declared the school's mission: "Education—Integral, Intellectual, Social, and Religious."

Luke caught the eye of a lone guard who ambled by. "Good evening, senhor. We're looking for Padre José's residence, as he invited us to spend the night. Would you point us in the right direction? I may have misunderstood where he lives. He serves as a parish priest in the Salesian mission," Luke said, exhausting all the information he recalled from Vera.

"Ah, Padre José, he's a good man. His parish is out of town, but I believe he's conducting vespers at São Gonçalo tonight. Please tell him that João says hi," he replied, giving the driver quick instructions.

After a half-mile weaving through back streets, the cabbie dropped Luke and Tatiana off at a colonial church with a tall bell tower and a statue of the Good Shepherd on top. Luke paid the driver and left with Tatiana, climbing the sandstone stairs and stepping inside. They sat on a wooden pew toward the back and relaxed. A few dozen parishioners in working clothes were scattered around the church under subdued light. The priest was finishing his homily about "loving your neighbor" and acknowledged the new arrivals with a nod.

They took Communion and waited in the short line to greet the slim mulatto in a Roman collar. Taller than his sister Vera, the priest stood five foot seven, had a shaved brown head, weathered skin, and a twinkle in his eye.

"*Boa noite*," he exclaimed. "You must be little Vera's friends. I'm Padre José, serving as a substitute priest. Welcome to our parish in Cuiabá. Do you mind returning with me to the nave so we can lock the doors and douse the lights? We must manage our finances carefully during difficult times. I'll show you to our accommodations in the back where we can have a cup of herbal tea." He gave Luke a tight hug and Tatiana two kisses on the cheek and led them inside. He turned off the lights and left two candles burning on the altar, which glimmered off pale blue walls and a simple bronze crucifix.

Luke and Tatiana followed him out the back door into an attached rectory and the small space allotted to the visiting priest. The room had a single bed, a wooden table, and a chair on a parquet floor. Two straw mats were rolled against the corner, and a wooden crucifix stood sentinel on the wall. A lone red rose in a vase decorated the chipped ceramic basin, and a mirror reflected weak light overhead. An open window let in humid air and the chirrup of an exotic amphibian outside.

"Excuse the rustic surroundings, but Vera insisted that you stay the night to get a sense of our mission here. I usually spend most time in the villages ministering to the tribal children who have few resources for school or daily life. Recently, workers imported from the North have asked me to visit them in their fenced compounds on the soy plantations." Looking down, Padre José added, "The owners and the foremen are not too welcoming.

"By the way, we have a common bathroom in this wing, just two doors down. I'll find pillows and cotton spreads for you, though it doesn't get cold at night. Please excuse the simple mats made by our villagers. Would you like to use the restroom, Tatiana?" Padre José inquired, pointing her down the hall. He left Luke to extract a toothbrush from his Air Force garment bag and to figure how to arrange themselves overnight.

Padre José returned with pillows, spreads, and a jug of warm chamomile tea. Tatiana reappeared in a pink dressing gown going just below her knees. She stacked her day clothes on top of Luke's and her suitcases in the other corner. The priest poured their tea in small paper cups and welcomed them to sit on his single bed.

When they finished tea, the priest offered a short prayer, asking protection for the visitors and for the indigenous people. They said the Lord's Prayer together. Tatiana rolled out her mat facing the window. Luke did likewise, pointing in the opposite direction.

As Padre José was about to turn off the light, Tatiana's phone buzzed twice. She checked the WhatsApp screen and stared at the message for a minute.

"Is everything all right, Tatiana?" Luke asked.

Still staring at the phone, she didn't answer right away. "Tudo bem, Professor. Just a message from a new friend. Good night."

The padre turned off the lights. It took Luke a while to go to sleep in his new surroundings. Throughout the night, he heard a croaking frog, a snoring priest, and a restive student tossing and turning right next to him.

CHAPTER 21

TWO MESSAGES ARRIVED WHILE LUIS WAS NIBBLING on the continental breakfast in this four-star hotel connected to the Convention Center. Five years ago in this Santa Rosa neighborhood, he'd attended an equestrian conference and purchased a yearling from a local family. The horse had done him well, so he was intrigued by the thoroughbred auction that Queiroz had advertised. Luis looked at his iPhone and saw that the senator's middleman suggested getting together at the poolside café around one o'clock.

The other message was from that alluring Brazilian. She had already arrived and was doing mission work with some church group outside of town. Not his cup of tea. However, she said that she'd text him when they arrived back tonight. His hopes and libido soared. Couldn't he relive some of his favorite stories in *The Arabian Nights*, right here in the Brazilian jungle?

According to his local contact, a bodyguard would arrive by noon. Outside, Luis glimpsed the Arena Pantanal stadium, where his Colombian team had once competed in the Copa America. Though tempted, he decided not to wander around town, which he didn't know well. Instead, he'd work out in the fitness center, which shouldn't be too busy this time of day. Always on guard, Luis placed his Glock inside the Patagonia gym bag and walked down seven flights of stairs. Relieved that no one else was in the center, he got on the boring treadmill, set it at medium speed and let his mind imagine what it'd be like to bed that Amazonian firebrand. He'd seen her interview on TV and felt attracted to her hot-blooded temperament. She was his type of woman.

After twenty minutes, a young man entered with his own gym bag, which he put down next to another NordicTrack. Luis Carlos decided that his time was up and opened his bag to towel himself down. Glancing over his shoulder, he noticed that the youth was watching Luis's every step as he departed the center. The elevator arrived empty, so he took it up to the top floor and reentered his suite.

Luis showered and dressed in a dark-blue polo shirt and tan Levi slacks and sat by the window looking out to the stadium three blocks away. As it was around noon, he mixed himself a Campari and tonic to get a leg up on his visitor who liked to order expensive wine. Queiroz was typical of all underlings, as well as soldiers of the Cartel; he wanted to get as much as he could as fast as possible in his allotted time. Understood.

The bedroom phone rang, but Luis did not answer it. Why should he, as no one knew he was here, save the Brazilian middle-man and his local handler? They were instructed to always text him beforehand. After a few minutes, he heard a knock on the door and grabbed his Glock.

Another louder knock and a deep male voice asked, "Senhor Luis?"

Holding his G-18 at the ready, Luis opened the door a crack, keeping the hinged lock on. "*Sim*," is all he said to a sturdy, dark-complected man, dressed in an ill-fitting suit, an off-white shirt, and loose black tie.

"It's twelve noon, senhor. Senhor José told me to report for duty as your escort today and to serve you wherever needed. Tudo bem?"

Ah yes, the bodyguard, how could Luis forget? Perhaps his fantasies about that Indian maiden had clouded his memory. Luis could never let his down his guard. "Tudo bem. Please just patrol the hall for the time being. I should be heading out by one o'clock. Thank you for coming," he stated, double-locking the door.

The Colombiano lay down on the bed, Glock by his side, and fell asleep. His iPhone began buzzing on the nightstand, but he was dead to the world.

Knock, knock on the door again.

Luis's eyes popped open as he grasped his gun.

"Senhor Luis?" came the voice from outside. "You have a visitor."

The clock showed one fifteen, so he got up and approached the door. Repeating the same procedure, he stood to the side and slid it open, He peered at his escort looking concerned and saw Queiroz leaning against the hallway's wall.

"*Momento*," Luis replied. He gave himself the once-over in the mirror and left the G-18 inside his gym bag. Pushing open the door, he placed the Do Not Disturb sign on the handle.

Walking briskly over to the senator's fix-it man, Luis greeted, "Tudo bem, Queiroz?" They gave each other a loose hug and sized each other up.

"Let's head to the poolside bar for some refreshments and con-versation," Luis said, leading the way. They took the elevator to the pool floor and found a table in the back under a parasol. The Colombian sat down with his back to the wall and Queiroz on his right. The bodyguard sat at the adjacent table on his left scanning the area. All they saw were young kids and two mothers splashing around in the curved pool. A waiter in light green shorts and T-shirt took their drink orders: Campari and tonic for the host and Cabernet Sauvignon for his guest.

They discussed the horse auction the next day, and Luis said he'd planned to participate online. They also complained about their soccer teams in Colombia and Brazil, as well as Cuiabá's mugginess, even in winter. When their beverages arrived, they got down to business.

"Senhor Luis, we have some hardwood ready to ship this very week. The loggers are storing hundreds of board feet of jacarandá and massaranduba in a warehouse in Marabá, Pará. As you're aware, the city has two rivers running through, as well as five roadways, including BR-150 heading directly to Belém. We need more protection to transport the wood to our partners' warehouse near the port on Guajará Bay. The wood is valued at a million dollars, and your cut would be a third. Can you provide us help?"

The Colombian listened carefully to Queiroz, whom his jailed cousin had once considered reliable. Luis had never dealt with him. This would be the first of several shipments, he surmised, and it would not involve drugs, which was a plus. Since that federal cop had been reassigned from Manaus, Luis had discovered that the heat was off on wood smuggling but still on for cocaine. Brasilia had reined in the federal police and inspectors, making transshipment of hardwood less risky. "Will you provide any reliable escorts," Luis asked, "besides some of my own? We have a friend inside Customs in Belém who can process the paperwork for export abroad. Where is the wood heading?" he inquired, paying close attention to Queiroz's body language. He didn't fidget which was a good sign.

"We know a couple of cops in Belém's policia civil and retired cops in Marabá. All can be hired for five hundred dollars a day. The buyer is an Italian furniture company, which will send a representative to accompany the shipment from Belém to Naples."

"I'll have to get on this right away. I was under the impression that you'd planned to ship through Manaus like the previous time. As I understand it now, our job will be to provide muscle on the ride to Belém's port, protect the hardwood until its release by Customs officials, and ensure it boards the freighter. Our normal fee would be 50 percent freight on board. How does that sound?"

Queiroz looked like he'd sucked a lemon and shifted in his seat. He nodded to the waiter to top off his glass and asked him to leave the bottle. Attempting to keep his voice low, Queiroz countered at 35 percent.

After minutes of back and forth, they settled on 40 percent and toasted the beginning of a new commercial relationship.

Just as he began to relax, Luis noticed that the same young man at the gym had arrived with another man. They both carried bags. He caught his bodyguard's eye and nodded toward the twosome who sat three tables away.

"Queiroz, it's been a pleasure to come to this understanding with you. Now, I'll have to leave for another engagement. Please enjoy the rest of the wine and order lunch on my account. Let me text you later today after the arrangements are made."

The Colombian rose, as did his escort, who stood between the two young men and his boss. Luis tapped his new Brazilian partner on the shoulder, forced a smile, and headed to the emergency exit and down the stairs.

Luis hoped he wasn't becoming too paranoid. For sixty-four years, he had stayed alive by following his gut, often taking the path of caution.

Furthermore, he never liked coincidences.

CHAPTER 22

TATIANA DID NOT SHOW. LUKE'S STAR STUDENT disappeared in the middle of the night.

Vera had arrived on Monday, and the two women had stayed in one room, and Luke and the padre in another. But no one heard or saw Tatiana slip away.

On the evening of their arrival, Luke recollected her strange behavior when she received a text from a new friend but shared nothing more. Yesterday, when they had visited tribal villages, Tatiana was sneaking peeks at her iPhone. He had noticed her texting surreptitiously under a low-hanging jacarandá budding purple flowers. Afterwards, he'd asked her if a friend had arrived in Cuiabá, receiving only a "maybe" in response. Tatiana had met with the village chief and engaged in active conversation with the women and children. She had shared her story and taught a few words of English. She seemed pleased, as did her native audience.

During dinner at the mission cafeteria, Tatiana had played with her food and excused herself early. Although she had joined them for vespers, she did not socialize afterwards but instead had retired to her room "to catch up on sleep."

When Vera turned in at eleven o'clock, her roommate lay facing the wall on the straw mat breathing lightly. The social worker, a deep sleeper, did not hear Tatiana leave in the early morning hours. Tatiana's suitcase was still in the corner, but her travel bag was gone.

Luke texted and called her several times on WhatsApp, receiving no reply. Given Tatiana's peculiar conduct, Luke guessed that she had snuck out to visit her friend and didn't want to explain. Maybe she had discovered a new lover on the study mission. He decided not to alert the police or to search the town, which he barely knew.

Thanks to the welcoming Salesian fathers and deacons, Vera and Luke spent another night at the rectory. Early morning, the two joined them for a simple *café com leite* and freshly baked bread. Teresa's animal shelter was near the Pantanal, so Luke joined Padre José, Vera, and a visiting nun on the twelve-hour ride to the Pantanal hotel near Brazil's famous wetlands. They crossed quickly into the neighboring state of Mato Grosso do Sul as the sun rose over the hills.

Midway, they stopped at another village, hosting the remnants of the Guaicurú nation. Two centuries earlier, their warriors were considered "the Apaches of the Pantanal and the Chaco."

When questioned by Luke, the priest explained: "The Guaicurú combined with other tribes and stood their ground against early Europeans invading the region by river and land. In battle, they formed guerrilla bands, setting ambushes and raiding adversaries when they least expected it. The warriors reputedly charged into battle naked except for jaguar skins, clubs, lances, and machetes. Crouching low on their horses, or riding on the animals' sides, they avoided becoming easy targets to European marksmen. They didn't use saddles or stirrups, guiding their mounts only with reins.

"The Guaicurú coalition proved so ferocious that the Portuguese decided not to fight them head on. They adopted a 'live and let live' policy as long as indigenous warriors hunted Spanish enemies instead. In that way, Brazil expanded its territory to its current borders and lived in relative peace for a while. Sadly, European disease did not honor the accord and spread throughout tribal areas, leaving hardly a thousand alive today."

The padre led them to meet the village chief, whose chapped lips formed a tentative smile. He invited them to sit on wooden benches under the thatched roof in the open-air communal hall. An older woman served herbal tea, brewed in a cast-iron pot over the outdoor fire. The priest and the chief exchanged ideas about dealing with the drought and how to keep young men from leaving the community.

The chief told more stories about his people's past and their relationship with the Terena nation, whose skill in agriculture enabled them and European settlers to work together. Then his lips turned down, to explain current concerns: "The main problem today is the vigilante miners and loggers who swoop down on our land, cut our trees, or go upstream to pan for gold. Also, bosses from the ranches keep promising riches to our young men and women. They lure them away to work in the fields. We often don't hear back from them," he lamented, looking out on twenty mostly middle-aged women and young children. A few boys were kicking around a battered soccer ball on the dusty playfield. Their abodes circled the communal lodge and were a smorgasbord of wood and mudbrick huts, covered by tin rooves. Some had installed glass windows, but most had not.

The chief led the community to a wooden table and a dozen benches under a large mango tree. The priest placed a white cloth over the table to transform it into a makeshift altar. Vera handed him the loaf of mission bread and led the hamlet's congregation in liturgy. The people sang the "Gloria" with gusto and voiced the Lord's Prayer in unison. Padre José broke and consecrated the bread into the *corpus Christi*, and everyone knelt on the sparse grass. One by one, each came forward for Communion, the priest placing the host in each of their mouths. For Luke, it was the most heartfelt worship he had witnessed.

When Mass was concluded, the padre delivered school supplies to the chief's niece and a used sewing machine to his sister, the local seamstress. Exchanging hugs and promises to stay in touch, the Salesian visitors thanked their hosts and returned to their minivan. Luke looked out the window and returned the waves of the chief, the women, and their children enveloped in a cloud of dust. He wondered what his life would be like had he been born in this village instead of Seattle. Would he be working on the soybean farm like most men or even be alive today?

Back on the two-lane highway, they viewed smoke spewing from a nearby hill. Padre José observed that it hadn't rained in weeks and the forest and underbrush were tinder to any untoward flame. A small herd of deer-like animals were running away from the brushfire. The priest decried, "As the weather becomes unpredictable, both humans and animals get confused. Look at these marsh deer with their black legs charging toward us. Their usual habitat is the wetlands, but when the marsh dries out, they wander in search of water anywhere. We hardly know from one day to the next if wildfires or flashfloods will pursue all earthly species, causing us to flee. For the indigenous people who for centuries lived off the land, unpredictable weather makes survival very difficult."

The padre, Luke, Vera, and the nun journeyed in silence most of the way. As they crossed a stream, movement caught Luke's eye. A furry brown animal and two young 'uns were splashing around a small pond. Their snouts were elongated, and the creatures had the look of a big hairy rat. An off-green meadow swept up from the stream, and a copse of palms dotted its summit. The priest pulled to a stop and viewed the animals frolicking in the slow-moving creek. "Professor, let me present you to Brazil's capybara, the largest rodent in the world. As long as they find water and forage, they are able to survive our changing environment. The little ones are considered quite tasty in a barbeque, but the big capybara is often used for breeding."

The mother stood briefly on its hind legs and ushered her kids into a clump of amaranth bushes, hiding under pink flowers. Luke was able to get a quick shot on his Galaxy to show Seattle U's students what they'd missed.

They drove on toward the town of Miranda, one of the gateways to the Pantanal. Luke looked back from where they'd come and noticed a light red glow. Night fell abruptly, and a waning moon peeked above the rolling hills.

Two hours later, they entered a small, sleepy town with few pedestrians on the street. The main activity centered on its Shell gas station and a fishing club where three residents sat in wicker chairs telling yarns. Arriving at their hotel, the foursome were relieved to find a pleasing lodge with a covered entrance and red tiled roof. Its outside patio sported wooden tables and a few visitors downing

Brahma Chopp beer. Luke's stomach lurched as he whiffed the aroma of manioc fries with parmesan sprinkled on top.

The men checked into their ground floor room, and Vera and the nun into theirs next door, pleased that the A/Cs were working. Returning to the patio bar, they joined tourists in tossing back draft beer. It'd been a long day. Everyone ordered the catch of the day, grilled *dourado* from the Miranda River, accompanied by a vinaigrette lettuce-and-tomato salad, beans, and rice. A homemade flan was included for dessert, and Luke paid the bill, less than twenty dollars. The four traded small talk and planned tomorrow's venture into the wetlands to visit Teresa's refuge in the Pantanal.

Padre José also shared, "I've become the itinerant priest for the mission. I'll be leaving again this weekend to substitute for another cleric on the island of Marajó, in the Amazon delta. Since you'll be ending your mission in Pará and enjoy pastoral settings, you'd be most welcome to visit me across the river. You have my WhatsApp, so please let me know."

Luke said he would, especially once he discovered the whereabouts of his errant student. Around ten o'clock, he felt exhausted and stifled a yawn. The long trip and tension of Tatiana's disappearance weighed on him. He decided to turn in. His companions wished him "boa noite" but remained outside to exchange news about the latest incursions in tribal lands in their respective regions.

As Luke opened the door to his room, his Galaxy began buzzing, alerting him of a recent message. He looked down and saw Tatiana's 206 number and the words: "Professor, excuse my early departure. I'm with a new friend. He's going to take me to Marabá and Belém in his plane. Don't worry. I am fine but need a time-out. I picked up my luggage from the mission. See you in Belém. Please don't worry. Kisses, Tati."

Luke called her back but received no answer. He walked outside to the verandah and paced back and forth. This was not how they had planned the last leg of the study mission, with some mystery man in the mix. How could he understand or anticipate the whims of this student, unpredictable as a tropical storm? Though she was a young adult, the safety of every Seattle U student remained his responsibility.

He kept breathing deeply to slow his heart rate down, finally going inside to brush his teeth. Lying down on his single bed, the clean sheets and firm mattress felt great after two nights on the floor.

Despite such comfort, it was Luke's turn to toss and turn throughout the night. His bad dream returned, with him suspended in that glass cage shouting to Tatiana below to watch out. But she didn't look up or heed his warning.

CHAPTER 23

In Flight to Marabá, Pará
Wednesday Morning, August 25

"DON'T PATRONIZE ME!" SHE SHOUTED, causing Luis Carlos to throw up his hands. Her new lover did not want an airport scene with passengers and attendants looking on.

Last night, he had invited her to join him and two business associates in his Cessna 172 on a flight to Marabá. Still enchanted by her new friend, she hadn't thought of asking about the other passengers and had assumed they were involved with horses too. She had accepted his invitation without question and jumped into bed.

When Tatiana arrived this morning, she was shocked to see who one of his associates was—no other than the fix-it man of that senator who disrespected indigenous rights. Her lover, noting her brewing anger, informed her that he was obliged to fly him there to ensure that the deal went off. He added, "My beautiful one, this is no concern for you. Business is business, and I must see this through. I promised an important man in Brasilia that I'd do so. Let me conclude this affair while you enjoy the pool at our hotel. We should only be there overnight."

After her pouting and stomping around, Luis appeared apologetic. Despite her misgivings, she agreed to go.

Luis sat in the pilot's seat with her right next to him in the cockpit. The fix-it man and the bodyguard sat in the back. After checking the instrument panel and receiving the control tower's approval, Luis revved the engine, cleared the runway, and took off into a light wind.

It was thrilling to fly in this small plane. Her pilot and lover tipped the wings to view a winding river, a small lake, and cattle grazing below. The savanna's fields soon melded into forestland pierced by makeshift roads. At the woodland's edge, a fire was smoldering next to ploughed fields of soy. From the forest, a logging truck was barreling down the road, laden with timber, kicking up dust in its wake.

"Shouldn't we report this fire to authorities?" she asked, as flames licked edges of the grove. Recalling the hotel's map, the woods below should be the National Park of the Xingú nation. "Luis, this is Xingú land, and that truck is taking away their trees. We should do something!"

The pilot looked out the window of the Cessna 172 but didn't respond, scratching his head.

"Can't you call someone on your radio? This doesn't look right," she exclaimed, her black eyes warning of trouble.

Luis sighed and asked the young bodyguard, whom he called Cuiabá, to let the control tower know about the burning land on the tribal reserve. The older unshaven man simply shook his head.

Tatiana resented the older man's haughty manner and his relationship with the infamous politico. She had never imagined being on this single-prop plane with him flying to Marabá for a business deal. That gruff man and his smooth boss were the avowed enemies of her people and all the tribes of Brazil. Caramba!

Then remembering that Professor Shannon would be worried that she hadn't replied to his texts, Tatiana promised herself to respond via WhatsApp on arrival.

Generally, she preferred the company of mature gentlemen and lost patience with men her own age. Though not loose in her affairs, she had enjoyed a three-month stint with a SU prof. While honoring her side of the bargain, the so-called divorced prof had not. One evening, she had entered the Chieftain Pub with a girlfriend and spied him holding hands with a dreamy-eyed coed. Tatiana had exploded on the spot. Her companion had had to restrain her when she had tried to slug her unfaithful lover. Tatiana had stormed out and like a machine gun spewed every curse word she recalled *em português*. It was such a scene that a sly reference to this "fiery blowup" had appeared in the school newspaper. Usually calm, Tatiana admitted she had to better manage her hot blood, especially after feeling disrespected.

Her new friend revealed that he too was a divorcé and had fathered two children. His youngest, Luis Junior, had just earned his MBA at La Javeriana and was working on his pilot's license in Bogota. His eldest daughter had her own life and family in Medellín. Luis confessed to travelling a lot but had no significant other in his current life.

Tatiana admired the way he touched her and made love to her, considering him a most seductive partner. He smelled good, knew the ropes, and was not rough. The Colombiano reminded her of a thoroughbred horse about which he raved so often. Her lover's gait and gallop won the race with her every time. She was really enjoying this break from her sexual fast of 2021.

During this whirlwind immersion in her native land, Tatiana admitted that Brazil may have cast a spell on her. Unbound by her mother's words or America's puritanical code, she was able to move to her own beat in the land of her birth. Having a secret affair appealed to her, especially with this man of charm and mystery.

She looked at the blaze below, recalling her other mission: to stand up for indigenous people and exact vengeance on her cousin's killers. What had Sonia declared at the Brasilia press conference? "We must be bold. We must stop the invasions and the fires on native land. We must seek justice for our people by all means possible." Yes, this was her real mission.

But why couldn't she have it all, a fling in the tropics and retribution for Paulino? When the time was right, she would ask Luis what he would recommend her to do in this situation. As a man of the world, he knew a way around dangerous people. Tatiana began plotting the moment when she'd question him. Afterwards, she'd find some way to track down her cousin's killers.

* * *

Two unsmiling men met their flight at Marabá's regional airport, heightening Tatiana's concern. Luis Carlos looked unhappy and rattled off in Spanish at one of his greeters, his anger growing with each word. He brusquely asked the other *en portuñol* to take her to their hotel in town. When her lover got excited, his Spanish overpowered his Portuguese, creating an exotic linguistic mix. No one looked pleased, so it was just as well she'd leave them so they could work out their business.

Tatiana gave Luis a quick kiss and entered the back seat of the Volvo. The well-built driver tossed her bags and the Colombian's suitcase in the trunk. He offered few words and brooked no smile.

They crossed a bridge over a torpid waterway, identified by a sign as the Itacaiúnas River. The downtown was a collection of mostly low-level structures, some whitewashed with red tiled roofs. The taller buildings were usually hotels, save a multi-storied edifice, which protruded starkly on the horizon. Few cars and fewer people moved about the streets. The digital clock read 15:00, followed by the temperature of 38 degrees Centigrade, or 99 degrees Fahrenheit. The A/C inside was laboring to beat back the heat.

The Golden View Hotel appeared abruptly in the cluttered city center. The mum driver took the luggage out of the trunk, gave it to the wizened doorman, who greeted, "Welcome to Marabá." Tatiana looked back to thank her chauffeur, but he had sped off in the Volvo without a word. Strange man, she thought. His gruff manner made her recall the big cowboy who had spoiled her dinner in Brasilia.

In contrast, the doorman was a loquacious sort and a great PR agent for Marabá: "Did you know that our city of two rivers is the fastest growing in the state of Pará? The July holiday just concluded, and all hotels were filled with tourists from the South— especially São Paulo. They love our beaches along the Tocantins and our relaxed life style. You and your companion should enjoy the sunset at one of the riverside bars overlooking the river. Don't forget to try our local açaí caipirinha, which is supposed to be healthier for you."

"It sounds delightful, senhor. By the way, what was that white high-rise I saw in the distance as we came into town? It seems out of character with the rest of the city's architecture," Tatiana asked this font of information.

"Ah, that new development is called Crystal Tower. It features luxury apartments for the rich and famous. Some allege that it's financed by Colombian drug lords, trying to launder their illicit gains in Northern Brazil. It's supposed to be ready this year but stands out like a sore thumb," he replied as he led her to the front desk.

After she had checked in, the doorman carried the bags to the top floor and showed her into the panoramic suite. The swimming pool glistened below with a few guests sitting under parasols. Tatiana hadn't swum during her trip, so exercise would do her good. She tipped the man ten dollars and thanked him again.

"I am at your service, senhorita, anytime. My name is José and am available 24/7. I have a room near the reception. Be welcome," he wished, showing her a toothy smile of uneven teeth.

Hanging up a couple of skirts, a black pantsuit, and a low cut-dress, Tatiana left most of her bag unpacked. Her lover's carry-on suitcase stood upright, a zipped pocket ajar. Always curious, she opened one side of the Eddie Bauer wheel-on and discovered brochures about the thoroughbred auction in Cuiabá and others about that Crystal Tower development in Marabá. Digging a little further, she touched clips of ammunition for a gun. Oh, oh. What was her mystery man's real business besides horse trading and racing? With menacing men in his entourage and bullets in his suitcase, maybe Tatiana should reconsider her impromptu affair. And how was he involved with the Crystal Towers, whose financing came from Colombian traffickers, according to the attendant?

Someone knocked on the door, so she stuffed the brochures and bullets back inside the bag and zipped it shut. Rushing to open the door, Tatiana found the doorman had returned with something in his hand. "Tudo bem?" she said.

"I'm sorry to bother you, but I forgot to give you the discount cards for the Batam Center on the waterfront. It's not far away and has an exhibit about Marabá. Here are two cards, one for you and your companion. Will he be arriving soon?" he inquired, raising an eyebrow.

"Obrigada, José. Yes, he'll be coming after his business is done. Thank you," she replied, wondering what that was all about. She removed the Do Not Disturb sign, putting it on the outside handle. Forcing a smile, she closed the door.

Feeling odd about the attendant's return and the menacing men at the airport, Tatiana attempted to put together disparate pieces of the last three days. Still perplexed and weary, she lay down on the king-size bed and fell asleep.

* * *

The reverberation grew louder, threatening to sweep Tatiana out to the River Sea. Matita Peré was closing in. As she ran through the rainforest, where would she find aid? She accelerated her pace and grasped her amulet, but heard a jaguar growling.

Both in her nightmare and in her bed, she thrashed around and called out loud for help, "*Socorro*."

The young woman opened her eyes as tears and sweat streamed down her cheeks. It was dark outside and confusion set in. Where was she now? The sound continued from a nightstand, and a neon screen was flashing. She turned and grabbed her cell. "Alô?"

"Is this my long-lost cousin? This is Luciana calling from Maranhão, tudo bem?" she inquired. When no response was forthcoming, the caller continued, "Alô, are you hearing me?"

Tatiana shook her head and replied, "Please excuse me, Luciana. I was just waking up from a weird dream. What a pleasant surprise. Are you calling from our village, or have you moved someplace else?"

"I left our homeland a year ago and am working as a domestic on a large ranch in Açailândia, in western Maranhão. It's not far from the Pará border. I heard from the CIMI missionary that you were in Brazil on a study mission. Then I saw you on TV. You've raised quite a profile since you left our tribe. It seems that America has been good to you. Congratulations," her cousin exclaimed, raising her voice as if in a song.

Tatiana paused, recalling the geography of her state of birth. "I think we're not too far away. I just arrived in Marabá on the study mission," she lied.

"How wonderful. Can we see each other? Oh, before I forget, a journalist in Belém has a lead on who killed Paulino. He said it's group inside the civil police and tied to organized crime. These are dangerous men and connected to big landlords and São Paulo gangs. They run illegal logging and real estate operations. I called to warn you not to raise your voice too loudly. These men are not nice people. Please take care, dear cousin."

Just then, another call lit up her screen. It was from Luis's cell, and she knew he expected her to answer it. "Luciana, how wonderful to hear your voice. I'll try to be more careful. Let me call you back within the hour, tudo bem?"

"Maybe a bit later? That will give me time to serve the family dinner and recharge my battery. Until later," her cousin said and hung up.

"Boa noite, Luis. Tudo bem?" Tatiana answered, hearing in the background men shouting and engines roaring.

"Good evening, Tatiana. It looks like it'll take longer to conclude business. Our partners are dragging their feet. I have to see this through, so I'll arrive late tonight. Please have dinner without me. I'll see you soon." He paused. A gunshot rang out and then another. "I have to go!"

The connection went dead.

CHAPTER 24

Federal University of Pará, Belém
Thursday Morning, August 26

LUCIO WAS GETTING CLOSER. His confidential informant inside the policia civil had heard that same detective brag how his posse killed the "troublesome Indian" almost two years ago. Sometimes, men who should know better cannot keep their mouths shut. They have to brag and show how macho they are to cohorts and to feed their egos of being tough. Now, Lucio had to come up with someone willing to testify in the public domain. Not easy to do in no man's land.

So far, he'd escaped their assassination attempts, thanks to friends, family, and fellow citizens of his hometown. But how much longer could he hold out, especially if he blew the whistle on this dirty cop? Though *O Globo* and *Folha de São Paulo* might shower Lucio with praise, the Ox Bench and local gentry would eliminate him. His daughters thought he should leave the country. Yet with so many lawsuits leveled against him by his enemies, the municipal judge and Brasilia's current administration would not let him depart. Lucio felt he was a political prisoner in the town of his birth.

At last, his friend in the Policia Federal was investigating the invasion of the Munduruku land. Hopefully his political boss would not sabotage the honest cop's efforts to uncover the truth. Such was the judicial process in his native land. He had to be wily and lucky to stay one step ahead of this greedy lot. His radar had to be on 24/7 or he'd be dead meat. Thankfully, his sundry allies had tipped him off.

Since Lucio had just completed presenting the introductory class of journalism, he thought a walk off campus would do him good. He did his best thinking out and about. Lucio advised the assistant that he'd stroll along the river and return in an hour. In the hallway, he greeted some students and left by the backstairs. Outside, the sun was warm but not harsh. Still, he clipped on his sunglasses and put on the Panama hat to protect his pate. No one was lurking in the parking lot, so he turned past the Technology Institute and headed for the pedestrian walkway along the Guama River.

This must be the most beautiful university setting in the world, he thought. White herons paraded on a spit of sand and stretched their long necks in search of minnows. A steady breeze ruffled the palm trees and created a chop over the lethargic river. In the distance, a pair of scarlet ibis were poking the shoals for a crab or mollusk. Lucio's captain friend of the ferry was docking a powerboat on the nearby wharf and waved. Breathing in the August air, Lucio reveled in the moment. Though a religious skeptic, he almost gave thanks to God.

Bzzt, bzzt, bzzt shook Lucio out of his contemplation. The modern world and its instruments intervened again. "Oi," he answered. "Professor Shannon, it's good to hear your voice. I wondered what happened to you. What, you've lost a student in Cuiabá, the one who gave the TV interview? Ah, maybe she just enjoys a little tropical intrigue. Or a Brazilian lover? . . . Yes, if she calls me, I'll find her a place to stay at the university. . . . Understood. As the responsible professor for the mission, I'd be concerned too. When might you arrive? . . . If you don't mind a newsman's clutter, you'd be welcome to stay at my home. No problem at all. It'd be nice to trade notes on what's happening in my vast country. It sounds like you've had an eventful visit. . . . With pleasure, Professor. If she sends a text, I'll let you know. Stay well and see you soon. Ciao."

Cuiabá, Lucio mused. He'd visited that city three years ago on his way to the Pantanal. The city had the smell of cattle and smugglers, not his type of place. Visiting the wetlands had been the highlight of the trip. He had loved the multitude of birds flitting about and mammals cavorting in ponds and streams. A jaguar had caught his glance for a second before returning to its leafy enclave. But that had been before wildfires had burned kilometers of their precious reserve. So many of these birds and animals died needlessly because of human foibles. Lucio shook his head.

The seven deadly sins still abounded in his homeland, despite the call of clerics and pastors to turn the other cheek. How could they, given the country's history, based on Portuguese thirst for land, gold, and slaves? This was his Brazil, for better or worse. For years, his vocation was to call to account those who abused the public's trust. That was his raison d'être. Despite the threats, he would continue on.

Lucio stood taller and quickened his pace.

* * *

THE ASSASSIN ARRIVED A DAY EARLY to get the lay of the land. He'd checked out the neighborhoods that his quarry would likely frequent: the waterfront, the stables, and the university. He had already viewed the chief target earlier at a different location but understood that Belém would be his ultimate destination. The hit would take place in the capital city of Pará. It would send the message his client desired. The lesser target would not make him rich but would make some powerful people happy.

He'd been approached by his handler on one of his websites. He'd done service for the group before. The professional hitman had sniffed around and concluded that the offer was serious. Last week, he received half the stipend in US dollars, not depreciating Brazilian reais, and agreed to the contract. The handler had provided a series of photos, bios, maps, and possible routes in and out of Belém, having surveilled both targets on and off for a month.

The only fly in the ointment appeared last night. A pair of detectives from the policia civil had prowled the sites his primary target would likely visit. Though less wily than himself, the undercover cops had carefully examined two warehouses along the waterfront and another in the industrial district. It was not a cursory inspection. He decided to go back to his contact to ask about police involvement with his prey. Collateral damage would draw attention to any incident and make his escape more difficult.

As he closed in on his thirtieth year, he reminded himself that protecting number one was his primary goal.

CHAPTER 25

On the Road to Dom Eliseu, Pará
Thursday Noon, August 27

TATIANA WAS IN OVER HER HEAD. Despite her wish to have it all, the events of the last two days shook her confidence to its core. Her lover was in danger, as were those near him. When she had discovered that his business was dealing illegal drugs and other commodities, her dreams were shattered. With time on her hands, she researched his background and uncovered his connections to the infamous Colombian Gulf cartel. Google helped out a lot. Being a horse trainer and racer was his public façade. Luis Carlos dealt with rough people who couldn't care less about her. So much for her tropical fling and the storyline she aspired to tell fellow students at SU. That is, if she made it back to her adopted city safe and sound.

When Luis called that he wasn't returning to the hotel the night of the gunshots, she decided to act. Calling her cousin in that rural town in Maranhão, she arranged to meet at a road junction called Dom Eliseu in rural Pará. Early Thursday, she hired an Uber to take her there, via Road 222, a secondary route to Belém. Tatiana was able to slip by the snoopy doorman and told reception that her companion was on his way but that she had to leave; an emergency had come up. She left a note to Luis Carlos, confessing that she really enjoyed her time with him but his business spooked her. She felt afraid. Maybe they could see each other in Belém.

The two-hour ride in the Uber was uneventful. Another passenger joined her. The young man was a student from the Federal University of Southern Pará, majoring in journalism. He wanted to become an investigative reporter, calling bad actors to account. Squinting at her an extra moment, he asked, "Weren't you on TV with some student group from the States?"

Tatiana confirmed that she was part of the mission to ascertain the impact of Big Ag on Brazil's native forests and people.

"The soybean farmers are a powerful lot, even in my hometown. Be careful," warned the student.

The driver was monitoring their conversation as they came into a small town, whose sign gave its population as thirty-nine thousand. The university student got off at his family residence, a large colonial home on the outskirts and wished Tatiana his best. The Uber chauffeur dropped her off at Hotel Araujo in the town center, asking "Tudo bem?" Tatiana thanked him and lugged her bags into a warm lobby.

Her cousin Luciana had arranged the reservation, thanks to a friend who worked on the front desk. The clerk hadn't yet arrived, but the receptionist gave Tatiana a second-floor room in the three-story lodge, looking out on the dusty street. A horse-drawn cart carrying sugarcane plodded along, and a few motor scooters putted over hexagonal tiles on the town's main avenue. As the sun rose higher, pedestrians took flight, and no breeze ruffled the spindly palms. Fortunately, the A/C worked fine, even though the heat pushed through the thin panes.

After the rollercoaster of the past forty-eight hours, Tatiana dropped her bags and tumbled down on the lumpy bed, falling into a deep slumber without dreams.

A rap on the door woke Tatiana. Luciana opened the squeaky door and rushed in to give her cousin a tight hug and kiss. She was Tatiana's height with black hair streaked with gray, a beige bandana covering the top. They caught up about friends and relatives in their Guajajara village. She was glad to hear that the chief was still standing erect and providing tribal justice, despite his advanced years.

When the sun declined toward the west, they took a walk around town with the temperature still a hot 92 degrees Fahrenheit. They dined at a homespun café with three locals and treated themselves to a *paçoca de carne seca*, a special Northeastern dish of shredded, salted, sun-dried beef with mandioc flour, and chopped green peppers. Chitchatting about their homeland, the two women deplored that more people had left the Guajajara nation than had been born this last decade. They looked at each other as prime examples of the exodus.

When the guava and country cheese arrived for dessert, Luciana raised the topic of their cousin's murder. "Be careful, Tatiana. These men have guns and still invade our land, chopping down trees and anything in their path. With Paulino's death, we lost our chief protector. Now crime syndicates from the South are involved in trafficking our trees and even our young men and women. One of Paulino's recruits was recently wounded by a submachine gun in our own homestead. As you've become a TV celebrity, they may go after you as well. These invaders play for keeps and have the backing of the Ox Bench. Atenção, cousin."

Over sweet herbal tea, Luciana gave Tatiana a note with the reporter's name, number, and university address in Belém. This long-time resident had investigated Paulino's murder and discovered links to the policia civil. "He recently visited the chief and residents in our village and received first-hand information. Friends back home confirmed that the journalist also suffered threats from the big landowners. As you're headed to Belém, you may want to meet with him on the sly. The Ox Bench has its spies everywhere. Take care," Luciana cautioned again, looking at her watch.

They settled their accounts with the middle-aged waiter and stepped outside, where the sky was turning from red to purple to deep blue. The temperature was still warm, but a slight breeze came and went. Approaching the corner, they stumbled upon a macumba offering with three candles blazing near a dead rooster and glass of cachaça.

"Caramba, cousin, are they still killing these poor creatures to exact revenge?" murmured Tatiana, sidestepping the corner sacrifice. She felt a chill rise inside her, even though the outside air was warm.

"Unfortunately, yes. People here are a superstitious lot. They still spread rumors about Matita Peré stalking victims at night or during early morning hours. For some, if you don't feed her crows, they will pester townspeople all night long. Then she'll stalk and cast a spell on her victim. Welcome back to our strange world in the middle of nowhere. Quite different from the United States. Now, I must go. My special friend at the hotel is planning to take me out to have some fun," she said, with a look of mischief and delight. "It's really boring where I work."

Returning to the hotel, they traded hugs and kisses. Luciana stayed in the reception area, and Tatiana tramped upstairs. She'd left her iPhone in the room and noticed three messages: two from Luis Carlos and one from Professor Shannon.

She opened the professor's first. The professor was on his way to Belém and would stay in the home of a federal university prof who had new information. He asked again for her to call or text him. "I am most concerned for my favorite student," he added. That was nice.

The two texts from Luis were both apologetic and angry in tone. She decided not to respond to any of the messages right now.

Instead, Tatiana slipped into the narrow double bed and tried to fall asleep. She planned to rise early the next morning and take the first bus heading north. Breathing deeply, she wondered what awaited her in Belém. Tatiana would text her professor on the way, asking for forgiveness. She didn't want any more surprises or Ox Bench visitors. She would tell the world what happened to her martyred cousin but would do so abroad. It was too dicey to do so safely in this part of Brazil.

Before shutting her eyes, Tatiana heard a clawing sound outside her window and then a crow caw. Tossing and turning on the uneven bed, she finally drifted down to a dream-filled sleep.

Her cousin never returned. Tatiana hugged a pillow, wishing that her lover was nearby. Instead, she sensed another presence in the early morning hours and asked how she could keep her spirits up and those of Matita Peré at bay.

Unable to sleep, Tatiana searched the shadows in the room, desperately awaiting the break of dawn.

CHAPTER 26

Recife to Belém's International Airport
Friday Noon, August 27

YESTERDAY, MURPHY'S LAW STRUCK AGAIN. Luke Shannon
fretted that a Gaelic curse had followed him to Brazil, punishing him for past transgressions. Or maybe it was his Catholic
guilt, which haunted him when things went sour.

The visit by the Ox Bench cowboys had initiated a series of
misfortunes, followed by Tatiana's disappearance in Cuiabá. Her
cryptic message made Luke worry more so he decided to go to
Belém, hoping that she'd reappear. As there was no direct flight,
he took Azul's connecting flight yesterday at three in the morning
to Recife's Guararapes/Gilberto Freyre airport. After a three-hour
layover in that city on the hump of Brazil, passengers boarded to
catch another flight north to the capital of Pará.

It was not to be. For over an hour, he and his fellow passengers sat trapped inside an old model 737 without air-conditioning. Outside, a couple of mechanics fussed around the left wing's
flap, trying to make it work. They did not succeed. The passengers
deplaned in a sullen mood, receiving superfluous explanations by

an attendant. Luke had to retrieve his air force garment bag and wait in line with angry travelers at the reservation desk. Nodding off from his early morning departure, he barely heard the harried attendant speak above the din. Jostling in the crowd, Luke accepted her offer of a hotel room overnight and a guaranteed seat Friday morning to Belém. Boarding the packed shuttle bus, he arrived at the Costa Mesa Inn, which he'd learned was paying its IOUs to the airline with budget-priced accommodations.

The motel wasn't too bad, and his room had a functioning A/C overlooking a shallow pool. After dumping his bag, Luke recalled his visit to the local Bacardi Rum's distillery during his banker's days. On a lark, he telephoned the manager he'd met years ago. His assistant remembered Luke but said his friend had retired. She gave him Oscar's cell phone, saying, "He lives near the ocean. You may find him there."

Indeed, Luke found his Bacardi friend on the beach.

His former client shouted over the pounding surf, "Wow, Luke Shannon, tudo bem? Long time, no hear. . . . Yes, the family's fine and you? . . . I think I saw you on TV last week about some study program. So now you're a professor, introducing American students to our crazy country? . . . Sorry you're stuck in the airport. It'd be great to see you again. Please join me and my family on Recife's favorite beach. We're right in front of the Grand Mercure on Boa Viagem under three parasols. Our attendant knows how to concoct Bacardi's wicked *caipirissima*. Speaking of which, I remember that you quaffed several down a few years back. You may enjoy. We'll be here until sunset. . . . *Excelente!* See you soon."

One little victory, thought Luke. It'd be great to see his old friend on tropical shores. Except for quick strokes in the Brasilia pool in Brasilia, he had not had time to swim in the open sea.

Plunging into the Atlantic Ocean would reenergize him. An optimist, he nurtured hopes that today would mark a turning point for his up-and-down mission. Donning a Seattle Sounders cap and a Hawaiian shirt, he appeared very much the gringo. Luke didn't care. Seeing his old amigo and swimming in the sea perked him up. If Tatiana was having fun, so would he.

Maybe Luke's Irish luck was returning. He arrived in the lobby just as the shuttle was about to depart for Boa Viagem. He boarded it with glee. After a five-minute ride, the bus turned onto the vast beach. Luke forgot how its seashore stretched for five miles, twice as long as Rio's Copacabana. The trade winds blew through the open windows, and the digital clock read 14:45, and the thermometer a comfortable 81 degrees Fahrenheit. The beaches were half full, as this seaside city reluctantly entered fall. If only Seattle's autumns were so pleasant.

Luke looked out on the scene and felt alive. Disembarking with two tourists, he crossed the mosaic sidewalk and loved the feeling of sand underfoot. Behind, Mercure's five-star hotel stood high on the boulevard, much ritzier than its budget cousin in Brasilia.

Meandering by volleyball games and kids bouncing soccer balls on their knees, Luke wove through a sea of yellow umbrellas to the surf. The turquoise waters enchanted him as they had in Cuba's Varadero. Hopefully, the undertow would not be as strong. He unbuttoned his shirt and breathed in the ocean air. Closing his eyes, Luke felt the breeze on his cheek and celebrated a moment of peace. He listened to the waves, children laughing, and the calls of vendors along the shore.

"Is that Professor Shannon, the reformed banker?"

Luke opened his eyes and turned toward the nearby voice. As he did, a pelican skimmed the water just yards away, and a one-mast *jangada* sailed the trade winds over breaking surf. A stout five-feet-eight man with indigenous features approached him with a wide smile. His bare chest and balding round head were nut brown, and his remaining curly hair alternated between salt and pepper. A ball in hand, he tossed it to a young boy and gave Luke a hearty hug. "You don't look too bad, amigo. Are you still swimming? I still remember you body-surfing on this very beach twenty years ago. It's great seeing you again," he exclaimed, slapping Luke on the shoulder. Pointing to a dozen family members, he said, "Let me introduce you to three generations of the Ferreira tribe. Here is my friend who quit banking to become a prof. He's also a fan of *futebol* and wears his hometown cap."

Soccer always provoked lively banter, making Luke feel right at home. He boasted a bit about the Seattle Sounders, which had won two MLS cups, and listened to their debate about Brazil's best team. Over *caipirissimas*, made from Bacardi light instead of cachaça, with ample lime juice and sugar over ice, Luke felt no pain. The unpleasant memories vanished for a while. They bought some barbequed shrimp from a young boy in tattered shorts and munched on manioc fries. It was a grand festa.

One of Oscar's grandkids wanted to learn to swim, so Luke volunteered. His tried-and-true method of having the child float on his or her back always did the trick. Once the boy gained confidence that he wouldn't sink, he began splashing around. His siblings and cousins joined in the merriment. Luke dove under the waves and did the butterfly fifty yards out. Feeling the undertow, he returned against the tide, not wanting to repeat his near drowning in Cuba last year.

Under the family umbrella, Luke asked Oscar if Big Ag was as strong here as in other Brazilian states. He learned that sugar and nuts were Recife's primary exports but not soja.

"We've avoided the clashes they're having up North," Oscar said. "I met a few big boys on my last visit to Belém. They're an arrogant bunch and hire men with guns. Atenção, amigo."

Shadows crept over the beach, and Oscar's family prepared to leave. They invited him for dinner, but Luke declined. Three hours sleep the previous night finally caught up with him. Exchanging hugs and kisses with the family, Luke accepted Oscar's offer to take him back. After loading up his SUV, he dropped Luke at the airport inn. Exchanging another hug, his friend implored, "Stay away from the Ox Bench, my friend."

Luke said he would, thanked him, and returned to his room. He showered but could barely keep his eyes open. In less than a minute, he fell asleep, having neglected to plug in his phone.

Tatiana's text message travelled somewhere in outer space but didn't land on Luke's Galaxy that night.

* * *

LUKE WAS ABOUT TO BOARD ANOTHER 737 and discovered his cell without juice. He found one charger in the departure area, occupied by another phone. The woman saw him pacing and diplomatically removed hers as the airline announced last call. Luke plugged his in for two minutes, yanked it out, and ran to the gate before a closing door. He was the last one on board and felt many eyes drilling him. It was a full flight. He excused himself and grabbed the last seat. As the plane was pulling away, he turned on his Galaxy only to be told by the stewardess to shut it down for takeoff. When she announced it safe to turn on electronic equipment, no signal registered on Luke's phone.

He sighed and closed his eyes until he was awakened by the

landing plane. The stewardess welcomed them to Belém's Val-de-Cans and Julio Cezar Ribeiro's International Airport. A mouthful of names, Luke thought, as he viewed a modern, newly constructed terminal pass by. The Azul flight arrived almost on time, and the passengers got up before the plane reached the gate. They grabbed their carry-ons and charged toward the front exit.

Luke followed them into the modern, high-ceiling airport, bathed in light. Its struggling A/C tried to dispense cooler air below. At baggage claim, he retrieved his luggage and entered the main concourse with passengers and family members rushing about. Remembering that his Galaxy needed a fix, he plugged it into a charging station, discovering two texts from his wayward student and the Belém journalist-prof. Tatiana said she was on a hot bus heading north to Belém from some rural town; ETA this afternoon. Lucio simply asked, "Where are you?"

Luke texted the Belém journalist that he had just arrived.

Lucio texted back, "Professor, come to the Federal University of Pará. My home is under surveillance. Atenção." He gave the building name and room number and asked him to arrive within the hour.

More intrigue, feared Luke. His mini-vacation on Recife's beach vanished as if a dream. Sensing he was about to run another gauntlet, he breathed deeply and called Tatiana on WhatsApp video. He waited a minute, but no one answered.

Where was his elusive student and what awaited them in Belém? He grabbed his bags, cell phone, and a Yellow Cab and decided to find out.

CHAPTER 27

On Route BR 316 to Belém
Friday Afternoon, August 27

FINALLY. TATIANA CAUGHT A GLIMPSE OF A SIGN announcing Pará's capital after putting up with the tired Mercedes bus that traipsed through small towns and dusty junctions.

Fortunately, one municipality, Paragominas, had piqued her interest. It was the second-to-last stop and located near a bauxite mine. A decade ago, the region had the highest deforestation rate in Brazil. A fellow traveler told her that the previous mayor, Adnan, had cajoled local ranchers, environmentalists, and small farmers to come up with a community plan. He had pleaded with all his constituents that it was time to redeem their past. After a year of back and forth, the mayor achieved agreement among all the players. Together they announced a program for sustainable development and for preservation of old-growth forests. "A win-win," exclaimed the local and the national press.

In São Paulo, Tatiana recalled her conversation with the former minister. Marina considered this out-of-the way town a stunning success, concluding, "Brazil needs more mayors like Adnan. He had the vision and determination to bring all elements together. Only in that manner will we succeed in safeguarding Brazil's environment."

In a recent series in *Revista Piauí* that Tatiana had read, its author João pointed to the mayor's consensual approach. Against all odds, Adnan had persevered with his disparate constituents, resulting in a comprehensive plan. This unsung hero deserved all the acclaim for his good works in Paragominas. It could be done, she mused, generating a ray of hope.

As the bus chugged into Belém, Tatiana checked her phone and found a missed call. It was from her professor, and she reached him on the second try. Luke told her to take a cab to the Federal University of Pará near the Guama River, where the journalism prof had secured a place for them to overnight. Apparently, the Ox Bench had lookouts monitoring the prof's home and the shopping mall he liked to frequent. Hearing mention of that group, her heart rate jacked up.

After a two-day respite in the countryside, Tatiana had to reacclimate to the urban scene and whatever came next. The mention of the Ox Bench pushed her back to that horrible incident with the cowboys. She didn't want to cross paths with their likes ever again. But how could she avoid them in this city, which exported their soybeans and beef and bowed to their power?

Since Tatiana hadn't replied to Luis's texts, she promised to do so after meeting with both profs. They all had to be on the same page so they could accomplish their mission and stay safe from nasty men. Her pulse rose as the bus crept by the Worker's Plaza and entered its stall. She took three deep breaths and was the last to leave. Tatiana and the profs would need all the allies they could muster to survive the final leg of the trip.

Maybe her Colombian lover could help. She hadn't been able to consult with him since his business turned south. What was Luis up to at this very moment?

* * *

Riding was Luis's passion and his escape. He rode his thoroughbred hard, trying to release his anger and his angst. As he scanned the track at his cousin's hacienda, he revisited the unexpected shoot-out two days ago in Marabá.

Little had he expected treachery or such incompetence on the part of his new business associate. The bona fides of the two guards who had appeared at the airport should have been checked out beforehand. Instead, they were merely hired guns, contracted by a friend of his so-called partner. Queiroz had admitted as much. Fortunately, his G-18 had done its job, stopping another threat in his zigzag life.

The Colombian had insisted that Brasilia's fixer clean up the mess, including the deceased gunman and the wounded off-duty cop. Luis had had to act quickly. Calling in favors from another distant cousin, Luis had secured two reliable escorts to accompany the trucks hauling hardwood to Belém. The whole affair had cost them another day, as well as unintended consequences. He hadn't asked the fixer what had happened to the wounded man. He later learned the cop was on the take from São Paulo's PCC, an alarming sign.

Importantly, who in his or Queiroz's organization had leaked details of their flight and the wood transfer in Marabá? Too many questions without answers. When he had cruised his Cessna over the verdant forests and the yellow fields of soy, his mind had reviewed all involved in his Brazilian organization. No one had immediately come to mind. Still, a traitor lurked nearby.

Landing in Belém's international airport, he had proceeded to his private hangar, where two crew-cut men had waited at the gate. They had given the correct password, *para frente*, mentioning the name of his cousin. Together with Cuiabá, Luis now had three personal protectors. Hopefully his growing entourage would not attract too much attention.

After parking his Cessna inside and giving the mechanic instructions, Luis and Cuiabá had entered the Land Rover Discovery parked on the tarmac. The new escorts had sped off to the west and arrived at his absent cousin's extensive ranch, which featured a one-and-a-quarter-mile track. It was here where Luis enjoyed riding his favorite mounts. The Colombian had climbed on a high-spirited colt, which took off like lightning. Around the track they galloped, wind refreshing both horse and rider.

As the yearling completed its second lap, Luis found himself grinding his teeth. In vain, he tried to put out of mind his fire-brand lover. Collateral damage in his line of work. Still, this female warrior had fire in the belly and drew him in. He yearned to have an all-nighter with her beyond the snake pit of northern Brazil.

Slowing the horse's gait, Luis surveyed the vacant track and headed to the stables. Cuiabá nodded as he passed and followed him inside. The young man had proved himself brave and loyal in the shoot-out, wounding one of the turncoats while Luis took out the other. Luis had tipped him ten Bens on the spot and promised him a position in his organization.

At this moment, all Luis wanted was to complete this hardwood deal with an unreliable partner and then get out of town. An R & R in his hacienda in Antioquia would suit him fine, maybe with Tatiana by his side. He could also invite his daughter and her growing family as they loved an open-pit country barbeque. Who knows, maybe his son would make amends and join them too? Luis had thought about enticing Junior with a fiesta to celebrate his new MBA in international finance.

Handing over the reins to the stable boy, Luis followed Cuiabá outside and stayed in the barn's shadow. Luis saw one escort waiting by the nearby Rover, scanning the long driveway. The other was behind the wheel, revving the engine. Nothing untoward that he could see, so Luis strode the two meters and entered into the back seat.

His trusted guard stayed outside an extra second looking at the ceiba tree fifty yards away. Luis thought he heard a twig snap, as did his guard and the escort, who jumped inside. They roared down the curving driveway, leaving a cloud of dust in their wake. The automatic gates opened just in time, and they skidded onto the paved road heading to the city center. The Colombian and Cuiabá frowned at each other but didn't say a word. A band of *urubú* (vultures) circled overhead, looking for prey.

The driver set out for the safe house not far from the port area downtown. His cousin often stayed there and had a loyal housekeeper named Rosa living on premises. Luis breathed deeply as a bead of sweat gathered on his brow. Remembrance of the sound of the breaking branch still spooked him. He'd stayed alive so far by following his sixth sense, which now sniffed trouble.

They arrived at the safe house and drove twice around the block but didn't spot surveillance. They slowed to let Luis's new right-hand man get out to reconnoiter. He returned confirming that the Colombian maid was in the three-room apartment; she said no one had been nosing around. Luis went inside, flanked by the two escorts, and approved the locale, especially its direct view toward Belém's docks. The A/C worked well, and his cousin's domestic was bi-lingual and spare with words. Luis liked that, after all the *merda* he'd heard from Queiroz.

As the shipment should have arrived, he tasked Cuiabá to visit the storehouse and check it out. First, the bodyguard texted the fixer, who asked him to come to warehouse number three.

Luis's new second-in-command walked the seven blocks to the wharf and found the depository, which had two wide truck entrances at either end and a side door for pedestrians. He noticed several nearby buildings whose roofs could be used for a sniper's roost and took note. After circling warehouse number three, he texted Queiroz and entered the side door.

He gave the fixer a loose hug and observed the other hired escort holding an IA2 automatic rifle used by the Brazilian military. Two forklift operators were lifting cut logs into two containers twenty feet long, eight and half feet high, and eight feet wide. The older man had a nervous tick in his right eye and appeared jumpy. Queiroz said only that he spotted the policia civil making the rounds on the wharf. After the shootout in Marabá, he was still uneasy.

They exited by the side door and walked a hundred yards to the *MSC Alexandra*, flying the Italian flag. Walking up the gangplank, they encountered the captain on the quarterdeck. He spoke a mixture of Italian and Spanish and indicated that the containers should be ready to load from the dock Saturday at 17:00 sharp. The custom's paperwork should arrive beforehand. They thanked him and returned to the warehouse, where Cuiabá reported back to his boss.

Luis breathed a sigh of relief as it seemed the preparations were in order. He thanked his cohort and said he was on his way to meet his Customs agent. The Colombian had known the man for five years and texted him from Marabá that he needed another accommodation regarding a hardwood export. The agent had sent him a positive response. Arriving in Belém, Luis had texted the official again and asked him to meet at a café around the corner, while Cuiabá was inspecting the warehouse.

Shadowed by his two bodyguards, Luis entered the neighborhood café and noticed the bartender and a man in his cups at the bar. The Customs agent was seated in the back. Over Brazilian cognac, they exchanged family news and concluded their transaction. The Customs man approved and signed the bill of lading and certificate of origin of the exported wood. In return, he received a small brief containing ten thousand dollars in newly minted bills, equal to 1 percent of the FOB value. They both downed another cognac, shook hands, and went in opposite directions.

So far, so good.

As the sun dropped toward the west, Luis felt his phone vibrate and saw his son's youthful face gleaming on the screen. He answered it on the third ring. "*Buenas tardes, Junior, que tal?* How is life in Bogota? Its politics appear more raucous every time I read the *Semana.* Did you already walk down the aisle at la Javeriana? . . . I'm sorry I couldn't attend. My hearty congratulations. . . . What? You're flying into Belém? When and why? . . . So, you received your pilot wings as well as your MBA? . . . You needed a change of scenery and wanted to celebrate with me. . . . OK. I'm glad your uncle lent you one of his Cessnas. By the way, I just arrived here myself but am embroiled in a dicey deal. Tell me where you plan to stay, and I'll call you later. I'm sorry that I can't meet you tonight but I can send someone to pick you up at the domestic airport. . . . If you'd like, yes, Uber should be reliable, but make sure to check the driver's identity card. . . . I look forward to seeing you too. Stay safe, my son."

His heart sped up. All Luis Carlos needed next was for Tatiana to reappear and create a three-ring circus in the wildest region of Brazil.

CHAPTER 28

Federal University of Pará, Belém
Saturday Morning, August 28

THE TWO PROFS HUDDLED OVER the Nespresso machine, which
was bubbling away on the countertop. Outside, a few cumuli
crept forward, and a flock of white heron took flight. A riverboat
and a cargo vessel headed in opposite directions along the slow-
moving river, shimmering under the rising sun. Luke moved his
neck around to remove the dogged crick; he'd spent another night
on the floor. Tatiana was still sleeping on her futon, purring like a
kitten. Lucio's corner office had become their makeshift headquarters in the capital of Pará.

"Please excuse the accommodations, Professor. While the
heat is on, we must be flexible. After what each of us has been
through, it's best to keep a low profile. I've asked the university
guards to make their rounds more frequently." Lucio sighed while
sprinkling a touch of cinnamon on his dry cappuccino. Luke followed suit.

Just then, Tatiana's cell buzzed on the countertop, where it was
charging. Luke looked down and saw the Colombiano's stern face

flash on the video display. So this was the mysterious lover she had promised to divulge. When she had arrived bedraggled last night, she had begged off telling her story until morning. "Let me just say that the last forty-eight hours have been the most dramatic in my life." After that pronouncement, she had yawned and fallen asleep. Luke really looked forward to hearing her account.

Unfortunately, it seemed Luke's dream had been prescient about the two of them. By adding a drug lord to the equation, as well as the Ox Bench and Lucio's enemies, Luke hoped the next days would not become a Molotov cocktail.

* * *

THE ASSASSIN'S SOURCE WAS INCORRECT regarding the timing of the target's flight, causing him to arrive late at the ranch and miss his chance. Now there were too many possible venues to cover, and he was an army of one. He needed backup and lookouts in Pará's spread-out capital. After alerting his handler about the policia civil snooping, he received a text offering to connect him with the syndicate's inside man. His preference was to operate solo, usually taking a week to methodically set up a firing nest and two ways to escape. Now, however, there were too many moving parts, and his victim was alerted. If his target departed Belém without prejudice, there would be all hell to pay.

He texted back asking to meet their inside man. Within thirty minutes, his handler replied that he should encounter someone called Silva at a trattoria appropriately named Capone Ristorante at 13:00 near the docks of Belém. The syndicate's man would be carrying a copy of today's *O Diario do Pará*, as should the hitman. His meeting name would be The Jackal, and he should pay for lunch.

Dirty cops. They always wanted someone else to pay for lunch, cocaine, or sexy women. This guy had better know his stuff and have eyes and ears around town. The young hitman had to find the right spot to take down his prey. For that to happen, he needed intel about the target's next move. To successfully execute the contract, he could not afford amateurs to muddy the waters. He simply needed one clean shot and two routes to get away.

Walking around the block as the equatorial sun beat down, he imagined the kudos he'd receive in the underworld if he performed as well as in his six previous jobs. This could be his lucky seven. He decided to trust his handler and texted back, confirming that the Jackal would appear at the anointed time and place.

Over him, dozens of vultures rode the heat waves, searching silently and relentlessly for quarry below.

* * *

"OI, LUIS, TUDO BEM?"

What music to Luis's ears. It'd been three days without a word from Tatiana. Given the tension from this deal, her words gave him an electric boost. Even he, the survivor of many ups and downs, needed emotional support—especially now. But the clock was ticking, and he couldn't meet up with his fiery favorite at this moment.

Then an idea came to him. "Tatiana, it's great hearing from you. My business is almost done but will take the rest of the day and night to put to bed. What would you say about meeting tomorrow, escaping to a quieter place across the river? It's on a rustic island where I've raced horses on the beach—I think you'd like the pastoral scene. . . . Ah, you're with the professor hiding out at the university. . . . So, he's got his troubles too? At least you were able to reconnect. . . . There's another professor in the mix? Should I be a little jealous? . . . Ah ha, he's not your type. Good for me.

"By the way, my son paid me a surprise visit here in Belém. We were planning to fly out together tomorrow to the big island. He'll be my co-pilot. Please consider joining us as Junior is a sharp kid and a newly minted MBA. He has a passion for the underdog, just like you. You may enjoy trading notes about your favorite causes. . . . Great, so you will consider coming. Let's speak tomorrow morning. The dust should settle by then. . . . I miss you too. Wish me good fortune tonight. . . . Kisses back to you."

He hung up, pleased to have heard Tatiana's voice. Seeing her tomorrow would be his just reward. But first this dirty deal had to come out right. Were he a believer, he would offer up a prayer. But after breaking the Fifth Commandment forty-four years ago and several times since, he began to trust his wits instead. No longer did he depend on someone somewhere that he could neither see nor fathom. His G-18 and his sixth sense were his dependable allies and should guide him tonight.

Now, it was time to put them to the ultimate test.

* * *

AT LEAST, THE SO-CALLED JACKAL DIDN'T strike the cop as an amateur. The assassin's eyes conveyed no emotion as he methodically scanned people, doors, and windows as potential threats. Though still young, he was considered top gun by the syndicate, which kept both of them on retainer. An ally of sorts, for today's takedown in Belém.

The city of his birth was still his turf, and higher-ups knew not to cross him, despite his official position as only a detective. They understood who had directed the posse two years ago to eliminate a high-profile troublemaker, making wood harvesting mores difficult. So what if the murder caused headlines in the international press? Now with allies in Brasilia, the incident was slowly being swept away. Only that pesky local reporter insisted on remembering the martyr, that so-called "guardian of the forest." He must be an Indian-lover. The detective got so tired of protests by do-gooders about invasions of tribal lands. The Ox Bench and his syndicate wanted to develop the region and not dither on legalities or whining from abroad. That insistent reporter!

After taking care of business tonight with the priority hit, his Paulista overlords should be pleased. Whether this assailant would follow up on the secondary target was unimportant. He himself would ensure the reporter's demise. That irritating old man had escaped him twice, but not this third time around.

As they spooned sugar into their espressos in this trendy trattoria, he nodded smugly at the prospects of making that newsman beg for his life. He could hardly wait. But first they had to send a public message that no adventurer could encroach on PCC interests. With the demise of the Family of the North, the Paulista syndicate had entered the vacuum and reigned supreme. They didn't yield to competitors anywhere, including those with political clout or foreign connections. The Ox Bench didn't mess with the Paulistas, nor should upstarts from Rio or anywhere else. They had to be taught a lesson.

"*Chega!*" he heard himself say to the hitman. "Enough! You pay the bill. We'll see you next on the docks. Do your part tonight and I'll do mine."

With those parting words, the heavy-set man pushed his chair back, nodded at his cohort by the door, and departed into the fading light. In the harbor, he saw the vultures and herons battling

for dinner. He rubbed his belly in satisfaction from the tasty cappelletti à la Romanesco. Maybe the tempest among the birds fore-
shadowed tonight's events. He shrugged, unconcerned.

In a few hours, everyone in town and in Brazil would know
that he was the man.

CHAPTER 29

The Port of Belém
Late Saturday Afternoon, August 28

DELAY DID NOT FIT WELL WITH LUIS. His Rio fixer texted that the two containers remained on the dock, temporarily held up by authorities. Some civil police type and a different Customs inspector arrived, demanding to review their bills of lading and certificates of origin. The Italian captain was furious as he wanted to depart by sunset and not pay another day of dockage.

On receiving this news, the Colombian's sixth sense ratcheted up. Why were police and Customs showing up at this late hour asking about the containers' paperwork? It didn't smell right. Given what had happened in Marabá and the weird snapping sound at his cousin's ranch, Luis feared that someone was leaking data to someone outside. Or that he was being watched. Or both.

Luis texted his Customs' source and demanded to know what was happening.

No response.

At five, Luis arrived at the dock. His driver texted the escorts

206 | Stephen E. Murphy

to open the sliding door on his count, and Cuiabá drove the Land Rover Discovery through the warehouse's back cargo entrance but had to dodge seabirds swarming over fish dropped by a fishermen's cart. After closing the automated door, he turned the Rover around and pointed it toward that exit.

Luis noticed that the escorts inside were looking antsy. It had been an hour since Queiroz had left to parley with the captain of *MSC Alexandra*, the civil police, and Customs agent on the quarterdeck. Luis paced back and forth and heard the bickering of birds outside. His Rolex continued ticking; the minute hand moved past the sixth hour. Sunset was at 18:17 Pará time. If he couldn't figure out what was happening by then, he would abort.

Finally, he texted his troublesome partner, "Que pasa?"

The reply was simply, "More money. Returning to consult."

After giving his Customs agent ten thousand dollars yesterday and receiving no response just now, this request did not seem right. Luis checked his cell again. Nada.

"Cuiabá, get in the Rover and turn on the engine. Queiroz is returning, but something is off. Get your finger close to the door opener and to your gun. We may have to take off in a flash. Escorts, get ready for action."

Five minutes passed, and a hard knock sounded on the pedestrian door. The escort looked through the peephole and said it was Queiroz and another man who looked like a cop.

Luis went to the door and looked through the aperture, shouting to the fixer, "Who is with you?"

"He's from Belém's policia civil and wants to have a word with you. Please open the door."

Luis nodded to the escort, who cracked the door open, Glock in hand.

"Gentlemen, please come outside, policia civil," barked the other man.

"Why not inside?" shouted the Colombian, his nose twitching.

"We need to check your identity papers. It's better in the light. Your name appears on the bill of lading as shipper. Come outside now."

As Luis peeked around the door, the birds returned, scoring more fish on the dock. A shout rang out, and the squawking got louder. The Colombian felt something crease his right temple and shut the door. Blood began dripping down to his guayabera.

"Lock the door. Open the garage exit," Luis commanded, moving quickly to the Rover.

More shots pounded on the side entrance, and one escort stumbled and fell, leaving the door ajar. The other ran for the car, jumping into the front seat. Cuiabá had the motor running. Luis reached the open back door as another shot ricocheted off the Rover's right side. He dove in, grabbing the door by his foot. The automated gateway slowly slid open, and the plainclothesman emptied his semi-automatic into the roaring SUV. Like a scared mare, the Discovery burst out of the warehouse, scraping its right side and sustaining shots on its bulletproof windows.

A policia civil VW with a flashing red light blocked the top of the ramp. Cuiabá turned on a dime, accelerating north away from the depot. Another shot cracked the back window, and seabirds raised a horrendous cry.

Luis's bleeding worsened, and he felt light-headed. Leaning down on the back seat, he decided to pray after all. His sixth sense had alerted but had not protected him from danger. He was running for his life but now was in someone else's hands. Before he passed out, he thought of Tatiana and his son and what might have been.

* * *

Lucio, Luke, and Tatiana watched the shoot-out on TV, along with most of Belém; it had been captured by a sailor's smart phone from the Italian ship. They saw an argument on the wharf between the captain, a man in a policia civil uniform, and two older rough-looking men. The next clip showed the two old guys quarrelling outside a warehouse, one of them beating on the entrance and shouting, "Policia civil." When the door opened a crack, a shot rang out and then another. The birds screamed and took flight. They saw a man inside the entrance slump to the floor and the plainclothesman charge through. Outside, the other man dropped to the ground covering his head. The final clip showed a Land Rover bursting out of the far depot exit, roaring away from the ship. Heading north along the dock, the SUV sustained bullets on its rear window which cracked but did not shatter.

"I know that detective," affirmed Lucio. "He's the bad apple of the policia civil and the alleged organizer of the group that killed Tatiana's cousin. The Ox Bench, as well as the crime syndicate from São Paulo, owns him." Reluctantly he continued, "He and his henchmen have been tracking me as well. That's why we're hunkered down at the university. Let's hope they don't discover our hideaway. Still, we must plan to leave early tomorrow. It's not safe to stay in my hometown with that dude on the warpath."

Tatiana exclaimed, "I know the man arguing with the plainclothes cop. He is called 'the fixer' for an important senator in Brasilia. I rode in Luis's plane with him and overheard them whisper about some deal in Marabá. Maybe they decided to ship it out of the capital instead. Let's listen to the rest of the report."

The disheveled detective told the interviewer that he had received a tip about an illegal shipment of wood from the port of Belém. "This is a major victory against organized crime, especially with a foreign connection. We understand that a Colombian cartel was behind this transaction. We did our best to take them down. Unfortunately, two of them escaped. But we will track them wherever they are hiding. We will ferret out these thieves of the rainforest."

"What *merda*," shouted Lucio at the screen. "He is the biggest perpetrator of tree heists in all of Pará! Merda, indeed. He is also the organizer of the killing of innocents who stood up to the Ox Bench.

"My friend Alexandre or Saraiva, while in charge of the Federal Police, had a bead on him. The politicos in Brasilia removed this honest Fed because he blew the whistle on their own corrupt minister of environment. Can you imagine that? The cabinet member orchestrated many illegal wood exports, lining the pockets of authorities who looked the other way. The bad apples got their cut. Alexandre was forced out. Because of press reports, Salles had to resign. His current replacement just marks time, fearful of Brasilia's masters.

"This detective is part of that brood of vipers. He's a dangerous man and a pathological liar—he'll say anything to make himself look good. His greed knows no bounds. The powers that be don't cross him as long as he does their dirty work. Merda, merda, merda!"

The three sat in stunned silence. After a minute, Luke recalled, "Here's some good news. Padre José of Cuiabá should be arriving this evening by plane on Marajó. He is coming with some CIMI missionaries and will serve as a substitute priest in the town of

Soure. Tatiana and I stayed with him at the Salesian mission and found him a helpful host. During our travels to the Pantanal, he told me he was leaving this weekend for the big island. I read that Marajó is the size of the states of Connecticut and Massachusetts combined. He offered us a place to stay to escape the urban scene. I'd like to text him and take him up on his hospitality. What do you think?"

"A timely offer, Professor. Let me call a friendly skipper and see if he can secure a boat to take us there. Besides being a ferryboat captain, he navigates the well-to-do on yachts upriver. He often has access to their vessels for a small fee." Lucio rang his friend via WhatsApp and left a message to call him back with urgency.

"Knowing that cop as I do, he'll sic all his hounds on us and the two escapees. It's not safe to move around. Let's keep the curtains drawn and lower our voices. We must become invisible tonight. Let's hope my friend calls back by tomorrow. We should leave at first light."

They arranged their futons for another night in Lucio's office. Each spent minutes in the bathroom and gazed out the small window to the string of lights along the river. It was such a peaceful if ironic scene. Lucio then put a chair under the knob, locked the door and doused the lights. As they squirmed to find a comfortable position on the floor, footsteps resounded in the corridor outside. They held their breaths. Finally, the footfalls diminished, and silence returned. They let out a collective sigh of relief.

Luke needed sleep to gird himself for Sunday morning. He so wished that this mission would come to an end without harm. As he finally drifted off, the Ox Bench's menace and the plaintive tune of "Matita Peré" lingered in his subconscious.

Together, they hijacked his dreams and offered no rest.

CHAPTER 30

Belém to Soure, the Island of Marajó
Sunday Morning, August 30

CUIABÁ PERFORMED ABOVE AND BEYOND the call of duty, even though the Colombiano was down and out. His bodyguard had the presence of mind to order the escort to go over the seat and apply pressure on Luis's head wound, stopping the blood flow with a clean towel. Next, he called the Colombian maid for a doctor off the books. He followed her directions to a nondescript residence on the far side of town. The doctor and nurse were waiting outside, pointing the bullet-shorn SUV to the open garage, and closed the door.

Luis's cousin had used this couple's services and facilities before and considered them reliable. Both the Brazilian doctor and his Cuban-born wife had been on the cartel's payroll for years. They whisked the semi-conscious patient inside to an operating table where they washed and dressed his grazed temple. They injected him with antibiotics and applied a compress of Elastoplast around his wound. After an hour, their patient was stabilized and resting.

"Muchas gracias," mumbled Luis.

Cuiabá next texted the maid to deliver a new SUV to their hide-out. Rosa asked that they strip the Land Rover's license plate and VIM number before she arrived. Her plan was to swap SUVs and drive the scarred Rover to a locale well-known for thieves. Within the hour, Rosa arrived with a Volvo XC40 and Luis's emergency satchel of one-hundred-dollar bills. She gave Luis a kiss on his bandaged forehead, smiled at Cuiabá, and left in the forlorn Rover. Driving down side streets, Rosa astutely parked it in a vacant lot of abandoned cars. She then walked a mile to the safehouse, uncon-cerned with a derringer in her purse.

All went according to plan, despite policia civil cars chasing around, lights flashing, and sirens blaring.

Before nodding off to sleep, Luis called his son via WhatsApp and asked if he'd seen the evening news. Junior said he had and asked if his father was safe and well. His father demurred but requested that his son meet him tomorrow at 08:00 at the munic-ipal airport where Junior had left his Cessna Skyhawk. Luis reminded Junior to file a flight plan to Laranjal do Jarí, on the north side of the Amazon. His son concurred and wished him a full recovery.

The morning crept in quietly, save for the songbirds in the garden. The sun played hide-and-seek with cirrhus clouds and at 06:30 extended a ray of light to the compound. The Cuban nurse had coffee brewing and heated *pão de queijo* in the oven, releas-ing an enticing aroma. They ate with little conversation and licked their lips after consuming the special cheese bread. Accompanied with *café com leite*, they arose from the table in a better mood.

Despite the harrowing events of the last twelve hours, Luis felt gratitude. "Doctor and Senhora Miranda, thank you so much for sewing me up. You will be remembered. But now, we must flee while the policia civil sleeps. We will be in touch," Luis exclaimed, giving them each a tight hug and an envelope full of cash.

"Gentlemen, thank you for your standup efforts yesterday against treachery. You too will be duly rewarded. Be prepared for one more challenge."

Cuiabá nodded his head enthusiastically.

"Vamos, amigos," the Colombian said and entered the backseat of the Volvo SUV. Cuiabá started the engines while the escort searched the vacant street before climbing into the shotgun seat. Luis waved at the couple who shut the garage door and disappeared inside.

Quietly, the driver slipped out of the residential neighborhood on side streets to the Brigadeiro Potásio de Oliveira municipal airport. They had a moment of fright when a policia civil car trailed them to the main entrance. The blue-and-white VW stopped at the gate, and two patrolmen began checking passengers going in and out. Continuing past the terminal building, Cuiabá entered the frontage road and found no one in the hanger at 07:55. Only the omnipresent vultures circled overhead.

At 08:10, a lone man came walking toward them carrying an overnight bag. He was over six feet tall, had long dark hair, and wore sunglasses like his father.

"Junior," shouted the Colombian who struggled out of the SUV, holding onto its side.

His son ran to him and exchanged hugs, holding his father upright. "Papá, it's wonderful to see you up, even with your bandana," his son said, trying to make light of the flexible cast around his father's head. "I'm sorry to be late, but the Uber driver was hassled by the policia civil. Shall we check out the plane's instruments and get ready to go? I filed the flight plan last night to Jarí, as you instructed. *Vámonos?*"

They pulled open the hangar door and stowed their baggage in the Cessna.

The other escort had a side conversation with Luis, who explained, "Jorge will not be joining us this morning and is going to return the car to Rosa. I'll call her now to meet you at the Boulevard Shopping Center. You should use this burner phone to communicate with her. She will have your remuneration and bonus and will arrange for your return to Marabá, tudo bem?"

The escort replied in kind and received the flip top from his employer. While Junior was checking the instrument panel, Luis called and made arrangements with the loyal Colombian maid. Cuiabá reluctantly gave the escort the SUV's keys, as well as a light hug, saying, "Stay alert, Jorge."

Luis entered the fixed-wing Cessna 172 and sat in the co-pilot's seat, watching his son going over the final checklist. The Skyhawk came to life and slowly inched outside. Cuiabá and the escort closed and locked the hangar door, the latter entering the Volvo XC40. Cuiabá braced himself against the turbulence and squeezed into the backseat. Clearance came from the control tower for their nominal flight to Jari.

The stalwart Cessna roared to life and raced down the runway into a fickle breeze. The plane's tricycle landing gear wobbled briefly, but the plane was soon airborne over Belém, heading west by northwest. Junior tipped its wings toward the airport's roadway and viewed their SUV speeding in the opposite direction.

The single-prop plane soon crossed over the Bay of Marajó but shifted steadily to starboard. Its new heading was north, away from Jarí and toward the mouth of the Amazon.

* * *

Light filtered through the blinds and landed on Luke's face. His sleep had been ragged and his heart beat restlessly. His other two companions were still dozing as he heard the vibration of someone's cell. It came from the table near the reporter's sofa, so Luke rose to answer it. "Alo? Yes, Lucio's here. Who may I say is calling? Captain Pedro, *momento.*"

The reporter's eyes popped open at the sound of the captain's name. Luke handed him the phone as Lucio shook himself awake.

"Tudo bem, Pedro? Yes, we're just waking up, but I appreciate your calling back. We're in a bit of a pickle. You may have seen the TV footage of the shoot-out on the dock. That same corrupt cop after the wood smugglers is also after me. We're holed up at the university but need to escape as they'll likely come here too. We have an invite to visit Soure on Marajó but need a lift. Would you be able to take us there by boat this morning? The US prof and I can help fund your gas and rental. We have one of his students too who's been pursued by the Ox Bench, so we really need to disappear. . . . I understand you need to get the boat owner's permission. . . . Our invite there is by a priest at the Salesian mission, and we plan to stay there a few days. . . . Excellent. Please call me back one way or the other. Obrigado, meu amigo."

Tatiana was awake and followed the conversation, as did Luke. She rubbed the sleep out of her eyes and confessed that Luis Carlos was her secret lover.

"We figured as much," said Luke. "Let's catch up on the details later. We must get ready to leave right away."

She nodded without words and entered the bathroom to get ready for the day ahead.

Luke rolled up the futons and packed some clothes, notes, his passport, and remaining dollars and Brazilian reais into his overnight bag. He left his large air force garment bag in the corner. Travelling light was best when they were on the run.

Lucio also put a change of clothes in his small satchel and looked out the window toward the Guama River. No police boats in view; just the urubús and white herons battling for their morning meal.

As Tatiana exited the bathroom, Lucio's captain friend called back.

The journalist simply said, "Tudo bem," and hung up. To Luke and Tatiana, he said, "Pedro has agreed to pick us up in a half-hour at 08:00 at the dock near the university. It's a ten-minute walk but let's go in a few minutes after packing up. I'll put some Nespresso on to boost our spirits."

Luke was the last to leave the bathroom and grab a quick cafezinho. Lucio gave his two visitors ball caps to wear while he put on his Panama hat and sunglasses. There was no one in the corridor at 07:45, so they walked briskly down the five stories to the ground floor and peeked outside. A university policeman was cruising along the main roadway, so they waited five minutes until the coast was clear. They hastened toward the river promenade while morning joggers passed them by.

As they approached the university dock, a harbor patrol boat cruised close to shore, heading up river. Lucio and Luke ducked under a grove of royal palms and asked Tatiana to remove her cap and show herself off. No woman was mentioned in the TV report, so a female presence was a plus, they said. When the patrol went around the bend, they hustled along the walkway to the landing. A few minutes after 08:00, Lucio's friend arrived in a thirty-foot cuddy cabin cruiser in need of a paint job.

Captain Pedro threw a line to Luke, who secured the bow and stern, helping Lucio and Tatiana board. Luke noticed the cuddy cruiser had a well-used Yamaha 200 four-cylinder engine, which should run comfortably at 30 mph. He untied the lines, boarded, and sat next to Tatiana aft. Lucio went forward with the captain in the covered cabin and caught him up with recent events. The captain hugged the city's coastline heading north, past the wharf where the shooting had taken place. They passed another patrol boat, whose sailors ogled Tatiana sunning herself.

Turning to port just before Mosquito Island, the captain entered the open Bay of Marajó, eighty miles from the Atlantic Ocean. The breeze picked up, ruffling the water into six-foot swells, causing the boat to pitch and roll.

Tatiana had to hold on and caught some spray instead of rays. She looked aft and exclaimed, "Is that a patrol boat following us? It seems to be coming up fast."

Lucio grabbed the binoculars from the captain, trying to steady himself against the rolling deck. "Indeed, it is. The gray boat seems to be gaining on us with its superior horsepower. What can we do, Pedro?"

The captain checked the vintage radar and noticed the naval vessel closing in. Angling the cuddy cruiser toward the coast of Marajó, he battled the rising waves and increased the speed to 35 mph. The boat shook and pounded on the swells, some reaching ten feet. Surf sprayed over the cabin, dousing Luke and Tatiana. They hung onto the stanchions for dear life.

After an hour in pursuit, the distance between vessels closed to a quarter-mile. The captain steered closer to shore in search of calmer waters. Yet the patrol boat loomed aft only a football field away. As Pedro swerved inward, he suddenly spied a series of logs rising and falling below the surface. He swerved sharply to port to avoid a fallen tree and then to starboard, zigzagging through the obstacle course. Another huge branch appeared dead ahead, forcing the captain to steer a hard left rudder.

"*Massaranduba*" was the last word Luke and Tatiana heard before flying overboard and plunging into the bay. Luke surfaced and barely avoided another log barreling his way. He looked up and saw the cuddy craft slow down, dovetailing between floating trees.

"*Socorro*," a voice cried out, "I can't swim!" Twenty yards away, Tatiana was thrashing between the swells.

Luke did a rapid breast stroke, keeping her in sight.

"Help," she cried once more, trying to grab a large branch.

When Luke came within five yards of her, his prized student submerged under the rolling waves. Grabbing a deep breath, he dove toward her last position. Thankfully, the sun shone brightly overhead and illuminated shifting shapes underwater. Luke aimed for the contours of a woman's frame, desperately seeking purchase. Yet her arm movement slowed and her body continued down. With a final lunge, Luke grabbed her streaming hair. He pulled with all his might and scissor-kicked toward the light. He swallowed his contained air again and again, hoping not to black out.

When they reached the surface, Tatiana was barely breathing. Luke gasped but hung onto her long, black hair with his left hand. He began the sidestroke on his right side and escaped the remaining logs. Over incessant rollers, Luke bodysurfed toward the shore. A pair of gray porpoises surfaced to check them out but disappeared into the bay. Twenty yards ahead was a narrow, sandy beach, so Luke accelerated his kick on the next comber in.

At five yards, he touched bottom and grabbed his listless student, hauling her ashore. Inside the inlet, a porpoise surfaced again, as if to say goodbye.

The prof and student collapsed on the sand. Luke knelt and turned Tati on her side, opening her mouth to let water pour out. Ensuring that the tongue was free, he rolled her on her back and began CPR on her chest. After a minute, he began breathing into her mouth and pinching her nose and then watched her chest rise. Breathing in and letting air out, he coaxed Tatiana back to life. Continuing in steady rhythm, he saw Tati's eyes flutter. Suddenly, his prized student shot a geyser of river water into Luke's face, causing him to laugh. It was his first chuckle of the day.

As Tati tried again to open her eyes, Luke spied a man approaching along the shore. The wiry man wore shorts and a white T-shirt with "Policia" written in blue. Luke looked across the bay, searching for Pedro's cruiser. Instead, he saw the patrol boat hit a log boom and roll hard to port.

Putting everything else out of mind, Luke continued CPR on Tati.

CHAPTER 31

Fazenda São Jeronimo, North of Soure do Pará
Sunday Afternoon, August 29

FORTUNATELY, THE FOREMAN STILL WORKED AT the large farm, which hosted tourists on weekends. Tiago had done favors for his cousin and remembered Luis Carlos, reserving him the private bungalow hidden behind the day-trippers' space. The mini-compound overlooked the mangroves along the bay, whose exposed roots appeared like tarantulas seeking prey.

Junior's sangfroid had saved the day. When Belém's traffic controllers radioed about his course change away from Jari, his son created static with the hand-held receiver, saying "You're breaking up." He then dropped from two thousand to under two hundred feet to avoid radar signals, continuing north up Marajó Bay. He stayed mid-channel, clear of a patrol boat speeding north along the island. Five miles out of Soure's airport, he asked permission to land for mechanical reasons; approval granted. Dropping the Cessna Skyhawk on the tarmac with aplomb, Junior arranged space in a hangar for a week stay. Even the stoic Cuiabá was impressed, "Like father, like son."

Cuiabá rented an old Volvo SUV from the airport manager, depositing one thousand dollars in advance. He gave his contact address at a local hotel, where he'd just made a reservation. They headed north away from town to the ranch hideaway up the coast.

More Bens were exchanged with São Jerónimo's manager, who pointed them to the concealed complex. After the twenty-four-hour marathon, they dumped their bags on the bungalow's floor and lay down for a long afternoon siesta.

Luis arose feeling restored, despite throbbing around his temple. He sat in a wicker chair, letting the A/C roll over him and rewinding in his mind recent events. Suddenly, he remembered that he hadn't called Tatiana, as he'd promised. Where was she now?

He texted her but received no reply. After half an hour, he called her cell and heard a mature male voice answer. "Who is this? . . . Oh, Luis Carlos, Tatiana's Colombian friend. She is resting now and has had quite an ordeal. I heard her phone ringing, so answered. Can she call you back later? I think we're all planning to go to vespers tonight at the Catholic church downtown. Padre José, whom she met in Cuiabá, is hosting our stay in Soure. Tudo bem?"

The Colombian breathed a sigh of relief and said he understood and hung up. Still, last night's takedown involving policia civil cast a pall over this state where he'd dealt successfully for many years. But not in 2021. The world and Brazil had turned upside down. At least they'd escaped last night's setup. But who had ordered the hit?

* * *

The assassin slipped away after three shots—one at the target, whom he'd grazed, and the other two at the bodyguard who'd gone down. The damned birds had altered his aim. Within thirty seconds, he'd broken down his Heckler & Koch, which had always served him well. Into the backpack, it went, and he down the warehouse's backstairs and out the pedestrian door. Walking south away from the action, he heard shots reverberate inside the warehouse where the policia civil charged in.

He walked deliberately past police cars to hotel #2 to lie low and collect his thoughts. On the evening news, he saw the arrogant cop tout his action to save the rainforests. He almost threw up but hoped the syndicate knew what it was doing with this detective who loved to see himself on TV. After a double cognac and a package of cashews, he managed to fall asleep. No ghostly faces appeared in his dreams, a positive omen. When he awoke in the morning, his confidence was on the mend.

After a Nespresso hit, he asked himself if he should report back to his São Paulo handler. With unfavorable news, he'd rather not. Upon showering, he saw that he'd received a text from that detective's partner, whom he'd met briefly at the restaurant. The message read, "News. Call me."

Gruff, like his boss, the cop didn't exude airs. He called him back and discovered the detective was chasing the second target up the Bay of Marajó. More interesting was that a Colombian-registered plane had left Belém today for Jari but landed in Soure. A plane was awaiting the assassin at the municipal airport to take him to the big island to check it out.

"We have target #1's cell number and will be tracking any open calls. If we get one, we'll be able to locate where he's staying. But you should reconnoiter too. Tudo bem?"

The hitman agreed, put on his backpack, and wiped down his fingerprints. Leaving by the hotel's side door, he walked a block and took a cab to the municipal airport. By noon, he was airborne.

At the Soure airport, he was met by a pudgy constable. The policeman said that a plane with Colombian registry had parked in a nearby hangar. The visitors had rented a SUV but hadn't checked into their hotel in town. Someone reported seeing a dark SUV heading north toward the saltwater beaches an hour ago. An unmarked VW was available for him.

The assassin thanked the constable and headed north, where tourists were known to frequent. Reaching the Praia da Maluca, "the beach of the crazy woman," he stopped at a hotel whose Wi-Fi tuned in and out. Learning more about the Colombian's connections, he decided to dig more into his past to see what else turned up.

* * *

PROFESSOR SHANNON HAD SAVED HER LIFE. Tatiana hardly remembered anything but flying off the boat into the bay. She recollected him breathing into her mouth but surmised that it might have been a pleasant dream. Maybe at twenty-three years it was time she learned how to swim.

Later Tatiana learned that a fisherman had alerted a lifeguard of their plight. Together, they had rescued the forlorn swimmers and taken them to the dispensary, later to the Catholic church in Soure, and ultimately to the rectory door. Padre José had met and hugged them all, offering a prayer of thanksgiving. The priest had blessed the good Samaritans and invited them in for Erva Mate tea and mandioca cake in the petite cafeteria. The fresh pastry had been devoured within minutes, and Tatiana and Luke had been slowly nurtured back to life. Love of neighbor indeed. She and Luke had thanked their rescuers and then fallen asleep in the priest's bedroom.

Now awake, Tatiana looked around the narrow room and heard her professor breathing lightly from a futon on the floor. A knock broke her out of her contemplation.

"Good afternoon, Tatiana. Tudo bem? You look much better after a well-deserved rest. By the way, your Colombian friend called. He is also on Marajó with his son and another companion."

"Thank you, Professor Lucio. I had forgotten that Luis Carlos had recommended getting away to this tranquil island too. Did he sound well?"

By now, Luke had awakened and sat up from his niche, offering, "Tudo bem?"

"Tudo bem, Professor, how about you? I heard from the priest about your rescue of Tatiana and being brought here by the fisherman and the lifeguard. We've certainly had much more excitement than we bargained for. My captain friend dropped me off at a village just south of here and skedaddled across the bay. Fortunately for him and us, the patrol boat also hit those floating logs and stayed dead in the water for over an hour. They too lost a couple passengers, I heard, and radioed for help. It's best we stay put in this church. Let's hope the lifeguard does not share our whereabouts with anyone.

"As to your Colombian friend, Tatiana, he sounded all right, despite the circumstances. I believe he's holed up somewhere north near the bay," Lucio said.

Padre José stuck his head inside his bedroom. "Great to see you both up and about. However, it's time to make another move so as not to draw attention. A Salesian brother has an apartment closer to the airport, outside of town. He's not returning for another week and gifted us this refuge. It's down the street from the Three Brothers Bakery, whose owners are members of this parish. The bakery also provides fresh bread, pastries, and of course, pão de queijo. What do you say?"

They all agreed and picked up their carry-ons. Luke thankfully found his cell inside. After the captain had left Lucio and their bags at the village dock, the native son had cajoled a trucker to take him and their luggage by ferry across the Paracuarí River into town, ending up at the rectory.

Now, the priest met them behind the church in the beat-up Toyota SUV and squeezed them and bags inside. The A/C didn't work, so they rolled down the windows for a faint if humid breeze.

On arrival, they smelled the yeast emanating from the bakery, which was about to close. Luke bought the last of the cheese bread and Brazilian ham-and-cheese pastries called "hot knee joints," for their dinner meal. The padre led them upstairs to the one-bedroom flat, as music seeped out of the apartment below.

"Shall I see you at vespers?" he inquired. "I'd be happy to pick you up at 19:00."

Lucio answered for them all, "After what we've been through today, a prayer would do us all good, Padre. That's very kind of you. We'll be ready."

"One last suggestion," the priest offered. "If the policia civil is still searching for you, it'd be best not to make unencrypted calls from your cell. They may have tracking devices. If you need to communicate, use WhatsApp from the church premises, where several parishioners should be present. Understood?

Luke and Lucio nodded their heads, but Tatiana's expression was hard to read.

CHAPTER 32

Soure to Fazenda São Jeronimo's Private Compound
Monday Noon, August 30

LUCIO, LUKE, AND TATIANA AROSE FEELING FRESH, having slept on a bed or sofa in the Salesian's apartment. Last night's Mass had also been special, and even Lucio had joined in the Lord's Prayer. During their visit, they had detected no surveillance or patrol car following them.

The morning ushered in a sunny workday, and several people picked up their daily bread from the Three Brothers Bakery.

Tatiana had made a call on the sly at church and another from the apartment in the morning to the Colombiano. Regaining her adventurous spirit, she extended Luis's invitation to Luke and Lucio to visit his compound near the beach. The two men looked at each other and shook their heads.

"My dearest student, after all we've been through, why should we tempt fate again?" Luke asked, amazed at how Tatiana had turned her thinking around in less than twenty-four hours. After being chased by the patrol boat and barely surviving their hurl into the bay, he was hard-pressed to understand her change of heart.

Sneaking around this small town added to their collective paranoia. Neither he nor Lucio made any calls. He would have liked to find a secure Wi-Fi to report back to Seattle U. On second thought, it'd be best to do so after departing Brazil.

Tatiana pressed on, "He would like to meet you both and has offered something special for each of you. Please reconsider.

"Professor Lucio, he would like to give you an exclusive story about the corruption in Belém's civil police and Customs offices. Working in tandem, they enable the export of illegal hardwood and encourage the invasion of indigenous land. Some were involved in the slaying of my distant cousin, Paulino Guajajara. This story could have a major impact in your hometown, as well as throughout Brazil.

"Professor Shannon, his son is a recent MBA graduate from La Javeriana in Bogota, a respected Jesuit university. He knows the dean, who is interested in forging closer ties with schools like Seattle University. Junior could connect you with him. If so, you'd have something positive to propose to our dean at Albers School of Business and Economics. What do you say?"

Both profs looked at each other, shaking their heads yet broaching smiles. Luke responded for both of them, "You sure know how to press our buttons, Tatiana. Is Luis in a safe place? As you know, the police are still hunting for him and Lucio. We don't want to be caught in a crossfire to end our mission. My goal is to keep all of us safe, so we can live to fight for justice another day. However, the dean would be pleased by closer ties with that fine university."

"They're in a private compound behind the São Jeronimo ranch, a half-hour north of here. He also has a loyal guard whom I met at Cuiabá. Perhaps the padre could lend us his Toyota to visit, even for just an hour?" she beguiled, running her hand through her luxurious hair.

The professor and journalist couldn't resist Tatiana's entreaty. They reluctantly agreed. Lucio confessed, "You're quite the sales-women, Tatiana. Let's hope we don't walk into an ambush, my dear."

She smiled in response.

Luke called Padre José, who said he could take them there now, as long as he was back by six in the evening. Luke asked Tatiana and Lucio again, "Tudo bem?" His student shouted, "Yes," and the reporter nodded his head. They freshened up and went outside, where legions of urubús soared overhead.

Following the tempting aroma, Luke bought more hot cheese bread at the bakery for their hosts. The padre arrived in the groaning Toyota and pushed a squeaking door open. With all aboard, the priest coaxed the SUV forward, spewing purplish exhaust. They turned on Travessa Thirty-Four and passed a couple of bars hosting early patrons for an afternoon cachaça. On the way, Padre José pointed out São Jorge's retreat area, which also hosted tourists. "We're not far from the other saint's enclave."

Ten minutes later, the padre turned down a gravel road at a homemade sign. He passed several coconut palms and two large ceiba trees providing shade from the afternoon sun. No one was present except the circling vultures. He bumped along the road to a semi-closed barrier, above which hung a placard, Fazenda São Jerónimo. Exiting the Toyota, he pushed open the wrought-iron gate but noticed red-and-white pennants blowing in the breeze. By the wooden post on the left were the remains of an animal sacrifice, picked apart by vultures and rodents. A glass of cachaça still glimmered in the sunlight.

Shaking his head, Padre José explained, "It looks like followers of macumba frequent this place as well. As you know, Saint Jerome is the Catholic counterpart of Xangó, the god of war in the

Afro-Brazilian cult. He is known for anger and for vendetta. This is not a welcoming sign."

He crossed himself, as did Luke, but Tatiana's lip began to tremble. Lucio stared stoically ahead and said, "Let's get this over with."

They wound around a dirt driveway past a wooden wheel inclined against a large massaranduba, as well as a ladder leading up to a fort hidden in its branches. Pots of plants were scattered underneath, and a half-dozen faded shacks were strung together in the distance. A larger home stood sentinel on higher ground to the right. When the padre shouted, "Is anyone here?" all he heard in response was the cawing of a crow. Further up the narrow road, they crossed a wooden bridge over a mangrove, which extended through a dense forest toward the bay. Another pedestrian bridge went over the steaming sand into a copse of palms.

"Tatiana, maybe you should call your friend, as I don't have a clue where to go." They stayed in the vintage SUV with the windows rolled down, fighting off mosquitos, many attracted to Luke's gringo skin. Tatiana telephoned and said, "It's up fifty yards to the right."

At the Y, they turned under an arbor of Brazil nut trees. They heard no sound except for the Toyota's whines. Suddenly, a young man appeared beyond the grove, descending the stairs of a bungalow under a thatched roof. "Tatiana?"

Before the SUV pulled to a stop, she jumped out and exclaimed, "Luis Carlos Junior?" She saw a younger version of her lover with the same Mediterranean features, dark eyes, and wavy dark hair. He sported a spontaneous smile, unlike his father, and wore a tropical beige guayabera.

"At your service, Tatiana. I'm sorry it was hard to find. The foreman thought we'd be safer up here away from the tourists. It's so good to meet you," he gushed and gave Tati a kiss and a long hug.

"It's a pleasure to meet you too and congratulations on earning your MBA. Let me present you to Padre José, Professor Luke Shannon of Seattle University, and Professor and journalist Lucio Flavio from Belém." All three shook hands and gave Junior a loose hug.

At the screen door, a stocky man appeared, wearing a shoulder holster. "Tatiana and friends, let me present you to my father's mayordomo, who goes by Cuiabá. Let's go inside where the A/C is working and caipirinhas are waiting."

They followed Junior up the stairs and acknowledged the guard, who gave the visitors a once-over. In the living room, stood Luis Carlos, whose eyes lit up when Tatiana bounded across the parquet floor into his arms. They held each other for a minute, unashamed of their affection. Cuiabá closed the screen and the front doors and led the men past the couple into the dining room, where preparations for the Brazilian national drink were ready. Luke delivered the warm cheese bread as appetizer.

They sat around the rosewood table, listening to the Colombiano's son tell his story. Luke probed about his passions and discovered that Junior, like Tatiana, was a dedicated environmentalist, working to save his country's rainforests and indigenous tribes. He also forged relationships with the Nature Conservancy and a German NGO. His father and Tatiana joined them a half-hour later to share caipirinhas.

Lucio checked his watch showing three fifteen and asked Luis Carlos Senior, "Would you mind if I turned on my iPhone to record our conversation? My memory has been known to fail of late. I appreciate your willingness to blow the whistle on the dirty cops who tried to kill you and me. As we must return Padre José's Toyota to the church this afternoon, would you be willing to have a private conversation?"

"Please follow me, Lucio, and congratulations on your diligence. I've read your columns and posts. I respect your honest reporting. It's not easy to do so up North," replied Luis Carlos. He led them to two armchairs in the living room's corner facing west. Cuiabá followed them and closed the dining room door.

Luke, Tatiana, and the priest plied the son with questions of all sorts, including how best to counter invaders of tropical forests. They also touched on philosophical issues, such as one's purpose in life. Luke observed his favorite student nodding often, enthralled by the son's idealistic words. The young man would turn twenty-nine this year and said he wanted to make a difference for the good.

Junior also promised to introduce Luke to La Javeriana's dean, who was interested in student exchanges with American universities. Luke thanked him, and they traded business cards with email and WhatsApp contacts. The door opened, and Cuiabá waved them into the living room. Luke's saw the sun decline further to the west, filtered through a distant ceiba tree.

Lucio thanked the Colombian for his extensive interview, duly recorded on his smartphone, and gave him a hearty embrace.

Luis replied, "Let me accompany you to your car. Please publish this only after I am gone, tudo bem?"

Lucio concurred and joined the entourage going down the front porch's steps. Luke noticed that no birds were chirping, though the sun would soon set. Luis Carlos hugged Tatiana and said, "Get to know my son. You are both kindred spirits."

Those were his last words on earth.

A shot rang out and then another from the ceiba forty yards away. Everyone dropped to the ground, save Cuiabá who fired his Glock toward the tree. Silence fell, but smoke wafted from the mangroves.

A late afternoon breeze rustled through the trees, joined by the distant croaking of a frog. Then a keening surged deep within Tatiana and Junior, becoming a crescendo of lament. They baptized the fallen Colombiano with their tears and embraced him in their arms. Their voices rose to the palms and to the heavens.

Only the rufus-bellied thrush responded in plaintive song.

EPILOGUE

Monte Dourado on the Jari River
Tuesday Morning, September 7, 2021

THE BRAZILIAN FLAG FLAPPED IN THE BREEZE, its green, yellow, and blue colors reflecting the tropical scene. The verdant forest, which Luke had entered forty years ago, appeared closer and thicker now. Gold reflected off the bridge where Lucio was chatting with his friend, captaining a riverboat to Belém. The azure sky suggested another warm day as the dry season continued on.

Luke waved and stood solo on the shore.

Brazil's Independence Day would soon be celebrated by a diverse community on the western side of the river. It was no longer the American town in the jungle, where its original owner aspired to create the cellulose capital of the world. Today, Luke would be the only expat here, unlike the hundreds he'd met in 1981. Just as well, he thought. The town seemed more relaxed yet resilient as the village parade wound through the public square.

He wandered over to a large ceiba on a hill overlooking the river. Sitting under its thick branches, he realized this was the type of tree used by the assassin a mere week ago. That day had gone from tranquil to tragic in an instant, flipping their worlds upside down. It was time for Luke to reflect on the aftermath.

* * *

BLESS THE PADRE FOR COVERING LUIS CARLOS'S FACE, shattered by the high-velocity bullet, and having the presence to administer the last rites. Bless Lucio for consoling Tatiana amidst her river of tears and himself for hugging Junior, trembling and orphaned as a young man.

Bless Cuiabá, steadfast Cuiabá, who chased the assassin through bullets and brushfire, only to glimpse his escape through the mangroves in a low-bottom boat. Thinking quickly, he hooked up a hose to the bungalow's water pump. Together, they extinguished the blaze set by the shooter to cover his tracks.

Battling the fire proved therapeutic for all of them, taking their minds momentarily away from the tragic event. Afterwards, they sat on the porch and discussed what they should do before news seeped out. Junior shared his father's last testament, specifying that Luis Carlos be cremated with most of his ashes interred at his Colombian ranch in Antioquia, where he'd raced horses as a young boy. The rest of his ashes he willed be scattered over the Jari River, where he'd spread his wings as a young man. Luke recalled their own meeting across this river forty years ago.

It was Padre José's turn to spring into action, calling his fellow priest to get the number of the town's coroner and owner of the sole crematorium. He reached the proprietor and convinced him to provide this service without a public examination, in accordance with the deceased's wishes. The man reluctantly agreed and would await their arrival.

They wrapped Luis's body in bed sheets and placed his head

carefully on the front seat, his body running diagonally over the flattened back seat of the SUV's semi-opened liftgate. Cuiabá and Junior stashed their personal effects into carry-ons, putting them in the church's Toyota. Luke would drive Lucio, Tatiana, Junior, and baggage to the apartment and await word. Padre José and Cuiabá would take Luis on his final journey to Soure's crematorium.

Before leaving, they knelt on the ground and joined the padre in the Lord's Prayer. Then they rose and gave each other tight hugs and a final glance at the bungalow. As they entered their vehicles, the sun cast its vermillion wand over them before disappearing into the darkening forest.

That late August evening, they arrived at Soure's modest airport after it had closed operations. Continuing to the tarmac, they unlocked the hangar and slid the door open. Having gassed up the Cessna Skyhawk on arrival, Junior checked its instrument panels and gave a thumbs up. They all gave each other hugs and exchanged WhatsApp numbers. Luke, Lucio, Tatiana, and Luis Carlos's ashes would board the plane with Junior. The padre and Cuiabá would stay in town.

The last quarter moon provided pale light over the unlit airstrip. The young Colombiano started the single engine, feathered its propeller, and slowly moved the Cessna onto the runway. He was doing the ultimate no-no, flying at night without a flight plan or control tower signoff. Yet his father had done so on several occasions. The airstrip was long enough for jets, and no steep hills lurked nearby. But what else could he do, without raising alarm with local authorities and the policia civil?

Earlier, Luke had texted Sergio, whom he'd met at the attorney's luncheon in São Paulo. The current president of the Jari project was working in Monte Dourado this very week and invited him to visit. Luke agreed at once. Importantly, Sergio gave him the coordinates to its municipal airport and said that a traffic controller would be on station until midnight. Luke passed the data to Junior, who entered it into the Garmin G 1000 navigation system.

The Cessna's engines raced as it sped down the asphalt. The plane lifted off past the darkened tower heading due west over the immense fluvial island.

The air guide described flying over Marajó during the dry season as "monotonous" with little elevation or tropical storms. Hardly any light showed below, and Lucio and Tatiana nodded off in the back seat. Luke was up front and remembered flying in his dad's Cessna years ago. He noticed the plane's altitude at five hundred meters, a little over sixteen hundred feet, and its engine pressure in the green. After what they'd been through, a boring journey to Monte Dourado was just fine. An hour and twenty minutes into the flight, Junior made radio contact with the municipal airport.

At fifteen minutes to midnight, they saw the lighted runway, angling to the northeast. Into a prevailing wind of 10 mph, they landed on the first try and headed toward the nondescript tower, where a short, lean man greeted them.

"Welcome to Monte Dourado," he exclaimed. "I drove Senhor Sergio's SUV to pick you up and take you to a guest house this side of the river, tudo bem? You can leave your Cessna here overnight. Just put chocks under the wheels."

They sleepily agreed. Their guide led them into the quiet town along the Jari, once upon a time, the talk of the world.

The next morning, they met for breakfast over cafezinho, fresh açaí fruit, and *cajú* juice, made from the fruit hanging from the cashew nut tree.

Sergio came by to greet them and share his philosophy. "Our

approach is not top-down like in the past. Instead, we include workers, families, and NGOs in our decision-making process. As a community, we have turned the corner. Monte Dourado is an example of what Brazil could be if we all work together."

The visitors applauded Sergio and peppered him with questions. Later, he offered them a tour of Jari's facilities. Lucio accepted his invite, but Luke asked to join him later. He planned to accompany Junior and Tatiana to honor Luis Carlos's wish to spread his ashes over the Jari River. They agreed to join Sergio for lunch at the dining hall and gave everyone loose hugs.

Outside, a nut-brown man waited near Sergio's SUV and looked carefully at the American prof. "Didn't we meet when my father took you by boat to Monte Dourado? You were a young banker at the time. I heard from Senhor Sergio that an Americano would be visiting. You may remember me as Beto."

Luke did a double-take and exclaimed, "Great to see you, Beto! We did share a boat ride together a while ago. How have you and your family been?" He gave the shorter man a tight hug, heartened by their serendipitous reunion.

"Tudo bem. We have a family of four and little Beto should arrive any moment. Thanks to Senhor Sergio and his team, our jobs and health have improved. We suffered twenty years of hardship after Ludwig's project fell apart. Now, our children stay here; they don't move away to the big city. There's work in town and at the pulp factory downriver. Many families are growing mandioc and vegetables in their plots or harvesting cashews and açaí in the forest. It's a different Monte Dourado from when you visited forty years ago."

They gave each other another hug and promised to meet soon. Beto opened the door for Sergio and Lucio, waved to Luke, and drove toward the groves of eucalyptus.

The hotel manager's son agreed to take Luke, Tatiana, and Junior in his father's pram across to the waterway's east bank. Offshore of the town of Laranjal do Jari, once called the "shanty's edge," the three somberly spread some of Luis's ashes on the flowing river. Little by little, memories dribbled out as well as tears. When cumulus rumbled in and cloaked the sun, they crossed back to the other side. The rolling waves soothed them like a bossa nova song.

The mist turned into drizzle the closer the pram approached Monte Dourado. Jumping off the dock, they hurried to the lodge where they planned to meet Sergio and the group for lunch. Instead, the airport manager was present with a disturbing message.

"I received word that a policeman from Belém is on his way and should arrive within an hour. As a friend of Jari, I thought you'd like to know. Per your instructions, I gassed up your Cessna and checked the oil. It's ready to go."

Junior looked at Tatiana and she at him. Without words they walked rapidly to their rooms. Within minutes, they returned with their carry-ons, his father's money bag, and the larger urn of Luis's ashes. They gave Luke extended hugs and asked him to pass on their regards to Lucio and their host. Hurrying into the manager's VW, Luke's star student and the young Colombian waved briefly as the rain picked up. The van raced to the airport, carrying Tatiana and Junior to fates unknown.

* * *

As the ferryboat grew fainter, Luke replayed his last conversation with Belém's top journalist. Lucio for the moment was protected by the Federal Police, thanks to the friendly Fed who had arrived within minutes of Tatiana and Junior's escape north. Luke and Lucio had shared vivid details with the honest cop about the policeboat chase up the Bay of Marajó. However, they offered no words about the shootout at Luis Carlos's bungalow.

The federal agent mentioned that the corpse of the corrupt policia civil had washed ashore south of Soure, savaged by fish with sharp teeth. Fishermen speculated that the scavengers included piranhas, pirarucú, or even porpoise, though a few urubú hovered nearby.

Though not wishing death on anyone, Lucio breathed a sigh of relief. He also told the friendly agent that he had recorded an interview with a Colombian drug lord about corruption in Belém's Customs service, as well as its civil police. The federal officer was keenly interested and asked if he could speak with Lucio's source.

"You know that we reporters can't divulge our confidential informants, or no one would ever talk to us again, my friend. I'd be happy to provide you with the transcript before the story is published, tudo bem?"

They had agreed and parted company. The Fed was off to chase down smugglers near the Venezuelan border. Lucio and Luke bid him well and returned to the hotel's veranda to down açaí caipirinhas, which loosened their tongues.

After two deep swallows, Luke shared some news: "Padre José sends his regards. Cuiabá spent a couple days with him and then returned to Belém. He's staying with Luis's Colombian maid and seems to be enjoying his time. As your friend confirmed, the big news in Soure was the cop's body washing ashore, but there were no other repercussions. As the corpse's blood-alcohol level was high, the padre heard gossip that he fell overboard from too much to drink.

"As for my errant student and Junior, despite a flash storm over the upper Amazon, they arrived in Paramaribo, Surinam, that very afternoon. As she is Brazilian and he Colombian, they didn't need a special visa for entry. The couple overnighted in the airport hotel, though she didn't say whether it was one room or two. The next morning, Junior piloted the Cessna Skyhawk over the Orinoco River, arriving 'on fumes' at Puerto Carreño on the Colombian side of the border. After gassing up, they crossed the Andes and reached Bogota at sunset. They are currently in the city's Zona T, staying in some fancy, schmancy hotel, 'enjoying each other's company,' according to Tatiana. They've already spoken with The Nature Conservancy and plan to join forces with green groups in both countries to battle deforestation. Olé!"

"Olé, indeed, Professor! Good for them. Also, that's quite an escapade, worthy of the silver screen. Besides finishing your study report, consider finding a script writer to recount their daring adventure. I hear that Netflix, Apple, and Amazon are always on the prowl for exotic documentaries. A friend in Rio named Jorge may be able to facilitate," Lucio concluded, finishing his drink and ordering another round.

"By the way, several news organizations have expressed interest in my exclusive talk with Luis Carlos. Besides the *Folha* and *Estado de São Paulo*, international groups like Reuters and the *Washington Post* are searching for material about Brazil's wild North, akin to America's Wild West. Yet it's almost 2022!

"If I provide confidential information to the Feds, my friend offered a guard 24/7 at my residence in Belém. However, my daughters and I are considering hiding out awhile in the South, maybe in Florianópolis. What do you think?"

"Santa Catarina has lovely beaches and well-ordered communities," Luke replied. "It may be just what the doctor ordered. I once visited Florianópolis and enjoyed its clean beaches and courteous residents. It'd be a pleasant and deserved R & R," he said to the reporter, who looked needy of rest.

* * *

NOW ON BRAZIL'S INDEPENDENCE DAY, only Luke remained. He rose from his perch under the ceiba and shook reminiscences away. His right hip had fallen asleep, so he limped toward the lodge as a bell tolled once. He saw a young boy, dressed in his Sunday best, standing on the veranda and fidgeting with something in his hand.

"Professor Lucas?" he asked in a low voice.

"At your service, young man."

"My family and Senhor Sergio would like to invite you to celebrate my new brother's birth," he replied, offering the envelope to Luke with both hands.

Luke opened the handwritten note, requesting his presence at the christening of Roberto Souza III at the Jariloca Club at 14:00. It was signed "Beto." So his wife Carla had given birth. Luke smiled at the young boy whose eyes exuded the warmth of his father's. "With much pleasure. May I thank you by your name?"

The young boy stood up tall and exclaimed, "I call myself Daniel, and I am nine years old. My father named me after the founder of Jari." He politely extended his hand, which Luke shook gladly.

"My pleasure, Daniel. Please thank your father and family for the invitation and tell them I plan to attend." He gave the boy a tight hug and entered the lodge.

In his second-floor room, Luke showered and shaved and was pleasantly surprised that a freshly laundered shirt had been hung in the closet. As his beige slacks were relatively clean, he put them on with his Hawaiian shirt, checking quickly in the mirror. A reddish face reflected back, crinkled around his sky-blue eyes. His once brown hair was streaked with more strands of gray. This was Luke Shannon in 2021.

Leaving at one forty-five, he strolled through the town he had once visited as a young intern. The streets were plotted by numbers, as in the original village, but were now lined with massaranduba, banana, and palm trees shrouding hundreds of homes. It had the appearance of a small American town reshaped by the Brazilian tropics. Kids were kicking a soccer ball on the playfield, and the plaza's eucalyptus trunks were painted white to guard against ants. White rocks also circled the flower beds as in a typical village of the interior.

Luke heard the ruckus of a blue and yellow macaw overhead and saw its mate on a nearby palm. Beto told him that they were a monogamous breed and lived together for life. What an example, he thought.

Passing by a pastel First Baptist Church, Luke saw a lady explaining Bible stories to children under palm trees. Down the lane, workmen were painting the blue walls of Our Lady of Nazareth church, shaded by a Brazil nut tree. He wiped his brow, wondering where the club might be. He stopped at a new one-story building called the Center for Covid-19 and asked a tired-looking a nurse for directions.

"If you don't mind riding on the back of my colleague's scooter, he'll pass by the Jariloca Club on One Hundredth Street. Tudo bem?" asked the nurse with a smile.

Luke thanked her and hopped on the back of a well-used Vespa. In five minutes, they arrived at a spread-out country club, surrounded by a multitude of trees. The complex included a moss-tinged pool, where a few kids were splashing about and zooming down the slide. He thanked the young driver and wandered down an outdoor corridor, noticing photos of the club's thirty-year history. A different Monte Dourado in 2021.

Outside a small social hall, Luke bumped into Daniel, chasing a mix-breed dog out the door. "Momento," he said to Luke and managed to corral the canine. "This is Lucy, senhor. Please come inside where my father, mother, family, and the priest are waiting."

Beto beamed when he saw Luke. "Welcome, Professor. We have to christen my youngest in this club as the church is being repainted. Let me introduce you to Padre João of our local parish. Padre, this is the Americano I met forty years ago when he visited Jari. He is also a Catholic and friend of Senhor Sergio."

They exchanged loose hugs and small talk. Then Beto took Luke aside. "Senhor Sergio was called away on an emergency at the power plant and may be delayed for my son's christening. As you are a practicing Catholic, would you be willing to serve as his godfather instead? I admit it's very short notice and very presumptive of me. But the padre can stay only until 16:00. You would greatly honor my family and our little Beto III."

Luke looked at Carla in her wheelchair, cradling their infant son. A family friend began strumming a guitar and humming Jobim's classic tunes. The music took Luke back to his visit along the Jari River when the maiden had danced and sung, "Happiness is like a drop of dew on a flower petal. It shines quietly, then shakes ever so slightly and falls as a teardrop of love." That night forty years ago, he had murmured that same bossa nova poem to the jaguar in the forest.

Moved, Luke felt perhaps this was his purpose to be in Monte Dourado, Brazil, today and on this study mission in 2021. He heard the children's voices resound in laughter and the trill of a rufus-bellied thrush outside. The sun filtered through the open window, accompanied by a wisp of breeze. And Jobim's music filled the room in rolling waves.

Luke breathed deeply and nodded to the baby's father. He gave his rediscovered friend a tight hug but turned away to hide his tears.

After a couple of moments, Luke said, "Beto, the honor is mine, compadre. The honor is truly mine."

ACKNOWLEDGEMENTS

I ACKNOWLEDGE THE SACRIFICES OF REPORTERS, MISSIONAR-IES and indigenous people who have paid the ultimate price to do the right thing. On June 5, 2022, journalist Dom Phillips and indigenist Bruno Pereira disappeared in the Javari valley of western Brazil. They were collecting evidence of illegal fishing and plundering of native lands. Villagers provided leads to the Policia Federal, which arrested two men. But who ordered their murder? May their courage and testimonies bring change, despite threats from vested interests.

I thank the Brazilian people for extending their hospitality and friendship to me for over forty years. Living as a young professional in São Paulo and Rio de Janeiro took me out of my "American box." Life exploded in vivid colors, and I spread my wings to a bossa nova beat. *Obrigado.*

My father often invited his client of fine furniture to our Sunday family dinner. Bryan shared his adventures of chasing down rosewood and massaranduba along the Amazon, notwithstanding jaguars, piranhas, and smugglers. His stories ignited this teen's imagination, making me dream big. I learned Portuguese as a result. *Obrigado.*

For destiny's "invisible hand," which led me to Brazil's *Custódio de Melo* while in the US Navy and later to AIESEC's internship in São Paulo, I thank you for opening my eyes and heart. My first journey to South America, with classmate Allan, made us stretch and adapt to new cultural scenes. "Someone" watched over us on the byways of Ecuador, Peru, Bolivia, and finally Brazil. *Obrigado.*

I thank the dozens of Brazilians and *brasileirados* for their stories, many of which are included in my third book of odyssey and redemption.

I thank all Brazil's unsung heroes and heroines, whose actions show their love of neighbor.

Early support from friends in Rio, like José Luiz Osôrio, Harold Emert, and Ronaldo Veirano, helped me keep current on Brazil's dealing with the pandemic and tumultuous politics. *Agradecido.*

Shirleann Nold has read every single word of my manuscript and corrected me with vigor. Despite occasional hot discussions, I confess that she was usually correct.

Steve Yolen provided sage counsel throughout my research and writing, as well as entrée to a Brazilian publisher about translating *Brazilian Odyssey* into Portuguese.

New friends of the state of Pará furnished tips about the forces at play in Belém, Santarém, Monte Dourado, Manaus, and communities along the River Sea:

I credit Cristina Serra, journalist and writer, for her early advice about indigenous people under threat. Caetano Scannavino's and his brother's commitment to Saúde e Alegria in Alter do Chão has taught me what citizens can do to advance a just cause. Lucio Flavio Pinto exemplifies a reporter's courage to hold those in power to account. Sérgio Amoroso, CEO of Projeto Jarí, has invested over twenty years of his life to renew community and sustainable development along the Jari River. *Parabéns e agradecido.*

To these Brazilian friends and expatriates, I recognize your confidential testimonies and words to the wise, listing you by first name(s): Aidé, Aldo, Alexandre, Álvaro, Amorím, Andrew, Ángela (SP and Curitiba), Araquém, Ariane, Aron, Beto, Bianor, Brad, Bruno, Caio, Camila, Charles, Claudio, Cristina, Edgard, Edi, Eduardo, Ernie, Eugênio, Evaristo, Fábio (Santarem and Rio), Fernanda, Fernando, Flávio, Francisco, Gabriel, Geisimara, Gilderan e Gilson da CIMI, Giora, Gisela, Gregorio, Guilherme, Hermano, Hugo, Ilko, Isabel, James (Rio and SP), John, Johnny, Jorge, Padre José, Deacon José, Juscelino, Letícia, Lídice, Lorenzo, Luciana, Luis Carlos, Luis do CIMI, Luis Fernando, Luiz B., Marcelo (SP and Rio), Marcos, Marina, Marta, Mateus, Matt, Mauro, Michelle, Milagros (RO and SP) Nelson, Nilson, Olivier, Olívio, Paulo (RJ and SP), Paulo Roberto, Pedro, Perdigão, Peter, Phylis, Plinio, Drs. Renilton and Ricardo, Richard, Rilton, Ronaldo, Rogério, Rubens, Samy, Sérgio, Sônia, Steve, Tatiana, Teresa, Thiago, Vera (Brasilia), Vera Aparecida (SP), Walter, Werner, and William.

A special thanks to Thomson Reuters' team throughout Brazil, especially Brad, Fabio, Gabriel, and Stephen, for their advice and introductions.

Information from these forestry experts provided timely insights to keep the author on track: Marcelo Ambrogi, of IMA Florestal, Luis Fernando da SOS Mata Atlântica, Dr. Claudio Pádua e Plínio Ribeiro da Biofílica. *Obrigado.*

Federal policeman Alexandre Saraiva and philanthropist Teresa Bracher assisted my understanding of Brasilia's current policies and their impact on deforestation. Richard Lapper's *Beef, Bible and Bullets* offered context about Bolsonaro's election in 2018. *Grato.*

I am grateful to Seattle University for being able to share insights with students about Brazil and Latin America and for authorizing missions to Brazil and to Cuba. I thank the lay missionaries of o Conselho Indigenista Missionário, for their dedication on behalf of native people, as CIMI celebrates fifty years of engagement—especially in Brazil's northern, northeastern, and *cerrado* regions.

Thank you, all authors, who have reviewed many pages of my book and have shared your thoughtful critiques.

Putting *Brazilian Odyssey* to print was made possible by Julie Scandora, line editor and cognoscenti of *The Chicago Manual of Style,* and by Melissa Coffman and Scott Book of Book House Publishing. Their commitment and steadfastness were material in getting it published stateside in a timely manner.

Pam Binder, president, Pacific Northwest Writers Association, gave encouragement all along the way to keep me writing. Thanks to her and all the PNWA family.

Thank you, brother Terry, for your wise counsel to reduce "world count" and for students and professors at the University of Washington and Seattle University who heard me out in impromptu readings. Thank you, nephew Jason, for guiding me through social media for both *Havana* and *Brazilian Odysseys.*

Thank you, Vicki, for putting up with your reclusive husband these past two years, as I traveled the winding road of research, interviews, and writing. *Merci et bisoux.*

Thank you, readers, for picking up this book.

AUTHOR'S NOTE AND BIOGRAPHY

Y ES, I ADMIT TO BEING THE young banker who recommended the loan to Ludwig's grandiose project over forty years ago. As "young and eternal," I unwisely entered the forest at dusk, saved by humming Jobim's song to a jaguar ready to pounce. Thanks to Beto's father, I crossed the river from Monte Dourado to the ramshackle village on stilts, water rushing underneath. In a rustic bar, I heard the Xingú maiden sing "Sadness never ends, but happiness does." In that same cabana, Luis Carlos introduced himself to me. Twenty years later, we crossed paths at the Jockey Club of Rio de Janeiro. We have not seen each other since.

Late 2019, I began interviewing dozens of Brazilians about a new book of odyssey and redemption, taking place in this tropical country where I lived many years. Several expressed concerns about Brazil's diminishing rainforests and degrading public services. Others decried invaders of indigenous lands and killing of innocents who got in their way. Several lamented the election of "Trump in the tropics" and a democratic process at risk. When the pandemic struck in 2020, many felt the pall of death among family, friends, and neighbors.

Thus, this second of a series (the first being *Havana Odyssey*), depicting Professor Luke Shannon, is dedicated to Brazil's unsung heroes, who have helped their fellow citizens navigate the pandemic, deforestation and favoritism from "above." People like Alexandre (Saraiva), Beto, Caetano, Claudio, CIMI missionaries, Padre José, Lucio, Marina, Plinio, Sergio, Sonia, Teresa, Vera, and Werner really exist in Brazil today. This book is my legacy to them.

During the calamitous years of 2020 and 2021, many ordinary Brazilians stepped up to help their countrymen and women survive. My third book recounts this contemporary story through the eyes of these champions who receive little notice in mainstream media. I have melded their testimonies and actions into Luke Shannon's storyline. All characters are cited only by their first name(s) in order to shield them from another's harsh words.

As an adjunct professor in Seattle University's Albers School of Business and Economics, I have co-led study tours like the one discussed in *Brazilian Odyssey*. Presently, I do one-off lectures on Latin American business in hopes that they pique student interest in our neighbors south of the border. In one such class, I met a student named Tatiana with indigenous roots, who brought to my attention the assassination of Paulino Guajajara on All Saints Day 2019. May the "guardian of the forest" rest in peace.

* * *

Stephen E. Murphy has lived and traveled south of the border for decades and is fluent in Spanish, Portuguese, and French.

He enjoys long-lasting friendships in Brazil, Chile, Colombia, Cuba, El Salvador, Mexico, and Panama. Professionally, he held executive positions in BankBoston, Paramount Pictures, and the Inter-American Development Bank. For the first Bush administration, Murphy was appointed Worldnet Television director, US Information Agency. Under President George W. Bush, Murphy served as regional director, Inter-Americas, for the Peace Corps.

At Miami Jackson High School, Murphy taught economics in its academy for at-risk students. The *Miami Herald* and the *Wall Street Journal* recognized his efforts to teach inner city kids about the stock market and how their picks beat the S&P 500 in 1995. Returning to his hometown, Murphy has taught courses on Latin America Business at Seattle University and consulted for firms expanding to the Americas. He mentors students and young professionals in Havana, Miami, Rio de Janeiro, and Seattle and serves as chapter advisor to students of the Phi Kappa Psi fraternity, University of Washington.

In 2016, Murphy published *On the Edge: An Odyssey*, a memoir about the turning points in his life. His second book, *Havana Odyssey* (2020), was based on sixty-five interviews with Cubanos in country and abroad, honoring the promise made to Ana Maria, the niece of Cuba's deceased "Hero of the Republic." In addition, Murphy has published articles on Brazil in the *Brazil Herald*, *Puget Sound Business Journal*, and *Quarterly* of Seattle's Trade Development Alliance.

Murphy has conducted readings of his books in three countries in more than sixty venues, including Books & Books (Coral Gables, Florida), Livraria da Vila (São Paulo), Livraria da Travessa (Rio de Janeiro), and La Biblioteca Nacional de Cuba. Currently, he is conducting research for a new book, *Colombian Odyssey*.

He lives in the Seattle area and still loves swimming in open bodies of water all over the world.

Seattle University mission to Brazil, Rio de Janeiro, 2001. Author is on far right.

Made in the USA
Las Vegas, NV
17 July 2022